For the girls:
Gigi, Shelley, Ann,
Sue, Meg, Margaret, Karen

Praise for *Her Daughter's Eyes*

"A debut novel as gutsy [and] appealing . . . as its heroines. But it is the plight of the teenage sisters, in all their clever foolishness, that strikes at the heart."   —Publishers Weekly

"A modern-day depiction of familial disintegration with offbeat twists and luminous sparks of hope."   —Booklist

"A well-written, thoughtful debut. . . . The understanding portrayal of her teenaged heroines—stubborn, careless, and fiercely honest—is remarkably astute."   —Kirkus Reviews

"An exquisitely poignant look into the heart of a troubled family. A beautifully etched portrait of loss, love, and family strength."
                      —New York Times bestselling author Deborah Smith

"Beautifully written. . . . [A] wonderful novel."
                      —New York Times bestselling author Sally Mandel

"Poignant, sharply introspective, and thought-provoking. Every parent of a teenager and indeed every teenager should read this work with care."   —New York Times bestselling author
                                       Dorothea Benton Frank

"A haunting, compelling debut novel that takes the reader on an emotional roller-coaster ride."   —New York Times bestselling
                                       author Kristin Hannah

Written by today's freshest new talents and selected by New American Library, NAL Accent novels touch on subjects close to a woman's heart, from friendship to family to finding our place in the world. The Conversation Guides included in each book are intended to enrich the individual reading experience, as well as encourage us to explore these topics together—because books, and life, are meant for sharing.

Visit us on-line at www.penguinputnam.com.

OTHER NAL ACCENT NOVELS
BY JESSICA BARKSDALE INCLÁN

Her Daughter's Eyes

Jessica Barksdale Inclán

THE
MATTER
OF
GRACE

FICTION FOR THE WAY WE LIVE

OUACHITA TECHNICAL COLLEGE

NAL Accent
Published by New American Library, a division of
Penguin Putnam Inc., 375 Hudson Street,
New York, New York 10014, U.S.A.
Penguin Books Ltd, 80 Strand,
London WC2R 0RL, England
Penguin Books Australia Ltd, Ringwood,
Victoria, Australia
Penguin Books Canada Ltd, 10 Alcorn Avenue,
Toronto, Ontario, Canada M4V 3B2
Penguin Books (N.Z.) Ltd, 182-190 Wairau Road,
Auckland 10, New Zealand

Penguin Books Ltd, Registered Offices:
Harmondsworth, Middlesex, England

Published by New American Library, a division of Penguin Putnam Inc.

First Printing, May 2002
10 9 8 7 6 5 4 3 2 1

FICTION FOR THE WAY WE LIVE

REGISTERED TRADEMARK—MARCA REGISTRADA

LIBRARY OF CONGRESS CATALOGING-IN-PUBLICATION DATA:

Inclán, Jessica Barksdale.
   The matter of Grace / Jessica Barksdale Inclán.
      p. cm.
   "Conversation guide included."
   ISBN 0-451-20575-8 (alk. paper)
      1. Cancer—Patients—Fiction. 2. Female friendship—Fiction. 3. Women—United States—
Fiction. I. Title.

PS3559.N332 M38 2002
813'.6—dc21   2001058713

Printed in the United States of America
Set in Simoncini Garamond
Designed by Ginger Legato

Acknowledgments

This novel could not have been written without my friends Gigi Cummings, Shelley Grant, Ann Cavalli, Meg Bowerman, Margaret Wade, Karen McDonald, Sue Graziano. Despite everything, we make a great team. My writing group read this novel in so many forms, and without Julie Roemer, Marcia Goodman, Keri Mitchell, Joan Kresich, and Gail Offen-Brown, I wouldn't know what to do. Again, Kris Whorton read this manuscript with thought and care, going always above and beyond the call of duty. My love and thanks to Susan Browne. Carolyn Nichols at NAL put in time with several drafts, really pushing me toward the story. I will miss you, Carolyn. And Ellen, I look forward to our work ahead. Pam Bernstein and Jonette Suiter at Pam Bernstein and Associates are great advocates and I appreciate you both.

Finally, my husband, Jesse; my boys, Mitchell and Julien; and my mother, Carole, have been there for it all, my fan club, my great loves. Thank you.

the seasons constant,
the wonder of light
coming over us

—Seamus Heaney, Beowulf

If there were a ghost in the room, *it would look like an eighteen-year-old girl, a girl just off to college. This ghost would be wearing a basketball uniform, one from the mid-seventies, nylon but not baggy, the shorts cut at the hamstrings. She is laughing, pulling her red hair back with a rubber band, adjusting her socks, tying her shoes. Her arms are tan and long, the flesh full and round and muscular. Even now, her jaw is pointed, angled sharp, decisive, though fuller and gentler than in life, certainly not sharp enough to make you step back with horror at the sight of this apparition. In fact, you want to move in, run a finger down the side of her face, remember what you never saw, not in all your days.*

The ghost picks up a basketball, and you remember your friend, the one you and your friends tried to save. When she had her strength, you saw your friend like this, picking up a ball, laughing, arcing the ball up and into a net. You saw her dribble and turn, curve away from an opponent, position herself to connect, and there it was, a score. This ghost knows nothing about these later games. She is on her way to college, ready for her first practice as a USC Trojan. She is going to roll up her childhood and stuff it in the closet.

Just as she turns to leave the room, you realize you would have had to have actually been there, here, back in 1975, back in this attic bedroom, in order to save your friend. You would have had to pull her arm, turn her toward you, and say, "Don't go. Come with me." After this moment, no one could have done anything at all.

The ghost leaves, and you sit on the dusty bed in the attic bedroom of your friend's mother's house. Downstairs, everyone—including your two best friends—is eating rolled and sliced buffet food and talking quietly, leaning against doorjambs, dabbing eyes. The afternoon sun shoots through the small window, the room a cave of early-winter light. And you sit on the bed, and forgive yourself, despite everything.

ONE

"**D**ON'T GO."

"You're being ridiculous."

"I mean it," Felice said. "Don't go." She held on to the smooth wool of Sean's pants, just to the side of his thigh, feeling the warmth of his body under her fingers. They sat together at gate 19 at San Francisco International Airport, huddled on two plastic chairs, their heads almost touching.

"I have to," Sean said, leaning back. "You know that. And anyway, the minute you leave here, you'll forget all about me. It'll be back to normal for you, the boys, James. You're really acting kind of weird."

"Excuse me?" Felice said.

"Well, you are. I told you not to come in. You didn't even have to drive me here. I mean, think of all the trips I've taken before."

Felice Gaitreaux looked up into the eyes of her oldest friend. For a moment she realized why all of his UC Berkeley literature students fell madly in love with him—men and women both, students slumped against their shared office door, swooning even as he reminded them about late homework assignments or essay due dates. When Felice said the same things to her own students, they looked down at their notebooks, scribbling madly, and then stood up and left without even a smile. Sometimes, especially lately, Felice wondered if she should finally request her own office, needing space away from Sean, who was so happy these days. But that was just as weird as moping about Sean leaving, which she knew she clearly was doing, when she hadn't moped once in the twenty years they'd known each other.

"What's wrong?" Sean asked.

Felice shrugged, her shoulders heavy with bones and sadness. "I don't know. Everything. James."

"What did he do?" Sean asked, distracted, looking over his shoulder toward his gate. *He's already left*, thought Felice. *He can't help me now.*

"He's just pulling away. From me. From the boys, and that's what kills me the most. He's never there. Not for swimming. Not for open houses. This spring he was like a ghost dad, a dad only in our imaginations. I barely see him anymore."

"Well, have you two talked about it?"

"Talked? It's more like I say something and he starts baring his teeth like . . . like a monster, and then I shut up. I swear, sometimes I feel like leaving, but it's the boys. They love him, Sean. And I keep thinking maybe he'll go back to normal."

"Aer Lingus flight 650 to Dublin will be boarding in five minutes." The tinny sound of the attendant's voice pulsed through the terminal. Sean pushed his hair back from his face, and Felice closed her eyes, feeling the movement of her heart, the blood circulating in her chest, the tears just under her skin.

"Listen, you aren't working this summer. You guys should plan to go away. Maybe just the two of you. I mean, what about counseling? You've been together so long. You've been with James almost as long as you've been with me!" Sean smiled, and Felice pressed back against her chair, knowing that he was right. She would fight for her boys. For Dylan and Brodie. For the family she and James had made.

The attendant called Sean's row, and he stood up, grabbing his briefcase filled with research on James Joyce, notes for his lecture series, and condoms for his probable adventures, all of which Felice was privy to. Over the years, she and James had gone to parties and dinners at Sean's Berkeley apartment, meeting Gwendolyn, Mary, Bryn, and Sue, woman after woman, each of whom Sean had initially claimed was "it," the one, his soul mate. And yet here he was, twenty years past college, alone, flying off to Dublin to spend another summer searching for what he'd always imagined Felice and James had.

"You be good over there. Call me if anything happens."

"You call me," Sean said. "I've given you my numbers. Call me if anything exciting goes on."

"Nothing good is going to happen this summer. I can feel it in my bones."

Felice walked away from the terminal into the dark tunnel leading to the parking garage, her eyes on the escalator, ground, escalator, the noise of travelers in her ears. She found her Dodge Caravan, her kid car, the car Sean called the vehicle from suburban hell, even though she lived in Oakland. "It might as well be the suburbs," Sean often said. "You drive this horrible thing, go to the club to swim and work out, and shop in the little cutesy Montclair shops. What's the difference?"

Felice put on her seat belt and looked out to the slat of open sky in front of her. *Maybe that's Sean's plane*, she thought, watching a jet head skyward. She imagined being able to pull it down—safely, of course—and make him stay with her. She thought about their one kiss years ago at Shakespeare's Wife, a coffee shop in Palo Alto. As his lips touched hers, slipping to an awkward angle on her lower lip, she realized that what should be there—the fullness of air and heat that came with passion, that came with a kiss—was missing. It was like watching a movie in black and white, all sharp angles and no warmth. Sean had pulled away, sensing it too, and they'd stared at each other, finally smiling, and then gone back to grading papers from the freshman composition classes they TA'd for. That was it.

She started the engine and drove the circles and loops until she reached the pay booth and then she slid out into the full sunlight. As she put on her sunglasses and accelerated onto the 101, she smiled, knowing that even if Sean was gone for the whole summer, she had her girls. She had Grace and Stella and Helen, her best friends. Every summer for over seven years, they'd sat together at the edge of the pool at Oakland View Swim and Tennis Club, watching their children learn to swim, slowly becoming friends, going out at night to movies, calling each other when a child was in trouble, when a husband or partner was completely unreasonable.

She stepped on the gas, knowing all she had to do was pick up the boys from school, drive to the club, and she would feel better about everything. Felice turned on the radio, let Brodie's favorite radio station, KLLC, spill into the car, and tried to not think about James, singing off-key all the way to Oakland.

"Mom," said Brodie, clambering into the car, pulling his seat belt across his body, his brother leaping in next to him. "I need to get a chicken."

"What?" Felice asked, pulling onto Thornhill Boulevard and then the freeway, heading south toward the club for the boys' swim workout.

"I need to mummify a chicken. With salt and bandages."

She grimaced. "Do you actually know how to mummify a chicken?"

"Of course I do," Brodie said, turning to her as if everyone mummified chickens on a regular basis. "Mrs. Dimond gave us instructions and everything. We have to cover it in salt and wrap it up and then dump more salt on it. Then we wait."

"Gross," Dylan said. "What if it comes alive and haunts us?"

"Don't be stupid," Brodie said. "It's for Egyptology week. The best chicken wins a prize."

"Ahhhh!" Dylan held out his arms in a mummy move. "Ahhhh . . ."

"Do you have to start it right away? God, I wonder what your father will say about this." Felice imagined James's disgust as he bent over the sink, saying, "What's this shit?"

She wondered if she could manage to tell him, "That's dinner," without laughing. She wondered if, once he learned about the project, James would be able to say to Brodie, "That's interesting," and mean it. She wondered if James would notice anything at all.

"Of course I have to start it. It's not Egyptology month. It's Egyptology week," Brodie said.

"Ahhh!" moaned Dylan, his outstretched arms banging against Brodie's headrest. Felice looked in the rearview mirror and saw his eyes were closed under his brown bangs, a laugh on his lips.

"Fine," she said. "We'll stop at Safeway after swim workout. But . . . a chicken! How are you graded?"

"Well, the ones that are mummified *best* get A's," Brodie said.

"How can you tell which chicken is mummified best?" she asked, trying to flick away the picture of chicken flesh, holding her breath in as if she already had a whiff of old meat and salt.

"Don't ask," Brodie said. "It's a long story."

"What are these teachers thinking?"

"Well, they can't assign us a human! Do you know what they did with the organs?"

"Yeah, yeah!" Dylan shouted, his eyes wide. "And the brain. They pulled it through their nostrils with a hook!"

"Dylan!" Felice said.

"That's what Mrs. Velasquez told us anyway."

Felice flicked on her turn signal and pulled off the freeway, turning left onto Cypress Road. "I'm glad it's only a week," she said, smiling at Brodie. "There's only so much about the brain I can handle."

Felice pulled into the club's driveway and almost sighed. She could already see Helen and Stella sitting at the edge of the pool—Helen in her ratty Chevy's hat, Stella tan and slim and sexy in her black bangled bikini. Grace was undoubtedly working out in the gym, as she always did once or twice a day, her legs all muscle and bone, her arms wiry and strong. Felice parked the car and the boys ran out, forgetting about the mummy, ready to play in the water with the kids until swim team started, eager to catch up to whatever Eric and Celia and Livie had already started. As she pulled out their gear—the towels, goggles, and fins—Felice knew that right here was where she should have been all day, the sun and warmth and her friends' voices lulling away all traces of the fights she'd been having with James.

As she walked up the path to the entrance, Felice caught brief bits of conversation, the wind blowing sound to pieces before she could understand. The air was a swirl of star jasmine and purple clematis, and she let her free hand rub the tops of Santa Barbara daisies, their petals soft and tiny under her fingers. A child pushed open the glass door and ran by her, laughing, and Felice caught the opening and slipped inside, breathing for what seemed like the first time all day.

Out by the pool, she nodded and smiled to other mothers and then looked to the spot she could navigate in her sleep. "God forbid anyone else tries to claim this spot as their own," Helen always said, and no one ever did; the slice of concrete between the fence and the baby pool was always theirs.

"Hey, guys," Felice said, heading toward the chaise longues Helen and Stella had out for them. "What's going on?"

Helen looked toward Stella, who stood up and walked toward her. Felice almost stopped, not liking how today was already different, how this afternoon no one had waved, beckoned her to hurry back, how no one was smiling or telling a joke. "What is it?" she asked.

Stella put her hand on Felice's arm. "Sit down."

"No." She didn't want any of it, imagining that her own dark feelings had created whatever she was going to hear from Stella. Maybe it would be possible to just walk backward, off the pool deck, out of the club, gathering her boys as she went.

"Hon," Stella said. "I tried to call you all afternoon."

"I did, too," Helen agreed. "Where were you?"

Felice sat down on a chaise, Stella's sun-warm body beside her. "I took Sean to the airport. What's going on? You guys are scaring me."

"Listen," Stella said. "Hon, this isn't good. It's Grace."

"No," Felice said again, feeling how small that word was. It needed to be a bigger word, longer, something that had more force. Maybe that's why people tended to say it more than once, turning it into a nononono, trying to build a fence around what they didn't want.

"Yeah," Helen said. "It's the cancer. It's come back."

"Oh, my God! No way!" Felice said, her words full of breath.

"We can't believe it either," Helen said.

"But Grace always said she was in remission. It isn't fair! Look how long she's survived!" Stella put her arm around Felice, who shook her head. "I don't believe it."

Helen scooted to the edge of her chaise, and the three of them looked out toward the pool. "Who can? She's done so well since her first battle. What was that? Eight years ago? Just before we all met. But we've got to get organized."

"What do you mean?" Felice asked.

"Well, we've got to get some kind of plan together. You know, who's going to take care of Celia when Grace has appointments and treatments? Who's going to drive her to school? All that. Between the three of us, we could probably cover just about everything." Helen began searching through her large black purse for a pad of paper and pen. "I can make a schedule."

"Wait. Where is Grace right now?" Felice asked. "Who brought Celia to workout?"

"Let's slow down," Stella said. "You haven't had time to even think about this. Grace called me in the early afternoon. She's at Stanford Medical Center having some tests run."

"So what do they know?" Felice brought her hand to her stomach and held herself tight, wondering what it would feel like to discover lumps under the skin, pockets of cancer, disease right under the fingertips.

"I guess the cancer from before—the melanoma that was in her liver or on her back or whatever—has metastasized into her lungs. There's a tumor. Or a lesion. Or something. Maybe more than one. I couldn't get it all straight when she called me. We had a really weird connection."

Felice bit her lip, thinking about Grace, her laughter that they could often hear all the way from the parking lot. When she first heard that laugh as she lay half asleep on a chaise, she'd imagined whoever pushed the sound into the air was a substantial person, heavy, tall, full of flesh. But when she'd opened her eyes and turned her head to the side, there was Grace, tall and lanky and pared as close to the bone as anyone she'd ever met. And while Grace's voice and body didn't seem to match, her laugh was like the rest of her, open, optimistic, interested in everything, even while all along there was this disease lurking inside her, ready to swallow her up.

"So what does Kathleen want to do? What's her plan?" Felice asked. Stella and Helen gave each other a glance.

"Well," Helen said, brushing a gnat off her thigh.

"She's working out right now," Stella said. "We didn't get much of a chance to talk with her. Hon, we will."

"She's working out?" Felice asked.

"Yeah," Helen replied. "Working *out*. Pain in the ass."

Felice wanted to stand up and shake off those words like clothes, slipping out of the situation and pulling on another. Kathleen, Grace's partner of seven years, was working out while Grace endured tests at Stanford. No one was taking care of Grace at all.

"So wait. Is her mother coming up?"

"You know Grace. She hasn't told anyone but us. So I'm thinking of calling Doris. If Kathleen isn't going to, and I know Grace won't, someone should. Doris needs to know."

No one said anything, and then the pool was full of noise, the children jumping in the pool for workout, Tony, the coach, blowing his whistle and barking out orders. Eric waved at Stella, and Livie pretended not to see Helen at all, but then laughed when Brodie and Dylan pushed her in the water. After listening to Tony, all the children began to swim in orderly lines, their hands flinging in arcs around them, their kicks random fountains. Just like that, life went back to normal, the day smoothing itself out despite Grace's illness. *Is there anything*, Felice wondered, *that could make it stop altogether?*

"I'd be dead already," Helen said. "I know it. I'd be flat on my back in bed, crying my eyes out and feeling sorry for myself. I'd have redone my will and called in the troops to take care of my every need. All of you would hate me by now."

Stella crossed her legs, swinging a tanned foot back and forth, a brass anklet jangling. "I know. Me, too. But that's not Grace. Apparently during the last bout of cancer, she took care of herself as long as possible. She called Doris only when it got really bad."

"So is remission a real word?" Felice asked. She turned to Stella, who shrugged. Felice could almost imagine Grace's cancer cells hiding behind organs and veins, waiting for a chance to jump out and attack.

"Shit," Helen said, finally finding a pen and a piece of paper. She quickly made a grid, marking the days and hours of the week. "So what are we going to do?"

"Will she *let* us do anything?" Stella asked.

"She can't do it like she did last time. I hate to say it—no, that's a lie. I want to say it. So here it is: Kathleen's not going to do what she needs to. Look at her now, inside on the StairMaster. So we have to pick up the slack. And we can call some of those women she plays weekend basketball with at Holy Names College. You know. The basketball league? I've met one of them. Drew. I think they even went to USC together."

For a strange second, Felice felt herself prickle with anger, silly with jealousy that her friends hadn't decided to help her in the same way. Here she was, her husband angry and awful. Just this morning she'd said, "Don't forget to pick up your dry cleaning," and James had flung out, "Shut up," as he'd walked to the door. Didn't they want to save her?

She knew she was being ridiculous, but she almost wanted to pull on Stella and Helen as she had on Sean that morning. She thought of another word that needed to be bigger: me. Memememe, a selfish fence Felice was building so she didn't have to see that Grace, one of her best friends, was really sick. Dying maybe. Felice leaned her hand into her palm and started to cry.

"Don't," Stella said. "Oh, hon. Don't do that. I've been crying enough for everyone." But Felice kept at it, even as she felt their hands on her back. As she wept, all she could think about was Grace in her chaise longue, smiling at her and then laughing out loud, her head bent back, her happiness above them all.

That night at home, James at work, the boys still red from the water and exercise, their hair barely dry from their showers, Felice served up a frozen pizza and a carrot salad. On the cutting board, a whole chicken sat salted and wrapped in cheesecloth.

"Gross!" Dylan picked up a shred of carrot with his fork. "What is this?"

"It's skin from the carrot man," Brodie said. "Mom killed him outside and peeled his skin for dinner. The rest of him is for tomorrow!"

"Jeez, Brodie," Felice said, putting down her glass. "It's carrot salad, Dylan. You've had it before."

"I'm not going to eat the carrot man!" Dylan pushed himself back from the table and crossed his arms.

"Fine. Just eat your pizza and drink your milk."

Dylan looked at her, making certain she was serious. "Okay," he said, picking up his slice of pepperoni pizza. "At least this is good."

In five minutes, both boys were done. They cleared their plates and went into Dylan's room for an hour of play. For the last few weeks they had been building a Lego village on the floor, a structure so large that Felice had to skirt the edges of the room just to make Dylan's bed and put away his clothing. As she sat at the kitchen table, she could hear them playing, taking up the voices of the small Lego people who lived in the village, imagining a world they created.

Felice stood up and carried the plates to the granite counters, the kitchen just remodeled the year before, a Sub-Zero refrigerator, granite, oak, skylight, chrome. Everything looked so good, straight out of *House & Garden*, but now she sighed, feeling as gray as the countertop and just as cold. Where was James? And did she really want to know? Felice turned on the tap and began to rinse the plates, thinking, *What is Grace going to do? What am I?* as the dead carrot man swirled in her sink.

Long after Brodie and Dylan had gone to bed, Felice sat up in bed reading, her eyes on the words, her mind somewhere out on streets and roads, in rooms she'd never been in, trying to imagine where James was so late. Finally, she heard his keys on the counter, his shoes on the hardwood, his slow walk into their room. Felice put down the latest *Beowulf* translation and looked up at her husband as he opened the door.

"Where have you been?"

"Where do you think?" He pulled his tie from around his neck with a slick hiss and flung it on the bed.

"Oh, I don't know. I just remembered you telling the boys yesterday you'd come watch them work out. Did *you* remember that?" Felice crossed her arms, the book a tent on her knees. For a moment she wondered if the words from the old poem—short, choppy, and violent, a terrible monster coming each night to kill everyone—were preferable to James's irritation, the shake of his head, the breath pushed between his teeth.

"Yeah. I'll talk to them in the morning," he said. "I had a meeting, okay?"

"So this big project is more important than your boys. Is that what this means? Do you realize what you tell them each day with your body? Your actions? What does it say when the last words they hear from you are 'Shut up!' "

James unbuttoned his shirt. "I was saying that to you."

"So *did* you get the dry cleaning?"

"Fuck you, Felice." James stared at her, and she realized,

again, how beautiful he was, even though he wasn't anything like the student she'd fallen in love with her freshman year, eyeing him for almost the entire semester in Western Civ before finding the nerve to ask him to study with her for the final. He had red hair, not as red as Grace's, more auburn, more brown, and not a freckle on his skin, his brown eyes a surprise if you saw his hair first. He worked out in the city at lunch, his arms and legs solid, his shoulders broad, and she could almost remember when she desired him.

"Nice," Felice said, suddenly so tired.

"Anything else you want to bring up? Do you have something else to say? Any more questions? Come on! I'm ready to answer. I'll tell you everything you want to know."

Felice ran her hand across her book's smooth dust jacket. When she was a child, she spent hours reading, not wanting to be caught up in the world of her household, the cleaning, the cooking, the fighting. She went out to the backyard with her brother, Gage, but she read while he played in the sandbox. It was easier to press herself between words and become something else, to go to other people's lives than to live her own. Like it would be now, James down to his boxer shorts, his hands on his hips, the truth just inside the barrier of his skin. Felice didn't want to know. Not yet. Not now.

At her silence, James shook his head. "Classic, Felice. You never want to talk about anything. You just sit there with a book. You're married to ideas, not me." James walked into the bathroom, and she heard him flip up the toilet seat and then the loud, angry stream of urine into the bowl.

Felice pulled her pillow under her head and curled up on her side of the bed. She'd read the words James had wanted her to hear a thousand times before. After all, she'd completed her dissertation on Guinevere, the great adulteress, and Felice kept inside the pain and sorrow of her betrayal of Arthur. Besides, Felice knew, it wouldn't take a Ph.D. to see that James was having an affair. He didn't smell like perfume; he didn't have lipstick on his collar; but the very air around him said goodbye.

James turned on the shower, and Felice closed her eyes, and the day, just like the truth about James and the truth about Grace, slowly slipped away.

That night Felice dreamed about a boy from her childhood. He was the same as he had been twenty-five, thirty years ago, the sleek brown boy with luminous green eyes, skin smooth and delicious enough to lick. Of course, when she was twelve or seven or five, she knew only that he was cute, older, the brother of a chubby boy her age. Her friend's brother, this boy with her now, had always been one of the older boys. A boy who paid no attention to her or her group of friends. A boy who became a lifeguard during the summers, applied to college, and then disappeared into his own life somewhere. By the time Felice was grown, her body smooth and sloped and curved, a lifeguard whistle around her own neck, she had all but forgotten him. And as she left the pool, disappeared into her life, she never thought of him. At all. Ever.

But here he was now, in her dream, the boy, in his orange Speedo, standing at the bottom of Sycamore Lane, the steep street her best friend, Rachel, had lived on. And there Felice was, in a black swimsuit, and when she walked to him, there was no surprise, only a sense of relief and recognition, his face smiling into hers, the love between them immense.

They didn't talk, but he convinced her they could swim the butterfly stroke up the road, even though there was no water, even though it was a road that made your calves ache while walking. And they moved together, arms, shoulders, back, hips, feet rolling like the hill they were climbing, perfect bodies against the terrain. Once, halfway up, she stopped, pulled on his arm, said, "I can't do this. I can't go on."

He smiled, said, "Come on. Of course you can." And they continued. They kept bending and kicking against the water/air under them, her dream ending with them stroking to the top, her eyes opening to the flood of joy at having finally found him.

Later still, the sky just turning gray, Felice awoke, her arms around James, his face pressed against her neck, his hands slipping up and down her sides, feeling her, really touching her. But as she tried to wake up, to truly feel their sex, it was over, James breathing harshly and then relaxing, turning away from her without saying her name once.

Felice turned to the clock, five a.m., and she knew she wouldn't fall back to sleep. She spun toward James, listening to his steady breathing. *No wonder,* she thought, realizing he'd been asleep the whole time. He didn't say her name because as he was in her, holding her, kissing her neck, he didn't know who she was at all. And she knew that, when he woke up, James wouldn't remember a thing.

James was showered and gone by the time she woke the boys, and when Felice returned from dropping them off at school, there was a message from Stella. As she dialed Stella's number, she wondered if this would be the first of many imperative phone calls, her fingers forever nervous on the numbers, knowing that this was how bad news was spread.

"What?" she asked as soon as Stella answered.

"She's fine. She's fine. It's just that she said no," Stella said.

"No?"

"Yeah. No. To everything. Rides. Food. Visits. The whole thing. She almost laughed at me."

"So what are we going to do? How long can she hold it together?" Felice asked. She picked up a rag and began wiping down the counter, colored marshmallow flecks of Lucky Charms everywhere. She eyed the shrouded chicken, bringing her nose close to it, smelling nothing but salt.

"I don't know. If I know Grace, she'll do everything herself until the last minute. And that can't be good for her."

Felice put the orange juice away, noticing James had drunk a small glass, taking nothing else, not even sitting down to read the paper. Maybe he had remembered what had happened in bed and couldn't bear to look at her. "So what went on the last time? You said her mother came up."

"I'm pretty sure that's what happened. I think her ex-husband, Roger, came up to look after Celia. But that's all I know. She never talks about it, does she?"

"No. It's all kind of vague. I even thought her cancer started on her face. But you said it was on her back."

Stella sighed. "I don't know. It was before we knew her. Obviously, we've got the story mixed up. You can't know everything about a person."

Felice nodded, her face moving against the phone, knowing that Stella was so right. For instance, how could James kiss her and hold her just after swearing at her? How could he love the boys and hate her? How could he want to leave but still be here? Felice swallowed, wanting to ask Stella these questions, but she couldn't, knowing that Stella and her husband, Aaron, were in the kind of marriage she herself had never had.

"Tell me about it," Felice finally said.

"You're not talking about Grace."

"I meant in general. You know."

"Yeah."

"So what about Kathleen?" Felice asked quickly. "Why do we think she won't help out? They've been together forever. She's practically Celia's other parent. She's bound to pick up some slack."

Stella was silent for a moment. Felice could hear the sound of AM morning shows in the background. "Oh, Felice. I wasn't supposed to say anything. Kathleen asked me not to. But just before this cancer thing, Kathleen was ready to move out. They'd had a huge fight, and Kathleen was starting to pack up. I guess it was about something that's been going on for a while. Grace's, um, habits. All the working out and stuff. The late nights at the gym. But barely a week after the fight, Grace found out about the cancer. Kathleen let me know she's not going anywhere now, but I don't think she'll be happy about all this."

"Oh. I didn't know about that. But Grace never says anything. Did you ever notice that she asks us all the questions? We never learn anything about her."

"I think Grace knows more about me than Aaron does. Really."

"I believe you. . . . So we've just got to keep an eye on her." Felice put her hand on her chest, full suddenly of a vision of Celia without Grace, of all of them without Grace. She realized she hadn't told James about this, and now she wondered if he would even care.

"I'm going to call Doris. Grace gave me her phone number once when she went home to visit," Stella said.

"That's a good idea. Pretty soon Grace'll be on some kind of chemo or something. You don't just bounce back and go on a twelve-mile run after that."

"I'd move my mother in. I'd have her on the phone in a heart-beat. I don't think I'd even have to call. She'd just know. I guess Grace and Doris don't have that kind of relationship."

"Grace never talks about her," Felice said, thinking back to their conversations around the pool. "I think a couple of times she's told me how ditzy her mother is and how, well, Republican, but other than that, nothing."

"Yeah. That's not much to go on. Listen, I've got to go. I'll let you know what Doris says, though. And don't worry. We'll get it together."

Felice hung up the phone and looked around her perfect kitchen. What would her children do if she was diagnosed with cancer, sequestered in hospital rooms, pumped full of solutions and poison drugs, her hair falling out? What would James do? Would he worry about her? Mourn for her? Would he turn to her as he'd done last night? Or would he be angry, his perfect banker's work life interrupted? He'd have to take days off to drive her to the hospital for treatments, tend to her as she threw up and then tossed feverishly in bed. Felice was pretty sure he'd forgotten how to care for the boys, this man who used to walk the hallways with them as they cried at night. Even with their current nights of fighting, Felice wasn't sure what he was going to do, how he felt. And she didn't know about herself either, still loving that boy in Western Civ, his red hair, his perfect body, the way he turned to her and said, "Can I borrow your notes?" That morning twenty years ago, Felice knew that James must be the one because she had the feeling—the exact feeling she had in her dream last night—that for the first time she was doing everything perfectly right.

TWO

ઉઝ

O N THE BACK PAGE OF HER WORN ADDRESS BOOK, Stella kept a
list of her friends' important numbers and dates, the names
of their spouses, and their children's names, ages, and
birthdays—most of the information long since memorized. She
rarely even looked at the page now, knowing Helen and Felice
and Grace so well that they would remind her themselves when
their birthdays were approaching, but she'd never dialed this
number before. She scanned through T, U, and V and found
Grace's mother's phone number. Doris. Doris White.

Stella tried not to think as she picked up the phone again and
dialed, knowing that what she was about to say was inappropri-
ate, rude, painful—all that was bad about phone calls on terrible
subjects rolled into one. "Hi," she imagined herself saying.
"Grace has cancer again." Doris would have every right in the
world to hang up on her; after all, Stella was no one to Doris. She
wasn't a family member or a lover or a doctor. Someone else
should call. Even though Kathleen said she would stay with
Grace, it seemed only her body was really there, not her heart and
certainly not her head.

"Hello?" a woman answered, her voice like a dried lettuce leaf,
brittle and almost transparent, ready to crumble at any minute.
As Stella listened to the echo of the voice in her own head, she already heard some kind of past damage and sorrow, and part of
her wanted to hang up, as she had in grammar school when she
made prank calls.

"Um, hi. Hi. Doris?"

"Yes? This is Doris."

"Doris, I'm a good friend of Grace's. We actually met once a long time ago for about a second. My name's Stella. Stella Steinberg."

Doris was silent for a minute, seeming to think. "Oh, Stella! Grace talks so much about you and all your friends. Helen and Felice, right? You three are so important to her. All those fun things you do. I feel like I know all of you really well. Grace says you all laugh and laugh."

Stella found herself gaping into the receiver. Grace only mentioned her mother now and then, casually, accidentally almost, as if the two of them rarely talked. But here Doris knew about them all. When had Grace told her? If they talked this much, why didn't Doris know about the cancer? And then Stella felt stupid, seeing that Doris probably already did know, and here Stella was, all nose and butt, trying to put herself into the situation.

"Oh, yeah. We are. We're really good friends."

"So what can I do for you, Stella? It's not Grace, is it? Or Celia?" Doris said, her voice quavering on the names.

Stella felt herself almost nod and shake her head at the same time. So Doris *didn't* know. "Well, it's not a total emergency. I just thought I should call you. I don't think Kathleen called you, did she?"

"No, she didn't. What is it?"

"It's Grace. There's something the matter with Grace. She went to Stanford, and I'm so sorry to tell you this, but I think you need to know. Her cancer has come back."

Stella pressed the phone against her ear, trying to hear clues from the other end, tears, sighs, the phone dropping. Stella finally heard tiny breath sounds and then Doris said, "It couldn't have come back, Stella. The doctors got it all the last time. They gave her almost a one hundred percent chance of nonrecurrence. And they don't like to say things like that, believe me."

Again, Stella shook her head. "Really? I thought she was in remission."

"Oh, no!" said Doris. "They got the spot off her nose and then dealt with some nodes, and that was it. She had some great treatment and a great doctor. What was his name? Karl, I think. Anyway, she was given a clean bill of health. That was over eight years ago!"

This mother didn't really know her daughter at all, Stella thought, remembering the conversations the four of them had by the pool, Grace saying, "I thought I was going to die. Sometimes I still worry about it." Grace told them about some spot that started on her back and moved inside, under the skin to her liver, every dark patch of skin suddenly suspect, the nonstop blood tests and protocols, and the chemo, interferon, radiation, herbal remedies, acupuncture, holistic doctors. Stella had never heard about the spot on her nose or the promise of nonrecurrence. And yet Doris thought it was over? "Well, all I can tell you is what Grace told me, Doris. She called me from the hospital. She went down to Stanford, and they found some spots or tumors—I don't know the word—on her lungs. She stayed over for treatment. I just know it's hard on her and on Celia. Kathleen isn't . . . she isn't . . ."

"I know they're having trouble. Grace told me about it last week. She even mentioned moving down south to be closer to me," Doris said. "But I'm sure I'm not telling you anything you don't know."

"I didn't hear anything about her moving. I just thought you'd want to know about the diagnosis. From what I heard, it's not good." Stella realized she was adding detail, trying to make Doris see how important it was that she got up here, took charge now that Kathleen didn't seem to care.

"I'll give her a call right away. This is hard to take in. I don't know what to think. I'm really surprised she didn't call me first, though. We just talked a little bit ago. She didn't even mention that she was feeling unwell," Doris said, "but thank you for calling, Stella. I really appreciate it. Grace is so lucky to have you."

Stella said goodbye and hung up, anxiety pulling at her mouth. She sat down at the kitchen table and began to cry, the way she'd been crying off and on since Grace first called her from Stanford. And truthfully, she'd hoped that Doris would somehow make everything better, but it was clear Doris didn't understand anything. Doris acted like Grace maybe had a flu or an infection, something that would go away with time and prayer.

Stella wiped under her eyes with her fingers. She'd found herself having to reapply her mascara and eyeliner almost every hour, often feeling like a raccoon, with dark circles drooping onto her cheeks in a weepy mask. She didn't know why she even bothered to look good, especially right now, and she put her head in her hands and rubbed her mascara into great black rounds.

Finally her tears stopped, and she stood up and pushed open the kitchen door, then walked toward the redwood planter boxes Aaron had built. She put her nose close to the mint pelargonium before pulling through leggy Snow in Summer with her slim fingers. She pinched the tops of the plants with her nails, feeling the juicy green on her skin, moving on to lamb's ears, fire penstemon, Spanish lavender, working one planter and then the next, the overgrown, the dead, and the spent at her feet.

As Stella worked, she thought how unfair all of this was for Grace. Once, she had told Stella that she was positive she could never live through chemotherapy again. "It was the interferon that was the worst," she said. "I had a terrible allergic reaction, and they had to restrain my arms because I almost scratched my skin off. I'd rather die than do that again."

So when Grace had phoned Stella from Stanford just days ago, the first thing Stella thought of was Grace's skin in loose itchy folds peeling from her arms. The call itself had been staticky and metallic, as if Grace were on a cell phone and not a phone booth in the hospital cafeteria. But Stella thought it was probably just her own hearing, her way of avoiding the fact that the cancer had shown up again as little tumors in Grace's lungs.

"Stella," Grace had said, "I need you to do me a favor. I'm at Stanford for tests."

"What's wrong? Why?"

"I've been having some trouble when I exercise. But listen, I need you to do something for me."

"Of course."

"I was wondering if you could call Kathleen at work. I need her to pick Celia up from school and take her to the club. I called just a second ago, and she's with a client. She couldn't talk."

"Hon, didn't you tell her where you were calling from? Didn't she know where you were going?" she asked, picturing Grace alone in waiting rooms, naked and cold on examination tables, poked with needles, bombarded with X rays.

"I didn't want to upset her. You know how she hates it when I bring up my medical history. So I really need you to call her."

"Of course I will. Whatever you need. But what's going on?"

Grace didn't say anything, and Stella imagined she heard cars, a police siren, loud voices in the background, the hum of the phone so intense. "It came back. The cancer's back."

"What?" Stella's lungs were suddenly empty.

"I can feel it. I've been feeling it for weeks. I'll be lying on my bed and it is pressing on me, heavy. And when I'm running or lifting weights, I can't get any air, like it's stuck there. So I called my doctor from before, Dr. Karl, and he got me in here for tests. I've got tumors in my lungs. It's not good."

Stella had felt more than air leave her as Grace spoke. Maybe it was hope and happiness and all the things she imagined life to hold. It was her vision of parents seeing their children grow up and children taking care of their parents as they grew old and feeble. It was the feeling that pushed against her throat when her husband, Aaron, came home and sat with their son, Eric, and her at the table, the glow of the warm light on the oak table, the soft heat in the air from the oven, outside street light shining on the smooth ash floors Aaron had laid himself. It was the way she felt at the club, surrounded by laughter as Helen told a joke, Grace slapping her thigh, Felice chuckling. It was watching all their children—Eric and Celia and Brodie and Dylan and Livie—swimming across the pool, little arms working so hard. It was everything that made Stella who she was, right now, and suddenly it was leaving, a leak, a hole, a tear in the fabric she had carefully pulled together. "Oh, God, Grace," she said finally, unconsciously and by rote crossing herself and finding her brain turn to prayer even as she listened to the electric phone noise. Grace had nothing but skin over bone, so intense was her fight against the cancer the first time. How could she possibly battle the disease again when she had no reserves at all? *Dear Mary, Mother of God, please help her, please help her*, Stella prayed, breathing in her own sadness. "I am so sorry. I am so sorry. What can I do?"

"Now don't get all in a twist," Grace had said. "I'm not even close to checking out. I've survived this before. You know that. I'm not going anywhere. And now there's so much they can do for me. I'm going to talk to my doctor in a minute. He's going to try to get me back into the drug protocols. There are so many new drugs they need to test. Don't worry. I just need you to call Kathleen, okay?"

"All right. Should I call anyone else? Your mother? You need someone to help you through this."

Grace fell silent again, and Stella imagined she was counting off who could know and who could not, considering how much vulnerability she could stand. Despite the fact she seemed so frail, as if she might suddenly tip over, Grace was strong. She knew how much pity she could take. "Just tell the girls. The 'pool honeys,' as Aaron calls us. I may talk to my college friend Drew, but I'll do that later."

"Sure, Grace. All right. But wait, hon. Should I come down and pick you up? You can't drive home by yourself after all those tests. Someone should be with you."

"I'm fine. I'm just the same as I was yesterday, but now I know what the shortness of breath means. I'll be home later, maybe tomorrow. Tell Kathleen I'll call her tonight from the hospital."

"I will." Stella paused. "I love you."

"I love you, too."

Grace had hung up, leaving Stella hanging on to the phone as if expecting further explanation. She rubbed her face, her own skin feeling distant, as if she was trying to revive another person.

Finally, she called Kathleen at her veterinary clinic. Stella listened to canned music while she was on hold, a series of songs featuring barking dogs. It was a wonder, she thought, that Kathleen kept any of her clients.

"Kathleen. It's Stella."

"What is it, Stella?" Kathleen said quickly, as if she were looking at a dozen charts and penciling in details: Doberman, age six, duodenal ulcers.

"I just got a call from Grace. She went down to Stanford for some tests."

Kathleen sighed. "She called you. She called you to tell you this."

"Well, she called you first, but she didn't want to leave a message with your secretary. They've . . . there are some tumors or something."

Stella heard papers flipping, a clipboard slammed to the counter. "Where is she now?"

"At the hospital, I think. Oncology. She's waiting to talk with that doctor. The one from before."

"Karl."

"You know him?" Stella asked.

"No. I never met him. Not once. Just the other night, though, I heard Grace talking to someone. She said it was Dr. Karl. She didn't tell me why."

"So I guess she needs you to pick up Celia at school. I could do it, though, Kathleen. I could do it for you."

For a moment all Stella could hear was Kathleen's breathing, slow and quiet, nothing like Stella would expect if she'd just heard the same news about Aaron or Eric or any other member of her family. "No. I'll do it. Listen, Stella, thanks. Thanks for calling. Okay?"

"Sure. And, Kathleen?"

"Yes?"

"If you need me, just let me know, all right?"

There was a pause. Stella heard dogs yapping in the background, the murmur of animal lovers' voices, *Good Tigger. Good doggie.* "I'm sure I will, Stella. Thanks. And, Stella?"

"What?"

"Don't worry. Don't worry about any of this, okay?"

She listened, stunned. When she'd first dialed Kathleen's number, Stella imagined she and Kathleen would cry together, wail at the unfairness of life, console each other over the months that were to come.

"Yeah," Stella mumbled, and Kathleen hung up. And as if nothing was out of order, Celia appeared for workout the next day, Grace showed up at the pool, her bags full of her workout gear, swimsuit, and goggles, and life went on, everything seeming normal when, in fact, nothing was at all.

Now, all the planter boxes neat and trimmed, Stella bent down and swept up stems and leaves with her hands, dumping them in the compost bucket by the door. She stood up straight and eyed her yard, wondering what needed fertilizing, how many holes Eric had dug to make caves for his army men. There was an overgrown scraggle of forget-me-nots by the fence, and the foxgloves needed to be cut back, their long wands of flowers dried and full of seeds. A yard was so easy, really. Yes, things grew wild and developed powdery mildew or a fungus, but there always seemed to be the right spray, the right solution, the perfect pruner for that wayward branch. Nothing about Grace was going to be easy—Stella knew that already. Her conversation with Kathleen had been as confusing as the one with Doris just minutes ago. Kathleen seemed curiously unmoved, uninterested, already gone. Doris either really didn't know or was pretending not to care. But in one way, at least, she was right—Grace didn't seem to be that sick. Coming home from the hospital after one quick night, the only sign of her diagnosis and treatment was the Band-Aids on her thin arms from IVs and chemotherapy. It wouldn't be the end of it, though. Stella knew enough about cancer to understand that.

Stella went back into the kitchen, propping the door open to let in more of the spring air. She opened the fridge wide and stared into it despite the waste of energy. There were enough eggs and fresh spinach and cheese, and she decided to prepare a vegetarian casserole for Celia and Kathleen, knowing Grace would never touch it, or anything, not just because she didn't like dairy products but because Stella had never seen her eat one thing. Not even eating was easy for Grace, because her stomach was a mess of scars from her prior treatments. *But at least Celia will eat tonight*, Stella thought. *At least I can do that.*

"How is Grace today?" Stella's mother asked.

"I called her this morning, and Kathleen told me she was out on a run," Stella said, blowing on the cup of instant coffee her mother had prepared for her.

"Oh, I forgot you like milk. Let me get you some." Joyce opened the fridge and brought out a carton of milk. "It's the lactose-free kind. For your father. But you can't taste the difference in coffee."

Stella smiled and moved her cup toward her mother. Her father ate hot dogs at ball games with Aaron and drank a forbidden glass of beer with his friends on the weekends at the local Alameda bar, but Joyce plugged on, guarding his cholesterol, blood pressure, blood sugar, and ulcer, buying olestra and Egg Beaters and imitation bacon. "It's fine, Mom."

Joyce put the milk away and sat back down. Aaron always said Stella looked just like her mother, both with the same dark eyes and surprisingly light hair. When Stella was little, she loved to sit by Joyce as she brushed out her long hair at night, the necessary one hundred strokes everyone believed would make hair healthy. Her mother would say, "Give me your wrist," and Stella would watch her dab liquid next to the cross of blue veins on Stella's thin wrist.

"Now smell," Joyce said, and she would close her eyes and breathe in, seeing flowers and spices and women in ball gowns behind her eyelids. Her mother would smile and then turn back to the mirror, rubbing Noxzema on her face, a perfect mask, and

Stella would ask for some, rubbing the waxy cream into her own cheeks, hoping that one day she could sit at a vanity table with her own daughter, surrounded by crystal bottles and amazing creams that would keep them both beautiful.

Joyce was still beautiful, her blond hair gray, but long and neat, swept up in a tight French twist at the back of her head. But instead of the red, orange, and black leather pumps she wore when Stella was a child, she wore blue Keds. Her crisp dress and apron had been replaced with a 49ers sweatshirt and soft denim pants.

"So what is Grace going to do?" Joyce sipped her coffee. "What about Celia?"

"I don't know, Mom. I really hoped Doris would come up right away. You know I called her. I asked Grace when her mother was coming up, but she didn't even answer me. I don't get it."

Joyce nodded. "I don't either, but you never know what goes on inside a family. It's like a private little world. But you'd think with cancer . . ."

"I know. I know. We're all freaked out about it. But Celia's fine for now. After all, Kathleen's still there. And Grace really seems okay, Mom. She's still working out and sitting by the pool with us. And can you believe this? Not a bit of her hair has fallen out! In a way, it's like there's nothing wrong except, of course, there is," Stella said, shaking her head.

"Well, it's all about attitude. Remember how long your aunt Dorothy held on. Ten years. Anything's possible with the right outlook."

"Helen said that, too, but I'm sure I would be dead already."

Joyce put down her cup. "No, you wouldn't. Look how well you recovered from Eric's birth."

"That's different." But Stella understood what her mother was saying. Eric had been overdue and big and her labor complicated, the eventual C-section messy, the blood loss enormous, the incision infected. Ten days after he was born, she came home, pale, depressed, anemic, exhausted, full of the knowledge that this was her one and only child. And even with that knowledge, Stella had been ready to offer him up to the first taker, so desperate was she for sleep. In a way, even though she had initially wanted three or perhaps four children, she was almost grateful she'd never have to be the mother of an infant again. "I knew I would get better, Mom. I knew Eric would eventually start sleeping. Or at least you or Aaron would cart me away to the insane asylum. But Grace . . ."

"I know. But these new treatments they're always coming out with can do wonders. Maybe she could get on some drug trial. She's at Stanford, after all."

"That's what happened before, and look how great she did after that. The doctor she had before, Dr. Karl, is helping her again. She told us he runs some special protocols, stuff like that. She's so confident. Every day she just goes on as if none of this were happening. But the rest of us. Celia. Kathleen. I can't imagine what it will be like without her. She's the glue. She brought and keeps us all together."

Joyce sat back in her chair. It had taken a while before Stella felt comfortable talking about Grace and Kathleen to her mother, much less her father, who still used words like *fag* and *dyke*. None of her family, including Joyce, had really liked Aaron at all when she first brought him home, short and Jewish to boot. "You're in love with a Jewish carpenter?" her sister, Stacey, howled. "A Jewish carpenter? Isn't that some kind of bumper sticker slogan? God, Dad is going to kill you."

Her father, Dave, a Catholic of long standing, shook his head. "How disappointing," was all he said. As he walked away into his bedroom, Stella wondered if he was going to pull out his rosary and pray, hoping for a Catholic carpenter, a Protestant carpenter, any other reasonably intelligent Christian carpenter, someone other than the Jewish one she'd found.

But Aaron, bright and funny, sat at her father's table despite Dave's glower, complimented Joyce's holiday ham, decorated for Easter with pineapple slices and cloves, and asked for seconds. "Ah," he'd say, serving himself another large slice. "The meat of my people."

He teased Stacey about her boyfriend Jesus Morales (Mexican but at least Catholic), and sat with Dave during 49ers games. At night, at Aaron's house, the house they lived in now, he made love to Stella, and she sighed into the darkness, hoping for more and longer and forever. And when Eric was a baby, after his bath, Aaron held his son against his chest, under his shirt. Eric gurgled and blew bubbles, and Stella would wonder how, after dating all sorts of men who only wanted her legs or breasts or face, she'd found Aaron, who thought she was beautiful, even at night when he couldn't see a thing.

Now Dave, retired and home all day, often called for Aaron instead of Stella, consulting his son-in-law on roofs, shower tiles, hardwood floors, and living room additions. It was as if her father's disappointment had turned into appreciation and love, the hard times of Stella and Aaron's early courtship all but evaporated. But Stella knew, if she thought about it long enough, she could still feel her anger at her father; she could imagine what she might have done, turning away from her family, ignoring her religion, her upbringing, her old life because she loved Aaron that much. *Thank God Aaron is a better person than I am.*

And even after all these years, Stella still felt her chest fill with amazement—the utter surprise and disbelief—that she'd been able to find someone to build a life for her, after all.

Stella sighed and nodded at her mother, knowing that Joyce had long ago fallen in love with Aaron and then Grace, wanting to know about Celia and even Kathleen. "What I mean, Mom, is that it's going to be as hard for Kathleen as it would be for Aaron, you know?"

Her mother bit her lip at the right corner as she always did when she was thinking. Sometimes Stella would see a slash of red lipstick on her mother's front teeth and wonder what she had been planning. "It is going to be hard for Kathleen. And Celia. If it happens. But you've got to have faith, honey. Just pray for Grace, and if she does well, so will everyone else."

Stella nodded and sipped her coffee, wishing she had some answer she could take up to Grace and roll out like a perfect map, showing her friend the way back to health. Usually, she was able to make things better, smooth over Eric's upset, caress Aaron into sleep after a hard day, fix her mother's anxiety over kitchen repairs or her sister's problems. But as she sat in Joyce's kitchen, Stella knew all she would really be able to do was watch.

After visiting her mother, Stella drove across the Park Street Bridge and up to Eric's school, where he sat on a bench like a toad, his arms folded around his backpack, his face closed and dark.

"What is this?" she asked after he was sitting down and buckled in. "Did you have a bad day?"

"Mom. It's not about school," Eric said, whining. "It's swim team. I don't want to go today."

"Why?" Stella looked in her sideview mirror and then pulled into traffic.

"I just don't." He turned to the window and crossed his arms over his chest.

"Well, that's not enough for me to take you home now, honey. You've got to give me a reason."

"I just *don't*!" Stella could hear the tears in his throat. She knew the corners of his mouth were pulling and twitching. In the year since he turned eight, he refused to cry, as if some man thing switched on and overcame him. Only as the last resort would he let the tears fall, and then he would wipe them away angrily with his fists.

Stella drifted in traffic, wondering what she should do. Part of her needed to get up to the club for herself, desperate to sit among Grace and Helen and Felice, wanting to talk about everything but the illness, needing to watch Grace and see how she was doing. Despite the cancer, there would be laughter and teasing and news, Grace's head thrown back, her laugh hard and strong. Except, Stella wondered, what on earth was she thinking? Weren't the club and the pool supposed to be for Eric? Wasn't that why they went up there every afternoon? It wasn't supposed to be about her.

Here her child was miserable, something big caught in his throat, some trouble with another child or maybe even Tony. What was the right decision? Stella pulled over, turning into a parking lot, and shut off the engine. She sat back in her seat and looked over at Eric, who was pretending to study the Safeway shoppers.

"Can you at least tell me why? Then I'll know what's bothering you. Maybe I can fix it."

"You won't want to," he said, bringing his hand to his face and rubbing tears he didn't want his mother to see. "You won't *do* anything."

She felt herself start, hurt that Eric didn't see how every minute of her life was about protecting him, helping him, making sure he was happy. She thought of the lists on her fridge of baseball camps and swim team rosters and art classes. She couldn't count the hours spent at his school, in meetings with teachers, teaching physical-movement classes to bored and snotty kids, helping the sisters with the yearly flea market. But why would he notice all that? Why would anything be more important to him than his feelings, the way he felt now . . . and now . . . and now? Just like a kid. Just like she had been.

"Try me," she said. "We don't have to go to swim team. I just want to know. And maybe I can help."

Eric turned to her, his face flushed and puffy. He looked at her for a few seconds and then said, "It's Celia."

"Celia? What do you mean?"

"You won't believe me."

"Of course I will, honey. Just tell me."

He scrunched his eyes tight and kept silent. Finally he said, "She's teasing me all the time. She says, 'You're a terrible swimmer' and 'You'll never be any good.' And then she calls me Eric the Floppy Backstroke King. In front of everyone. Even Brodie. She's *so* mean!"

Stella felt empty places, her heart, her lungs, her head. She felt Eric's own tears in her throat. She felt Celia's anger and sadness and frustration, and she shook her head. "Oh, hon. I'm so sorry. I'm sorry she's doing that."

Suddenly Eric was angry, whipping his head back to the window. "No, you're not! You don't care! You won't make her stop because her mom is dying! Because Grace is your best friend!"

Stella thought of Eric sitting on the living room couch watching television when she talked to Felice or Helen. What had she said exactly? She hadn't been careful. She hadn't, as she thought, kept Eric in mind all the time.

"I should have talked to you about this. I'm sorry. And we don't really know if she's dying," she said slowly. "She has cancer, Eric. She's very, very sick and taking lots of medicine to help her, so we don't really know what will happen."

"Oh," he said, spent and sullen, his hands now folded in his lap. "But she doesn't look sick, Mom. She looks exactly the same as she always has."

Stella nodded and put her hand on Eric's shoulder. "This isn't the first time she's been sick, honey. It's a cancer that she had before, so she hasn't really changed. She came out of it pretty well before, so we're all hoping she'll do it again."

"Really?" He looked up. "Will all her hair fall out? Will she be bald like Aunt Dorothy was?"

"Maybe. But I don't want you to worry about her. I want you to just enjoy swim team, and I'm going to say something to Celia. That's not nice. It's not even true. You've really come a long way this year. She's been on the team longer than you have, and she's not acting like an older swimmer should. But she is probably scared about her mom, and sometimes when you are scared, you do things you wouldn't normally do. Things that seem like you're another person altogether. Sometimes you do things that are really wrong. But it'll be okay. I'll take care of it."

Eric turned to her, grateful and only slightly wary. Stella imagined he was thinking about practice without insults and harassment, and part of her wanted to slap Celia across the face for hurting Eric; the other part wanted to hold her in close, tell her, as she'd just told Eric, that everything would be all right.

After making sure Eric walked out onto the pool deck, Stella went into the girls' bathroom to look for Celia. The bathroom was a dangerous place, humid from silly and loud half-hour-long showers, four or five girls to a single stall, slick from spilled shampoo and conditioner, the entire room echoing with giggles. The toilet seats were always wet, small bathroom accidents clinging on, near, or under the toilets themselves. Once a day, the dour janitor wangled her bucket through the door, slopping up the mess, filling the towel dispensers the girls had emptied to carelessly wipe up messes, piles of paper thick with sunscreen or lotion in every corner. At night, a crew of cleaning professionals arrived in a white van and peeled the dried towel mounds from the tile floor, bleached the toilets, hosed out the showers. Stella could only imagine what the boys' bathroom looked like. Eric told her that Dylan tried to flush a tennis ball down a toilet, the result a geyser of toilet water and tissue. Steven, the owner of the club, had told Dylan that, if he did anything like that again, he'd be kicked out for good. Felice hadn't even bothered to try to excuse her son, turning to Stella with raised eyebrows and whispering, "I'm just glad nothing exploded."

But now the bathroom was quiet. Celia was alone, sitting on the wooden bench facing her open locker. She had her swimsuit on, but was slumped over, listlessly pulling on her gym bag handle.

"Hey, Celia," Stella said, sitting down on the damp bench.

Celia turned to her and again, Stella was struck by how much this child looked like her mother, the same bright red hair and green eyes, a similar constellation of freckles on nose and cheeks, the same long bones. Stella looked down and compared her slim thigh to Celia's, and she knew that in months, maybe even weeks, Celia would begin her period, her breasts swelling into a training bra, her body lengthening and curving until she would look like Grace must have years ago. *In a year or two,* she thought, *Celia will have boys after her*, and Stella couldn't imagine how Grace would handle all that male attention focused on her daughter. But just as she thought it, she felt the prick of tears in her throat, realizing that Grace might not even live to see Celia's first date, much less junior prom, senior ball, or marriage.

The desire to live those moments was what kept Grace going, Stella knew, and the thought of all she herself would miss by not having a daughter keened through her belly. Every year, as she continued to not have a baby, that girl she wanted slipped farther and farther away, and the closest she knew she might ever get was in moments like this, with another woman's child.

"Hi," Celia said, looking down at her sandals.

"How are you doing?" Stella put a light hand on Celia's shoulder, feeling the girl pull politely from her touch. Stella thought of lime-green wisteria shoots so new that sunlight almost shone through them, and the way the wind would pick them up and curl them away from her pruning shears.

"Fine."

"How's your mom today?"

"Fine."

"I'm glad to hear that. That must make you feel good, too."

Celia nodded, her head bent down. Stella noticed Celia's toenails were painted pink, ten tiny seashells on the smelly tile floor. "Listen, if you ever want to talk, I'm here. You can call me at home. I know your mother has my number on your fridge, right?"

"Yeah." Celia stood up and stuffed her gym bag in her locker, closing the metal door with a clang.

"And, Celia, I just wanted to talk about Eric for a second. You know, he's pretty new to the team. I mean, he's nowhere near as good as you. Who is? And I guess what I'm saying is that he needs encouragement, not teasing. Okay?" She stopped, hoping that Celia heard what she was not saying, heard the "Leave him alone, dammit."

Celia turned to her, and Stella almost gasped, the blank stare on the girl's face too old a mask for this eleven-year-old to wear.

She wondered if it was just grief behind the dull eyes and hard mouth.

"Fine. Okay?" Without looking at Stella again, she picked up her towel and walked toward the pool exit.

"Celia?" Stella called.

Celia turned back, her face the same still wall. "What?"

"Remember, it's not only me. Helen and Felice are here for you, too. Anything you need—whenever—ask any of us."

"Okay." Celia walked out the door, her shadow growing longer and longer as she moved into the afternoon light.

Out at the pool, Grace sat with Helen and Felice. Tony stood at the edge of the pool with his hands cupping his mouth, yelling, "Hey, try getting off the bottom, Dylan!" The rest of the children seemed to be moving faster than before, their strokes sharp and precise, the mood definitely more serious. Stella walked over to the group and pulled up a chaise.

"Things seem pretty shipshape around here."

"We're hoping Dylan will get off the bottom of the pool," Felice said. "It's my goal for this summer."

Helen poked Felice in the shoulder. "We can't ask for miracles."

"That kid will end up being the league champion," Grace said. "Mark my words."

"Well, I'm counting on you to make it happen," Felice said. "But the rest of them are going at it."

"Just wait until later in the season when he has them working out twice a day," Helen said. "Then they'll all wish it was just easy spring workout again."

"Tony's killing them." Grace looked out toward the pool, smiling, and Stella thought of all the hard work Grace did herself, all the miles and miles on the StairMaster, all the asphalt hills, the laps in the chlorinated pools, the up and down on basketball courts.

"So I'm sure they already asked. How are you feeling?"

"I'm great! This protocol is awesome. I don't feel sick at all, and my hair! I haven't lost a strand."

"What happened last time you had the chemo?" Felice asked.

"That was a different story. Each time, just like that, after the third treatment, I'd wake up to a huge swatch of it on my pillow. I'd be too afraid to look in the mirror, knowing I'd end up with a scary comb job."

"Did it all fall out?" Stella asked, unconsciously smoothing her long blond hair.

"Yeah. I lost my eyebrows and eyelashes and pubic hair and leg hair. Everything. I looked like an egg." Grace laughed. "I felt like a newborn alien."

Stella looked at Grace's hair, which was still in seeming recovery from the chemo years before. There were no patches of scalp in her red hair, but it didn't shine the way Stella imagined it should, eight years out of chemo, all of it brittle and hard and thin, as if the drugs had burned through cuticle and sebum and cell to leave Grace with this permanent reminder.

"What's different this time?" Helen asked.

"There's a brand-new drug. Totally experimental. But it eliminates hair loss. I'm one of the first people to take it. If it works on us, well, then everyone on chemo will get it."

"Unbelievable," Felice said. "And it's sick that they don't give it to everyone right now. Think how much better people would feel."

"Drug companies. The government. Someone doesn't really give a shit about us cancer patients," Grace said.

"At least you have it," Helen said.

"At least," said Grace, nodding, running her thin fingers over her head, a single ruby hair shimmering as it fell to the pool deck. "It's my big perk."

They all laughed, and Stella knew that now, like then, Grace would struggle and fight and pull and laugh against all of this. Grace would show them all how to live even as she died.

THREE

⁓

"LOOK AT YOU."

Helen glanced up at her husband, Darryl, in the mirror, her mascara wand in her hand. "What are you talking about?"

"Can't you relax? I can see you planning."

"Who else will, Darryl? Are you going to go to sign Livie up for ballet? Are you going to bake the cookies for the open house?"

"Give it up, Helen."

"What?" She stood straight, her bare chest pale in the mirror. Helen blinked and looked at her husband, his towel around his middle, his blond hair slicked back in wet neat rows.

"Give it up. Look at you. How many things can you do at once?" He unfurled his towel, his ass red from the shower's heat and steam.

"One of us needs to take care of things." Helen picked up her blush and made quick rose strokes on her cheeks. She looked in the mirror and saw Darryl looking at her, his eyes heavy on her face and body. A quick shiver of shame pulsed through her, and she wished for her robe, not wanting to see her flat, nursed-out breasts, her nipples like two dark quarters.

She zipped up her makeup case and bit her lip, knowing that this conversation was really about last night, when she had turned away from Darryl as he rolled over on her side of the bed, trying to reach his arms across and under her. In the space between them, she could feel his erection. Before she even really knew she didn't want to have sex, Helen feigned sleep, pushed him away, made deep breathing noises until she heard her fake ones matched with his real sleeping sounds. But as he looked at her now in the mirror, she could see he wanted to strike back, take what he hadn't been able to get last night.

"All I'm saying," Darryl began almost wearily, slipping on underwear and then pants, "is that you seem way too preoccupied. And then that Grace stuff."

Helen put her hands on her hips, feeling her bones just under her hands. "Good Lord, Darryl. She has cancer. And I know something bad is going on between Kathleen and her, now of all times. We were just trying to arrange some help." She didn't tell him that Grace hadn't needed a thing from them and that Helen had finally recycled the lists she'd compiled of Celia's ballet, aikido, and ceramics classes, Grace's appointments at Stanford, and the times Kathleen would be out of town for veterinary conferences. Grace had assured them there was no need for driving and meal shifts or housework help. Even though Grace was on chemo and fighting off the disease and the cure, all Felice, Stella, and she could do was what they'd been doing all along. Be her friends.

Darryl put on his dress shirt and then his tie. "But all the calls. It's getting a bit ridiculous. I mean, she's up at the club. She works out when I do, and she's still there when I leave. How much help can she need right now?"

"You know she's trying to stay healthy. It builds up her immune system. It works for her. Her doctors recommend it."

"It's odd, Helen. Flat-out weird. For one thing, if I had metastasized melanoma in my lungs and it almost killed me before, I know I wouldn't be sitting out in the sun every damn day."

"She says the sun gives her energy," she said, suddenly realizing how strange the words sounded as they came out of her mouth.

"Right. Whatever." Darryl hung up his towel and took his shoes out of the closet. "Fine. But I think some of your concern for Grace could be redirected."

Helen wanted to say, "But we wanted to help." She wanted to say, "I just hope someone would care that much about me if I had cancer." But she knew that part of what he said was true. Grace was nowhere close to needing their help. There was so much else Helen should be thinking about—her child, her schoolwork, her marriage, her mother alone in her Florida condo, never visiting California because she was afraid to fly now that she was alone. So Helen was silent, turning back to the counter, dropping her makeup bag in the drawer. "I know. But it sounds so bad. It could spread. And now at least we know we can get organized."

Darryl put his hand on Helen's shoulder. "She's different than anybody I know. She may not want any help at all. She might not *need* anyone, ever."

After rushing Livie to school, stopping in to talk with the school secretary about teacher appreciation day, and driving across the bridge in the tail end of the morning commute, Helen sat in her class staring out the window, thinking for a moment about nothing.

"Are you getting all this?" the young man next to Helen asked, leaning over toward her ear. He smelled like patchouli oil, and he was fuzzy, ripe with dreadlocks and soft, tattered clothes, and pierced, a stud in his tongue, eyebrow, and nose. Helen looked him up and down quickly, thinking there were probably other bits of steel, hidden under his clothing, in the softest imaginable parts. Nothing on his body looked combed, smoothed, ironed, or pressed.

"I don't think so," she whispered. "I'm just not into all this today."

"I'm never really into this," he whispered back.

She smiled at him and then remembered some other smell, something dark and wet and tangy, something like old sheets from a known bed.

Turning from the white board, a black marker in his hand, their professor looked up at them, his eyes narrowed, and then he went back to his calculations, long felt strokes on the slippery board. Helen stared at his shiny bald head, wondering what it felt like, wondering if it were smooth or somewhat prickly, little nascent hairs under her hand. And how did one take care of such a head? Were there creams and ointments and unguents, lotions made especially for that thin, tender skin? Was there something the professor could tell her that she could pass on to Grace? Helen slid down in her seat a bit, as if trying to hide, and considered this personal hygiene dilemma.

"My name's Pablo Hernandez," he whispered again as soon as the professor went back to his work. "I think we had Program Design together last semester."

Helen turned to him slightly, remembering this fuzzy brown man, his funny asides, his nonchalance when questioned, his perfectly correct answers each and every time. "I know," she said, feeling a sudden surprising flush, starting from her groin. She almost stood up, but instead pressed her inner thighs together, willing this pulse to subside. "Helen Jordan."

"Do you want to get some coffee after class, Helen? An espresso or something?" he asked, and she almost snorted at the idea of them together, her with a daughter and stretch marks and lists full of dance lessons and car pools and dentist appointments. Her with a husband.

"Okay," she said, "but I only have a half hour or so. Maybe you could try to explain to me what this entire class has been about. And while we're at it, let's go over what happened last semester, too."

Pablo smiled and nodded, sat back in his desk, and began doodling on his notepad. Helen simmered at her desk, her thighs still firmly pushed together.

Later, at the student union coffee shop, Ultimate Grounds, Helen blew on her nonfat decaf latte, daring herself to look at Pablo. In line, it had been easy to talk and avoid eye contact. But now at the table, she had to look at him or it would seem rude. So she began with his arms, covered in flannel, and his chest, more flannel and a holey blue T-shirt, and then his face, bearded and brown with skin at his cheeks the color of her espresso. She brought her cup to her lips and looked up, into his eyes. They were brown with flecks of green, and he was looking back at her and smiling.

"So you don't like the class much, huh?" he asked.

"It's not a matter of liking it. I have to take it. That's all. There really isn't that luxury of *not* liking anything."

"Why?"

She shrugged. "It's part of the computer science major. You know. Java. Cisco. All that stuff. I have to take it. Don't we all?"

"But do you have to major in computer science? Don't you have any choice in that?"

Helen took another sip, realizing how right he was. She'd decided on computer science because Darryl told her it was the fastest-growing field. "You'll be able to get a job, no problem. We're right in the middle of everything here," he had said. "There will be places begging to hire you, probably before you even graduate."

So on her college application she had inked in the computer science box, believing she was doing the practical thing. But then she imagined not only getting a job, but a good job, a great one, one that would free her to leave, to leave Darryl, to support Livie in the same way she'd been supported since her birth. It wasn't about the family and two incomes anymore or Darryl's pride in her accomplishments; it was about freedom and leaving and letting go of all that seemed dead inside her. It was about busting loose and shaking off years and years, all the way back to childhood. But Helen didn't think that way too often or too much. Instead, she thought of her drives to State, the homework she did night after night, and the sacrifices of time and attention that Livie and Darryl made for a good family cause. And if she did conjure up, briefly, a life without Darryl, she smothered it with a new list, other ideas to help her forget.

"No. I don't *have* to major in anything," she replied, irritated.

She put down her coffee and stared at Pablo, who didn't try to duck her gaze. "It's a choice. Once I made it, I had to follow through. I made a commitment to my family."

He was quiet for moment. Then he said, "So, like, you're supported or something? This whole school gig is like just a hobby?"

She felt herself flare with nerves, and she wanted to strike the table or maybe even his arm or face. How could he say that? How could Pablo put her in a group of women who did things for *fun*? Helen didn't do anything for fun.

She closed her eyes and counted to ten, like she did when Livie irritated her and she needed a few seconds to figure out how to behave like an adult. Finally, she curled her hands into loose fists and held them between her knees. It wasn't his fault. To him, so young and ready to push out into life, she must seem ancient, bored, a woman with a child too old to need her much. Like Darryl, who saw her interest in Grace as a way of staying busy rather than a desire to help. There must be nothing on the outside that showed she was alive inside.

"No." She looked up at Pablo. "That's not it, really. It was my choice to go back to school. I didn't have to do it now. And . . . I guess, I didn't have to do it ever."

"How old are you?"

"What?" Helen brought her hands up to the table to fiddle with her cup. "Christ."

"How old are you?"

"What a question!" she said, a rush of blood spreading across her neck. "I'm thirty-nine."

"So maybe it's time, you know." Pablo leaned back in his chair.

She imagined standing up and giving Pablo a slicing glance. She imagined ignoring him in class for the rest of the semester. Instead, she looked out the window of the coffee shop, the flowers as vibrant as those in Stella's backyard, bergenia, rose, daylily, and bottlebrush, red and pink and yellow flowers thrust up and opened, the wind blowing them gently, the ferns nodding as if to Pablo's words. "I have a degree, you know. In business. I worked in an import company until my daughter was born. I traveled all over the world. I didn't always look like this. I wasn't always a mother." She took her last sip of coffee and leaned over to pick up her bag, which bulged with notebooks, her day planner, swim goggles, and ballet tights. "I think . . . I think you're really not in a position to tell me it's time to do anything. You don't know where I've been or what I've done or anything about my life at all. I'm trying . . . I'm trying to find . . . something."

Pablo closed his eyes for a second. "I'm sorry. You're right. Me, I don't know what I'm doing myself, I guess. Listen, that was really out of line."

"How old are you?"

"Twenty-seven. I took a bit of a detour during my undergraduate years."

"So what are you doing? Why are you taking computer science?"

"My dad, man. He just knows it all. He made everything for himself. He runs a chain of auto body shops down in Los Angeles. He started from nothing, so he expects all my siblings and me to take the business route. I guess it's like he doesn't want me to have to suffer in poverty before I find a place. So he just said, 'Get something that pays. Then find yourself.' "

"What did he mean by 'finding yourself?' "

"Oh, you know. I want to work in film, the typical 'I want to be an artist' thing. I majored in screenwriting at UCLA, but my dad said, if he was going to pay for my education, I had to take math and business classes, too, so they accepted me here despite my major."

How lucky he was to have all these questions when he was young, before marrying or becoming a parent, before his every move was so crucial to other people. *Why can't we learn not to rush? Why can't we be rumpled and soft and messy like Pablo for years and years until something truly calls us and our life really begins?*

She shook her head, reaching her hand out to touch Pablo, when she noticed the time. "Oh, I've got to go. It's been . . . nice talking to you, Pablo." She stood up, clutching her bag.

He didn't stand up with her, as Darryl would have done, trained so well by his mother, but Pablo smiled, and as she walked out of the coffee shop and toward her car, something old and forgotten began to split and crack open in her body, something powerful, something she couldn't name.

As she sat in traffic on the Bay Bridge, stuck behind a stalled Caltrans truck and a constellation of orange cones, Helen thought about Pablo's father's words and remembered her own father, Jackson, and all he had and hadn't said. When she reached for the peanut butter, the waist of her shirt rising up over her prepubescent stomach, he'd narrow his eyes and say, "Chubby Checker," poking a finger into her flesh. When she won a speech and debate team medal in high school, graduated near the top of her class, placed second at a track meet, he waved off any compliments given her by friends and family, shaking his head, his lips turned down, saying, "Oh, she's all right," without any false modesty. Her father meant it, and he knew best because he'd been watching her his whole life. She was just *all right*. And now, even when she was arranging help for Grace or working at Livie's school or acing an exam, she heard the same words, "She's *all right*."

That was the way Jackson had liked things, quiet and calm unless it was he who was yelling and tossing things around or laughing loudly with his head thrown back, no bumps either high or low. A half hour before he was due to arrive home from work, her mother, sister, and she would pick up books, bags, and cat toys off the floor, set the dinner table, turn off the television, and wait. It was impossible to predict what kind of day he'd had or what the traffic had been like on the 101. If Jackson was angry, if he'd been stuck behind a stalled car or an underling had screwed up an order or a secretary had spilled the coffee, he'd storm through the house, looking for something to trip on, something to hold in front of Babe's face, something that said, "You all don't even deserve me." Babe, Frieda, and she would try not to react, would be still and silent and calm as slim trees, just as he liked. "Don't say a word to your father," Babe would hiss out of the side of her mouth. "Let it pass. You know it will."

And it did pass, until the next time he exploded, teased, or joked. That was what he did, leaving all the other parts of family life, the serious discussions, the worries, the heartaches to the girls, as he called them, even Babe.

From an early age Helen had practiced the art of invisibility, figured out how to breathe shallowly enough to fool Jackson, to keep him moving past her. And now, when she was with Darryl, she knew she could avoid scrutinizing stares and glances, both of them innocuous and silent as they moved through cocktail parties or buffets or back-to-school nights. Darryl was handsome, even though his hair was thinning and his stomach wasn't as tight as it had been years ago. But whose was? That wasn't the point, though. It was their chemistry, something off and flat, nothing like the sparkle of Stella and Aaron, she with her go-forever legs and he with his confident smile. And they didn't catch eyes like Grace and Kathleen, Grace lean and tan, Kathleen short and strong and spiky-haired. And Felice always knew what to say, understanding the idea, the joke, the plan, and there was James, his arm loose across his wife's shoulders.

It was as if Helen had picked Darryl so her father wouldn't notice her or him enough to say a thing, no poking, teasing, or joking. No awful stares. And she still felt like that, even though Jackson was dead and gone, so far away from her. Like Pablo, she could still hear her father. She could still feel his finger in her side, imagine his gaze on the back of her head as she walked down the hallway. But sometimes with her friends or today with Pablo, she felt her real self slip out, angry, maybe funny, and wanting. Wanting something nice.

When Helen and Livie walked onto the pool deck, Livie squealed and ran to Celia, desperate to whisper a hot secret that she'd carried in her eyes all during the ride from school.

"What are you thinking about, missy?" Helen had asked earlier.

"Nothing," she'd said smugly, but now she was cupping her hand over Celia's ear, Celia breaking out in a rare smile and swinging her feet as they sat together on the bench.

Helen walked over to Felice, Stella, and Grace and placed her bag on a chair.

"What's that all about?" Felice asked. "I've never seen Livie run so fast."

"I have no idea. Maybe I don't want to know."

"It's about a boy," Stella said. "I can tell. They just pretend to hate them, but look how excited they both are."

"It's a crush of some kind." Felice rubbed sunscreen on her nose. "A mad crush."

"That's right. That's it," Stella said. "It's our drug of choice."

" 'What's forbidden is delicious,' " Felice said.

"Who said *that*?" Stella asked.

"I don't remember. But anyway, lust is a high. I remember when I first met James. I would drive to school with the head-phones on, listening to Van Morrison. James gave me that tape. I would just drive and drive, practically stuck in the night before. Before I knew it, I'd be walking into a class, and I'd think, *My God, what have I been doing this whole time?*"

"I miss it," Helen said, sighing, and there was Pablo again, his body under his soft clothing.

"I do, too," Stella said. "But I think it can kill you if it goes on too long. I think I lost ten pounds when I first met Aaron. I don't know if I was even breathing properly. The air was coming into the top of my chest. I felt dizzy all the time."

Grace shook her head. "Not me. I *gained* ten pounds when I met Kathleen. It's the fattest I've ever been. She couldn't stop tak-ing me out to dinner. I still can't go to Oliveto's without feeling sick. The idea of a marinated olive is enough to make me throw up!"

"I'll develop a crush on someone to get that high," Felice said, raising her eyebrows as Dylan jumped out of the pool and ran to her. She handed him a towel, whispered, "Go see what Eric's up to," and watched him walk away. "Like this graduate student in my Medieval Lit class last semester. He was really good-looking and older than most of my students, and I'd think, if I were twenty-five, twenty-seven, he's the guy I'd want. And I'd think about him sometimes to avoid thinking about James . . . and, well, life, and I'd kind of be hyperventilating before a lecture. It was really silly."

"What were you trying not to think about?" Grace asked Felice, and Helen felt herself flinch, knowing that Grace always asked the questions closest to the bone.

Felice shrugged. "Oh, the same things I'm trying not to think about now. Like where did all of that go for James and me."

None of them spoke, staring out onto the momentarily flat, glassy water, the fog spitting cold air inland. Two white-crested sparrows twirled by in the air, arcing up over the children in the pool. Helen used to feel that way for Darryl. She used to want him, his long white body, smooth and warm. When they first started dating, she could barely control herself, her hands almost itching for him, needing to rub against his flesh. And there was such a longing in her when she watched Darryl and Livie that went beyond sexual desire, all the way back to some sense memory of being held by her own father, his peppery skin, his Aqua Velva, the heat of his body pulsing, just living, against hers. *When did that happen?* Helen wondered. *When did I ever feel that?*

Stella sighed. "You know I love Aaron. But that longing for whatever that is, lust or something, doesn't go away. Like just this weekend. We went to the fireworks show at the marina, and there was this music. I saw this couple dancing. And they were really having fun, looking at each other like they really wanted to be with each other. Not even touching. They had these smiles. There was this . . . this aura around them that made them look, well, so incredibly beautiful."

"Hmmph," snorted Felice, as if, it seemed to Helen, she was flinging her sadness over her shoulder. "Like that didn't happen to us in the beginning of a relationship? Listen, lust is a defense mechanism," she said, looking at Helen as she spoke, as if she knew about Pablo. "It's a way to slog through something we don't really like. A class. A day. An outing with our families. We manufacture a feeling that is more exciting to keep us going, to keep us in the place we're in without going totally crazy."

They all laughed, but Helen wasn't exactly sure what she was trying to slog through. Was it her marriage that was stuck like glue on her back and breasts and head, keeping her with Darryl, keeping her with Livie, keeping her from herself? Or was her sudden attraction to Pablo real, true, something she should follow? She looked at her friends and wondered if they could see into her, watch the name Pablo throb on her chest like a neon sign, an open-for-business sign, a welcome sign in red and gold.

The next evening, Darryl was already home when Helen and Livie finally made it back after a dance class following swim team. He was standing by the answering machine writing down messages, an apron around his waist, Chilean sea bass in the broiler. Despite her relief that she didn't have to make dinner, Helen was angry with him, moving past him and ignoring his pat on her hip, irritated that she had to be grateful today. And she knew she should be grateful. So many women she talked to at PTA meetings, soccer games, and ice-skating lessons told her, over and over, that their husbands were never home, always traveling, never cooking, never cleaning, only sleeping and eating and fucking before heading out the door in their Armani suits. And sometimes they didn't even fuck at home, finding that elsewhere, too, their wives angry and sad and frustrated, wondering how to bring them home for that, at least. Even Felice told her stories about James's late-night homecomings, slipping into bed at eleven or twelve and then leaving the house by seven, jerked tight into his dark gray suit and serious tie, barely kissing her or the boys on his way out. Helen knew how Felice and James seemed not even to speak the same language anymore. She sometimes found Felice weeping in the locker room. Helen would move toward her, but Felice would wave her away, joking about her crying spells. As a husband and father, Darryl was nothing to complain about. But even so, here he was, cooking after a full day of work, following a recipe, taking care of family business. It pissed her off.

"Grace called." Darryl handed her a piece of paper. "I didn't save the message, but this is what she said."

Helen took the paper and read:

In hospital for treatment. Pick up Celia
from school tomorrow at three-thirty to take
to club. Everything okay.

"Oh, my God," she said, picking up the phone. "I saw her three hours ago! I don't understand. This is terrible."

"She seemed fine. I mean, her voice sounded normal." He opened the oven to check the fish. "She sounded like herself. In fact, she sounded great."

"Of course she did. But that's the way she always sounds," she said, dialing Grace's number at home.

Just before the fourth ring and the machine pickup, Kathleen answered the phone. "Hello." Kathleen's voice was stretched from a long day and chores, water sounds and dishes against porcelain clacking into the phone.

"It's Helen. I just got Grace's message. What's going on? Aren't you going to the hospital?" She felt all her words coming out at once, and she leaned against the kitchen wall, looking up to see Darryl staring at her.

"Hospital? What are you talking about? Hospital! This is all I need today." Kathleen seemed louder, filled with energy, an edge, something angry or irritable underneath her smooth tones.

"I got this message. It says . . ." She unfolded the paper and read it to Kathleen. "See? She wants me to pick up Celia tomorrow. I'm calling to see if you need anything else."

Kathleen was silent, water still running in the background. "Helen, Grace is at her friend Stephanie's in Santa Clara. From college. They played basketball together. She's visiting for the night. But hey, I'd appreciate it if you could pick up Celia, though. I have a long day tomorrow at the clinic."

"I'm confused. I saw her earlier at the club, so I don't know why I didn't hear any of this."

Kathleen was silent, breathing into the receiver.

Helen felt an urge to reach in and pull Kathleen's hair, wake her up to this life-or-death situation in her own home, wake her up to the care Grace needed. If she was sick enough to race down to Stanford after swim team, then there was something truly wrong, and Kathleen was mistaken or deluded or simply didn't care.

"I have no idea why she didn't tell you about Stephanie," Kathleen finally said in a monotone.

"But what did she mean, *hospital*?"

"Like I said, I really don't know. You must have heard the message wrong."

"But I didn't take it. Darryl did. My husband did. He wrote it."

"Listen, Helen. I don't know who got it wrong, but I know for a fact that Grace is at her friend's. She's been planning it for a couple days. I heard her talking on the phone about it. Stella has Celia. I really can't say anything else because I don't know why Darryl wrote what he did."

"Well, okay. I mean, I'm sorry about the confusion. So I'll pick Celia up from school. Right?"

"Thanks. That's really great. 'Bye." Kathleen hung up the phone, and Helen looked up at Darryl.

"This is so strange. Are you sure she said hospital?"

Darryl nodded. "Of course. Hospital."

"She didn't say *friend* or *Stephanie*?" Helen put down the phone.

"Gee, Helen, I think I know the difference between all three of those words." He turned back to his sea bass. "This was what I was talking about before. Look at you. So Grace made a mistake or Kathleen made a mistake. Who cares? No one's in trouble. Let it go."

"But I have to know what's going on. Don't you think it's weird? Kathleen says she's staying at a friend's house. Stephanie's house. And there's no hospital involved at all." Helen opened her bag and pulled out Livie's wet towel and swimsuit. "I don't understand."

Darryl shrugged. "You know, it's probably just a communication problem, but it's not my problem. She said *hospital* and she said *tests*, but she didn't say anything about a friend."

"I think you might be a bit more concerned about all this."

"I'm concerned, but not about Grace. At least right now. Grace always seems to take care of herself." He looked at her, the spatula in his hand. "So it's not Grace I'm worried about at all."

She stared at him for a second and then sighed and walked down the hall to the laundry room, the cold wet fabric in her hands, Kathleen's tired voice in her ears. That relationship was not going well, not well at all. *Grace must be keeping her health problems from Kathleen*, she decided. *There must be something Grace doesn't trust about Kathleen. A reaction, a comment, a look.* Grace probably made up the whole story about Stephanie to keep Kathleen away, apart, not connected, and it was Helen, Stella, and Felice she was turning to because they were the only ones she could trust. But if that was true, she thought, why hadn't Grace told them about the tests at the pool? Why this sudden message?

Helen sighed and carefully hung up the towel on the metal bar over the washing machine, arranging Livie's swimsuit next to it. Then she stood there in the dark room. *We have to take care of her*, she thought. *It's up to us.*

FOUR
⁊

WHEN GRACE CAME HOME FROM THE CLUB, Kathleen was well into her packing, open suitcases on the floor, her side of the closet almost emptied, half-full boxes of books on the kitchen counters, a sack of papers by the front door, certain photographs pulled off the refrigerator. Grace walked into the bedroom and threw herself on the bed and lay there, an arm over her eyes. Kathleen wasn't speaking, moving quickly between drawers and closet, throwing shirts and pants into her suitcases. Thank God, Grace thought, that Celia was staying at Stella's for the night.

"You're leaving now?"

Kathleen shook her head. "Let's not do this again. We've already talked about it for days. For a long time really. We'll talk later."

"When?"

"When you get back from Stephanie's house. After I have a chance to talk to Celia. Stop crying, okay?"

"How can you leave us?" Grace tried opening her eyes to see if the tears would stop, but they were full of water and she shut them again, feeling how easy it would be to simply sleep.

"I'm going to live at the clinic until I find a place," Kathleen finally said. "I've got that room and bath behind exam three. I've told all my employees. Everyone knows."

Grace was unsure she could move her throat to speak, the inside of her esophagus heavy and on fire, burning with fear and gastric juices. She didn't even think she could pull her arm from her nose and eyes because once she did and saw Kathleen working so diligently to leave, packing all the clothes Grace knew so well, she knew it would be true. Kathleen was really leaving. Even though Grace was sick. Sick! She could feel her stomach turning, pulsing into a retch.

Grace coughed and swallowed down acid and tears, lifting her arm slightly from her face. "You've told everyone already? How can you leave me now? Can't you see? Can't you see I need you?"

Kathleen didn't answer. Grace listened to the back-and-forth clap of Kathleen's shoes on the hardwood. No matter what she did, nothing was stopping Kathleen, her steps fast and decisive. "Kathleen! Kat! I have cancer."

Grace listened as Kathleen seemed to slow and then did slow and stop. She opened her eyes and looked at her lover, seeing first her smooth tan hands, the silver flower ring encircling her right ring finger, the rings they bought for each other.

"I know you have cancer. I know I promised to stay. I tried but I can't. It's not like I'm abandoning you, Grace. I told you that last night. It's not like I'm abandoning Celia. But I . . . I want something for me. That doesn't mean I won't support you and let you live here. It doesn't mean I won't pay the bills I've always paid. It doesn't mean I won't be with you until the . . . until it's time. I need to go. For me. I need to try to find some semblance of a normal life. I'm going to be fifty. I don't want to live like this for the rest of my life."

Grace stood up from the bed, her eyes suddenly dry. "You just use people up and throw them away. You don't care about me and how I'm dying. You don't care that Celia won't have anybody after I'm gone."

Kathleen put down a pair of jeans and moved toward Grace. "That's not true. I care about you both. But don't put that all on me. Celia has your mother. And her father, too. She will always have Roger. You know that."

"But Celia knows you best, loves *you* best. She looks to you for so much. How can you leave us both?"

Kathleen ran her hands through her short hair and then moved her hands to her eyes, rubbing them, it seemed to Grace, so she didn't have to look at her. "I can't live like this anymore. Really! The way we've been going on! You won't let me go to the doctor with you. I know it's the secret protocol and the doctors, but I'm shut out. I've never even talked to this Dr. Karl. I almost think he doesn't exist. There's no place for me because you won't let me be there for you. I don't know where you are half the time. At the hospital? At a friend's? Working out? People call and I don't know what to say. No matter what I do, I can't be there for you."

Grace breathed into the fire in her middle. "But I've told you! If you come to the hospital, you'll blow everything. I'm not supposed to be in the protocol. I'm too sick. Karl's only taken me as a patient because he knows me, because of the last time. The hospital doesn't even know. That's why I go in at night. If the hospital higher-ups find out, he'll get fired, and without him, I'd already be dead. Can't you see what I owe him?"

"But what about what you owe me, Grace?" Kathleen shook her head and then bent over a suitcase, arranging shirts, shoes, bras, T-shirts. "What about what you owe us?"

"What about me? How can you leave me now?"

Kathleen shut her suitcase and threw her purse over her shoulder. "We're not getting anywhere in this conversation. You're not listening. And I haven't left yet. But I will take care of you. Your friends will take care of you. Your mother will come up and take care of you. Roger will take care of Celia if you need him to. You are not being abandoned. You're still living in my house, Grace, and I'm still paying your bills. I'm as here as I can be."

Kathleen moved toward Grace as if thinking to kiss her, then stopped and turned away. "I'm going to the clinic. I'll be back later."

Grace's body seemed to stop, every part of her listening for Kathleen's return, the sound of a door reopening, footsteps leading back to this room. But all the noise seemed outside, away from her. Grace heard the roar of Kathleen's car, and then it was silent except for the squawk of a blue jay, the hum of a garbage truck, the thin beat of her skinny heart.

* * *

In the bed, one thin sheet over her body, Grace could hear the movements of people out in the hall, whispers and slight laughs, a telephone, a television, a cry for help or water, the muffled but deep voice of someone strong, someone calming someone else down.

Grace turned over, moved her eyes along the dark wall, following a flicker of light. The light seemed to be beating out a pulse to her, a one, a two, one-two, Morse code from another person in another room, someone breathing the same stale air, someone whose body drifted up and into a space above her body. She was familiar with this floating, having practiced it often as a child, looking down over her attic-floor room, the Barbies lined up on her dresser, pouting at her. She would move her eyes to the toy horse corral she'd made with Lincoln Logs and blocks, her plastic horses, Polka Dot and Adventure, still and perfect by their mounds of plastic hay. There was the quilt Nana Jean made for her folded on the rocking chair, the braided rug that used to be in the dining room, her posters of the Rolling Stones. And her bed, the movement, the fear, the moon a pale blue through the small window.

It would be so easy to let go, she knew. Just another breath out, and she could sail up and over everyone, into a quiet dull place and then a bright place where it would finally all make sense. She brought her arm up to her throat and began to urge that breath along her windpipe, but then she thought of Celia, and she clunked back into her body, brittle bones and skin, and she knew she would have to remember this night. And Grace did remember, all of it, and she slid down under the sheet, listening to the noises all around her, listening to doors opening and closing as she waited for sleep.

"Girl, I don't know what happened," Grace said, clutching the edge of her chair. "I really must have screwed up somewhere."

Helen sat back. "Come on! I really don't think it was you. Maybe if Kathleen was paying attention she—oh, never mind."

Grace nodded, silent, looking down at a blue vein throbbing just under the skin of her foot.

"There's too damn much going on. At least you're feeling better. That hospital stay probably did you good." Helen patted Grace's arm.

Grace closed her eyes and leaned back, too, feeling the sun, hoping Helen would relax and stop asking questions.

"Are those marks from the IVs or the chemo? They must have given you a lot. Shouldn't you have Band-Aids on them? Or at least cover it all from the sun with a shirt or something?"

"Oh," Grace said, her eyes still closed. "I have no veins left after all the treatments I received the last time. They collapse, you know. And it was a new nurse this time. I think she just graduated from Chabot College or something. But the head nurse finally found a place to stick. Anyway, I think the air is good for healing."

She waited for other questions, but there were no more, Helen caught up in watching the pool, Livie and Celia and now Eric and Brodie and Dylan splashing in the water, calling out *Mar-co Po-lo* in loud, rhythmic waves. Grace imagined Felice and Stella in the gym, pushing against metal, their bodies sweating to the pull of gravity and the resistance to it, their conversation punctuated with the whir of machines and the grunts of the men in the corner dropping weights to the floor, exhausted. She imagined Tony coming out to the pool deck with the lineup for the weekend's swim meet, the kids stopping their game, paddling over to listen to who was swimming freestyle or breaststroke or butterfly or backstroke. She heard groans and shouts, heard Tony give a motivational speech, urging team spirit, and she sailed back into college, into her basketball body, the ball under her hand, the floor under her feet, the net only moments away.

Grace heard only the slight rustle of a magazine, and then she slipped into the other place she could go, sliding inside her own body, somewhere between muscle and skin, away from her open ears and shut eyes, the sun pouring across her, the waves of light all she needed. Outside, all around her, she felt her friends, even now hearing Stella and Felice walk up and drop their bags, Helen pulling a chair across the wet concrete. She didn't want to open her eyes; she couldn't. It was so nice here, slipping along her own clean flesh, imagining the glistening clarity of her organs, everything infused with light.

"Is she asleep?" Felice asked, and Grace imagined that she shook her head, letting them know she was here. But how could she have? She was still somewhere under her own ribs.

"I don't think so," Helen said. "Did you hear what happened? She had to go to the hospital again."

"Already? God, this treatment is relentless."

"And there was a mixup. Grace called me to pick up Celia, and when I phoned Kathleen to see if she needed anything else, she didn't know what I was talking about. She thought Grace was at a friend's house."

"I don't know why I didn't pick up Celia," Stella said. "I had her all night. We really need to have that schedule back. Do you think we should rewrite it and make copies?"

Grace remembered that she had to be out of her body, part of life, especially now, when things were getting too complicated. "No," she said, pulling her self like stuck gum away from her insides. "I'll get it together with Kathleen."

"How are you doing?" Felice asked. "Sorry we were noisy."

"Well, damn, Grace," Helen said. "You can't expect to nap today. These kids of ours are too loud. It's not the mothers."

Grace opened her eyes slowly and yawned, forcing her energy into her head. "So what were you guys doing in there? Trying to win the StairMaster Olympics?"

"That's right!" Helen said, laughing. "I've heard all about that new event. They put all these StairMasters in a row and then blow a whistle. Everyone pumps and pumps for like, what? Two hours? The one with the most miles wins the gold medal. It's going to be a demonstration sport next time. I swear."

"What nuts!" Stella said. "But let me tell you, I'm a contender."

Grace felt a laugh push up her throat and she leaned back,

sound pulsing out of her mouth, the sun hot across her neck. Everyone else started to laugh, too, and in that second everything was as it should be, always. Exactly like this.

When Celia was almost three, Grace's dog, Jimmy, ate the d-Con a neighbor had left out for rats. She called Celia's baby-sitter and then pulled Jimmy into her car, briefly wondering if there was such a thing as an animal ambulance. By the time she reached the veterinary clinic she'd passed by every day on her way to work, Jimmy was convulsing and foaming at the mouth. Two assistants helped her lug Jimmy into an examination room, and soon she was watching Kathleen feel Jimmy's stomach.

"When do you think he ate it?"

"Probably this afternoon," Grace replied. "I found the package when I came home from work."

"Well, Jimmy probably has internal bleeding. That's what d-Con does. After we take X rays to determine the site of the bleeding, we'll start treatment, which consists of plasma transfusions and vitamin K supplements. It's a long recovery. And expensive. About five hundred dollars. But it's treatable."

Grace swallowed and tried to hide her mental calculations. Rent was due, and she had all her vitamins and acupuncture visits to pay for. But Grace knew how Celia would look at her if Grace had to say, "Sorry, baby. Jimmy's dead." So it wasn't really for Jimmy that she nodded her head and signed the papers. But she did love the dog, the way he almost rumbled with pleasure when she came home from work, the way he jumped when she pulled out the leash before a long run. No. It was for Celia and her still unbroken heart.

Grace hadn't really looked at Kathleen that first night at the clinic. She had been too busy with calculations and the almost-grief of her child. And really, Grace knew, she'd been too bruised to think of love, especially with a woman. Grace had only been with Roger, even though, she admitted later, she had often developed tiny, fleeting crushes on girls in high school and college, something she'd assumed was normal, something she assumed every woman did.

At night in dorm rooms, three girls on one bed talking, eating popcorn and Doritos, laughing about men or classes or professors, Grace felt a fullness she'd never felt before, a tingle that spread from her chest to her crotch, a burst of happiness as she leaned against warm friend flesh.

Yet later, long after she'd moved in with Kathleen, Grace wondered if those times had been signs of who she really was or she wondered, just for an instant, if all she wanted from Kathleen, truly, was that same dorm closeness, that acceptance, that lovely lull into sleep.

On later visits for Jimmy's transfusions and oral supplements, Grace felt herself drawn to Kathleen's humor, the way she looked at Jimmy as if he were a person, not a scruffy SPCA reject, the way Kathleen's small brown hands moved neatly over his cinnamon fur. Grace found herself wishing that she were Jimmy, needing that quiet stroking herself.

"I . . . had anorexia. When I was a girl," she said the first night Kathleen made love to her.

"What?" Kathleen pulled her face away from Grace's neck and stared at her.

She tried not to notice, but she felt Kathleen's body move slowly away, the skin of her chest, then hips, then legs pulling apart from her own.

Grace swallowed hard, already imagining the empty bed, the rush of air as Kathleen threw on her clothes. "I have to tell you. I mean, before . . . I thought I should tell you. I'm basically recovered, you know. I had it for years, even before the cancer. But now, between the chemo and the anorexia, I can only eat at night. It's really just a bad habit. It's like I started to think I had to get everything done in the day, just right, before I could eat," Grace offered, even while knowing that a habit is something that supposedly can be broken, and she'd never conquered this one.

"Oh," Kathleen said, growing still.

"I've tried everything, but the eating at night is the best I can do. And I *do* eat. A lot."

"What about therapy?" Kathleen moved to the other side of the bed, sat up and wrapped a sheet around her body.

Grace sighed, knowing the long story would only make Kathleen impatient. That whole part of her life didn't deserve any attention at all. And ultimately, her eating was simply a habit. It was simply about food, and Grace had managed to keep barely above one hundred pounds for years before the cancer, and now she was slowly heading back to that weight. People still stared, but Grace would mention she was a runner, an athlete, and they would nod, understand, say, "You sure look like it."

Grace looked at Kathleen. "Believe me, I've gone to therapy. But listen, I eat at night. Plenty. Rice and beans and soy milk. I'm not starving. I'm healthy enough. You should see all the supplements I take. I wouldn't have told you except things are . . . you know, getting serious. I thought it might explain things."

Kathleen leaned back, not responding. Grace felt tears under her skin and thought she should get up and leave, pick up Celia from the baby-sitter's, and take Jimmy to a different clinic. Grace could already feel the hole that Kathleen would rip into her life if she left this room right now. It was like all the leavings she'd ever gone through; it was like the way it had been at home, at night, doors opening and closing, people leaving Grace alone and scared. It was like her whole life, this minute, this minute when people decided to leave.

Kathleen sighed, unconsciously touching her own stomach over the sheet, her lovely, rounded flesh that looked so wonderful on her, thought Grace, imagining she could lean over and rest her head there. Would Kathleen let her? Or was she scared of Grace with all her bones so close to the surface?

Finally, Kathleen reached over and grabbed Grace's hand. "I can help, if you want."

"There's really nothing to do. I make sure I eat enough every day." *She's not leaving yet*, she thought. *Not yet.*

"You're so thin, though." Kathleen smiled. "Not that I don't like it."

"You do?"

"Of course. After all, aren't we here in bed?" Kathleen reached across the empty space and placed her hand against Grace's cheek. *She's staying*, thought Grace. *I can tell.*

"I want you to be all right. I know you could do it. Look what you did with the cancer."

"It was so hard, but I did it." Grace looked down into her lap.

Kathleen pulled Grace to her, holding her against her smooth skin. And Grace let the tears come, knowing she was wanted and accepted, finally.

"Kathleen left this morning," Grace said. She looked at Stella, Helen, and Felice carefully, watching their eyes and mouths. "She took her stuff. She's moving into the clinic until she can get another place."

"No!" Felice said. "Why?"

"What a *bitch*!" Helen threw her arms out and let them fall to the table in the club's café. "How can she do that?"

Felice shook her head back and forth. "I don't understand how she can do it. What is she thinking?"

"I don't know," Grace said, not understanding still how Kathleen could leave her alone. She was so sick. Maybe dying. Sometimes she couldn't even get out of bed. It took her all morning and half the afternoon to twist out of the bedcovers, pull her legs up and over, deciding to move, pick up Celia, head over to the club. Even now, her head throbbed and her stomach was a dull pulse under her heart. All she could think about was Kathleen, her voice, her body, her surety about everything. Without her, Grace knew, there wasn't much of anything left at all.

"I feel so alone," Grace said quietly, wishing the words back into her mouth even as she said them, not wanting to let out the pain that kept her connected to Kathleen.

"Of course you do." Helen slapped her thigh. "Shit! I don't get it, Grace."

"It's been so painful for her." Grace sighed. "She was devastated by my diagnosis. But it's been a long time coming."

"Shit," Helen said. "Pain in the ass."

"I don't know Kathleen that well," Felice said, "but she sounds just like a man. I'm not kidding. Leaving while the getting is good. Leaving without much more than a few promises."

Grace shrugged. "It's hard for her to watch me in pain. These last weeks have devastated her. I don't think she knows how to deal with it."

"Devastated," Felice repeated.

"It's not like she doesn't see it at work, for Christ's sake," Helen said. "Don't animals feel pain? Doesn't she know how to give shots and take care of them? You don't have to protect Kathleen anymore. What she did was weak, Grace. It doesn't work."

"It's her job to take care of you," said Felice bitterly. "It's what she should do. It's what she promised she would do. It's not like you weren't married. In all senses you were, and when you need her the most, she bails out."

"I don't want to say anything to hurt her," Grace said. "I've got to respect her path in life. But it doesn't seem to include me." She felt these words slip out and sail toward her friends. She felt how true they were, saw how scared Kathleen must really be, how much she couldn't deal with Grace's terrible health.

Helen and Felice shook their heads, and Grace looked over at Stella, who sat looking down at the table. Grace wondered what she was thinking about, wondered if Kathleen had called her and told her another side of the story. She felt a quick flare in her rib cage, wondering with whom Stella would side. Finally Stella said, "Well, it's going to be hard, Grace. You know we will do anything for you. Take care of Celia. Drive. Cook. Whatever you need."

"That's damn right," Helen said.

"You know I'm off this summer," Felice said. "Really. I'm not teaching summer school or going to a conference or anything. I took it off to be with the boys and . . . well, be at home more. So whenever you need something, morning or afternoon, I can help. All we're going to be doing is swim team and some art classes. James didn't want to plan a vacation or anything. I don't know why."

Outside, the sun arced over the San Francisco skyline, glinting like a hundred eyes off building glass. Below, in the bay, white specks of sailboats flitted in a slight breeze. Grace turned to her friends, these three women, and knew Kathleen was right. Whatever else happened, they would help. They would take care of her. They would be with her till the end.

The next night, Helen and Felice organized a girls' night out, with the kids eating pizza at Stella's, Aaron in charge. At the Elmwood Theater, Grace sat between Felice and Stella, Helen at the end of the row, watching a movie that had come out a couple of years ago but still played on in Berkeley at half price. The movie was oddly lit and very strange, people walking up and down a tiny office corridor like something from *Alice in Wonderland*. Felice was laughing and slapping her thigh, the sound making Grace giggle, seeing the scene as funny suddenly, when at first, with her own eyes, it looked off-kilter, wrong, like some bad vein in her own body.

"God, this is so weird," Stella whispered.

"I like it," Grace said, wiping her eyes.

"But do you get it?" Stella asked.

"I don't think we have to. It's just what it is."

Grace watched Stella from the corner of her eye, seeing her friend's confusion. There were things Grace knew she could never talk about with Stella, subjects that seemed to go over her head. Stella had the habit of confusing words, once calling a malamute dog a "malamud"; another time, she thought synchronicity had something to do with electrical current. Grace would see Stella's embarrassment and slide into the conversation and change the subject, knowing that inside, Stella was beating herself up, humiliated at yet another thing she didn't know.

But Stella was the only person Grace had told about the anorexia. They'd been sitting out at the pool, and Grace, watching Celia and Livie splash in the water, had said, "I've had issues with eating."

Stella had looked at her, shielding her eyes from the sun with her hand. "Well, who doesn't?"

"Mostly, I've got some really bad habits." Grace prickled with nerves as she spoke. "It kind of started in high school. But then college was the worst."

"Those teenage years. God! I think everyone went through some kind of body or eating thing. And even now! You've seen what I eat with Eric. Juice squeezes. Hot dogs. Microwave burritos. I'm lucky if I get a carrot stick down sometimes. If it weren't for Aaron, we wouldn't eat anything wholesome."

Grace had nodded, a full feeling bursting warm inside her chest. Grace didn't have to say anything else because she felt Stella's complete acceptance, and she closed her eyes against the sun.

The movie had quieted down, whispers inside a dark tunnel, and Grace leaned back against her seat. She'd known Stella the longest of anyone at the club and understood Stella held truths softly, taking them in and holding them close. Grace couldn't imagine Helen with some of the stories Grace could tell, all Helen's sharp edges, though Grace could talk to her about everything else. Felice would try to understand the story literally, wanting to offer resources, trips to the library, doctors' phone numbers.

Kathleen used to understand and let her eat what she wanted, until the end when she couldn't look into Grace's shopping cart, couldn't bear to watch Grace prepare a meal. "If I see one more damn packet of Sweet'n Low or NutraSweet, I'm going to go crazy," she would say, slamming out of the kitchen.

Kathleen had wanted to eat everything, to have it all there, on the counters, in the fridge, in the stove. She wanted to eat out twice, three times a week, snack on bagels and cream cheese, pluck Kalamata olives from the jar, dip steamed asparagus into garlic mayonnaise, watch cheese bubble on a lasagna, smell salmon grill on the barbecue. Kathleen wanted to buy hot dogs at baseball games, stop at fruit stands, dart into smoothie shops in Santa Cruz and Berkeley, wherever she was. She even ate in bed: chocolate chip cookies, ice cream, Tootsie Rolls. Grace some-times found herself holding her breath against the smell, feeling large and greasy and full of fat just sitting by Kathleen as she licked her fingers.

"Eating is healthy," Kathleen said. "It's not the problem, Grace."

"What are you saying?"

"I'm saying food isn't the problem. It's how you relate to it. Like it's the enemy, something to defend against, something to suffer through and then attack. The way you are, well, it's like fighting against life. It's disgusting."

As an actor sailed out of a tunnel and onto a rain-wet field, traffic whizzing by on a nearby freeway, Grace swallowed the same tears that had filled her throat when Kathleen had spoken those words. Disgusting. Disgusting.

Stella leaned over and whispered in her ear. "I still don't get it."

Grace shook her head. "Neither do I."

After the movie, the four of them sat at a table sipping mochas and lattes and Earl Grey tea. Grace had a glass of water in front of her, but sat back in her chair, her jacket bundled tight, a scarf around her neck, protection against the fog blowing in from the bay.

"Why don't you get something hot?" Felice said. "You look so cold."

"You know I can't drink caffeine," Grace said, her body tin-gling with the questions she could feel starting to spill out of the group. That was why it was easier to be with them at the pool, where eating wasn't expected or planned. There was food every-where else.

"Why? Does it keep you up? There's got to be decaf around here," Felice asked, turning back to look at the counter.

"Caffeine's not all of it, really," Grace said.

"I can't believe you're not cold," Felice said. She held her mug with two hands and leaned over the steam.

"I am. I mean, that's not it." Grace felt her hands pressing against her ribs, her fingers beginning to count the bones under her breasts, one, two, three, four, five, the floating sixth. "It's what happened with the radiation when I had cancer. It's not just the caffeine. It's anything in my stomach. I'll be sick."

Felice spun the mug on the table, the porcelain grating against the wood "Oh, right. I forgot."

Grace swallowed and then dragged out the old story. "My duodenum was damaged. Whatever goes in goes out all night long. That's why I eat at night right before bed. At least I'll be close by, you know. It was really bad last week for some reason. It comes and goes."

"I had no idea radiation could do that," Felice said.

"Even though they're trying to help, doctors really give you poison sometimes," said Helen. "Who knows how much damage these drugs do?"

Under her jacket, Grace moved her hand from her ribs and pressed it against her stomach, feeling the bowl of her hips, the circle of her spine. "I went through so many kinds of treatment when I was sick before. One of them was radiation treatment to the liver. There's only so much you can have in your whole life, and I'm at my limit. I'm not going to be able to have any this time. But anyway, I'd had too much by the time I went on the experimental protocol. It was too late for my stomach, you know."

"You did have it in your liver, didn't you?" Stella said. "I thought so. I thought that's what you'd told me."

Grace nodded, seeing that dark organ in her mind, the gray spot of the tumor. And now there were more, balls of light on the X rays, her lungs a universe of disease.

"Did the doctors ever tell you it might come back? What are

they saying now?" Felice asked. "It seems like they would have given you some kind of odds or something."

Helen shook her head. "They *never* tell you never. To save their asses."

"Really?" Stella asked. "They don't give you odds? They didn't talk about remission the first time?"

Grace shrugged. "Depends on what doctor you talk to. Sometimes they do, sometimes they don't."

"I can't believe that happened to your stomach, though," Felice said. "You could sue those doctors."

Helen put her arm around Grace. "Believe me, it's no fun eating with this one, let me tell you."

Grace smiled, relieved by Helen's comment and the laughs that followed. They all went back to their drinks, and Grace knew that there wouldn't be any more questions about her eating, at least for a while. Just then her stomach began to lurch, and she laughed, loud enough to cover the awful sound. At least later, because she'd done everything right, there would be beans. And rice cakes. And all the soy milk she wanted.

After the movie, Grace sat at the dining room table, a bag of rice cakes, six packets of Sweet'n Low, and two cans of green beans in front of her. It went like this: rice cake, half a packet of Sweet'n Low, five green beans, the beans bobbing swollen in the water as Grace plunged her fingers in to pull them out, sucking on each, feeling the smooth inside and swollen seeds on her tongue before swallowing. After the beans, she went back to the rice cakes, anticipating the sweet bitterness of the Sweet'n Low as she crunched through the crisp top of the rice cake. And then beans again, until both cans of beans and the rice cakes were gone, nothing but white flecks of Sweet'n Low on the table. Grace placed a thin finger softly on her tongue, and then brought her wet finger to the table, pressing it against the random grains, cleaning the table until not a bit was left.

FIVE

❧

"WHERE HAVE YOU BEEN?" Felice turned in the two a.m. darkness, seeing James's form against the closet door. "You didn't tell me you'd be this late. I called the office and talked to Sylvia, but she couldn't tell me where you'd gone. Or what time you'd be home. Or who you were with."

Felice heard the *thump, thump* of his dress shoes, the slip of his wool pants as they slid over his thighs, the clang of his belt buckle hitting the back of the desk chair.

"What's the emergency now?" he said calmly, moving toward the bathroom in his socks.

Felice sat up, feeling around for the bedside lamp switch and then turning it on. She'd been trying to talk to James about the championship swim meet all week, but she'd never had the chance, and the boys asked every day if he was going to come watch them. "Does it have to be an emergency for me to talk to you? Do I have to provide you with something alarming in order to get you home to me, to the boys? I needed to talk with you. Christ."

He came out of the bathroom, his face ripe with the red patches that always spread over his cheeks when he drank wine. "I told you this morning. I had a meeting."

"A meeting! Do you think I'm an idiot? It's two a.m. Don't you think I know you're not working? *Working!*"

"Here we go. What I do doesn't count. Same old story. So I have to take out some clients. No, that's not working. You just think I'm pandering, trying to sell, sell, sell. You never have given me any credit, Felice. So why should I tell you shit?" James took off his T-shirt and stared at her, the college boy she'd once known so far gone, she knew that if she could reach inside him, there wouldn't be a thing she'd recognize.

"That's not how I feel."

"Oh, right. Remember what you said to my boss last Christmas? What was it? 'Bayview is corrupt. Like every other bank in this nation' or something like that. You didn't think of me having to face him afterward. You just went on and on telling him how immoral we all were. You just look down your nose at me because what I do isn't art or education or science or literature. Because I work for a bank. Well, fine. I'm leaving you out of it."

"James. That's not . . . it's not you—it's the company. I know you work hard."

"I can't talk to you about anything anymore. Look at this. Why should I be here now? For this fighting?"

"You're my husband, James. You're the boys' father. No matter what you did or do. I still need to know what's going on. You know that. You can't make that go away."

James sat down on the edge of the bed and took off his socks, throwing them toward the bathroom door. She wondered how many times he'd put them on and taken them off today, imagining that other dressing, in another room. "You don't want to know anything about me. You made that clear a long time ago."

Felice bit her lip and closed her eyes. She couldn't believe she was having this conversation, one that seemed on the edge of truths she was afraid of. If she was smart, she would shut up now and fall back on her pillow, letting tonight, as so many others, slip into a bad dream. She would wake up in the morning, the only clues James had been here at all the steam in the shower, a juice glass on the counter, the empty spot in the garage where he parked his car. But there were his late nights and supposed business meetings and his home office, the office he locked, saying, "I don't want the boys getting in." He had a life of secrets in him, and for the first time Felice wanted to know what they were. "What are you hiding?"

"Excuse me?"

"What is it? Tell me. Tell me now." He looked back over his shoulder, his face so familiar, even in anger, that she wanted to weep. What had happened to them? Why did she get drunk at his business parties and say things she carried safely inside her the rest of the time? Why didn't she care about mergers and acquisitions? Why did she wish he'd read *Beowulf* or *The Canterbury Tales* with her, when he never had in college? When had she forgotten to ignore what she might have had with him or another man? "Just tell me."

James turned to her, words on his tongue, but then he pushed his hair back with his hand and closed his eyes. "I can't talk now. Turn off the light and go to sleep."

She moved toward him, almost lunging across the bed, but he stood up.

"Don't."

Felice stiffened, feeling her body move from wanting to touch him to wanting to hurt him. She swallowed down tears. "What about the swim meet on Saturday and Sunday? I wanted to talk to you about that. The boys are so excited. All of us have planned meals for each day."

James shook his head. "I can't believe you didn't teach this summer. What a waste. You've got too much damn time on your hands. I mean, really, Felice. You're starting to sound like Helen and Stella. At least Grace with all her weird stuff is interesting."

"Weird stuff? She's got cancer."

"The weirdest cancer I've ever seen."

Felice rubbed her face. "What? Forget it. That's not what I want to talk about. And anyway, the pool is for the boys."

"Is it really? Are you sure? The only thing I've heard you talk about all summer is Grace's illness. Like that's what matters. Now turn off the light and leave me alone."

He walked into the bathroom and closed the door, and she sat still, wondering how their marriage had come to this, late-night arguments that ended with James peeing. Why couldn't she say

more of what she felt? Why couldn't she do anything? For instance, she knew she could beat down the door and push James
against the marble counter. She could imagine herself yanking
down his briefs and smelling his penis and pubic hair for clues to
his other, secret life. And there would be clues—she knew that.
Even from here, she could smell the other woman. She hadn't
studied Arthurian romances for nothing—she knew the signs of
adultery by heart.

She could silence him if she would get out of this bed, and then
he'd apologize and change. No, he wouldn't change. That never
happened in any of the tales she'd studied and taught. But at least
she'd know he wasn't the boy she'd loved so deeply in college that
when she looked in her dorm room mirror, she saw him instead
of herself. If she could just move. It wasn't the bathroom door
keeping her out, but the stories on the other side and then the
things she would have to do once she heard them.

Her body was heavy and torpid and full of sadness, and as she
lay wondering into the night, the bathroom light a slash of yellow
under the door, she fell asleep.

James left in the morning without saying a word to her or the
boys. Brodie walked into the kitchen and looked at the counter,
staring at the empty juice glass, just as Felice had done. "Where's
Dad?"

"He had to leave early again. Lots of work." She bit off the lie,
wondering how she would be repaid for these untruths.

"Did you ask him about the swim meet? Is he coming?" He sat
down at the table, his tanned feet dangling over the floor.

Felice smiled and poured him some cereal. "I hope so. Hey,
Helen's going to take you two to Montclair Park. I better go wake
up your brother."

She walked into the hall and leaned against James's office door,
finding her breath somewhere in her throat, urging it down. She
heard Brodie's spoon clang against his bowl, and she thought
about Celia. Which kind of loss was worse? A parent who disap-

peared without a trace or one who vanished right in front of your eyes? She couldn't decide who was losing more, Celia or her boys.

The boys were quiet as they dressed and Felice packed up park gear, bread crusts to feed the ducks, and sandwiches for everyone. Dylan sat on his floor just looking at his Lego town and Brodie slumped on the couch watching cartoons on Nickelodeon. Felice was relieved when Helen finally came to pick them up, but then found herself trying to stay busy, desperate to keep last night's fight from replaying in her head. She started with the hardwood floor, pouring wood oil soap into a bucket of water, and mopping clean, straight wet lines back and forth. With all of this—Grace, James, the boys—it seemed impossible to imagine that in a couple weeks she'd be back editing *The Mediaevalist* and lecturing to hundreds of students. Even though she would never want another summer like this one, Grace sick, Helen absent, Stella preoccupied with worry, Felice knew that after this weekend's swim meet, everything was going to shut down, her old life taking her up again, and she nervously wrung out the mop, trying to picture who she was, a professor, someone who knew things, someone who commanded hundreds into bizarre reading and writing tasks and was obeyed! How could this be? she wondered, knowing that she couldn't get her husband to answer one single question, come home for dinner, stay for breakfast.

After finishing the dining and living rooms, Felice dumped the dirty water and walked into her office, full of student papers, books, and journal submissions, everything tumbled together, nothing like James's office. His locked office. Suddenly she knew what she had to do, and it seemed an easier solution than the one that had presented itself last night, her barging into the bathroom and sniffing out what was real between them. Felice went to the kitchen and pulled out the ice pick from the silverware drawer and walked down the hall to James's office, slipping the pick's deadly tip into the lock just as her brother, Gage, had taught her years ago when they looked for Christmas presents in their parents' bedroom. She slid it in, pressed, and the door clicked open, as she knew it would, and Felice walked into James's office. Exactly as she had thought, his office was organized, pristine, sterile even, no papers fluttering on the desk, no stacks of books on the floor. Just clean and clear Pottery Barn furniture, washed oak and metal, the computer a technological centerpiece on the desktop.

She sat down on his leather chair and tried to imagine what he saw as he sat there: the view of Oakland outside his window? Or, she wondered, swiveling, the wall? His diplomas? Did he even bother to look at the picture of her with Brodie and Dylan? Actually, the picture looked completely out of place here, too old for the feelings he seemed to have for them now with his slipping in and out, his late nights, his disinterest in the boys' activities. Why did he even bother to leave it here? Without thinking, Felice grabbed at the desk drawers, but they were locked, too, and she tried the ice pick, but it was too big to work these locks. Where would James hide a key? And then she saw her own face on the desk, and she felt it, as if she were calling herself awake, and she picked up the picture, and moved her fingers behind the frame. There it was. A key.

Felice went through all the drawers at once, pulling them open, staring at the files. She started with bank statements, annuities, 401Ks, retirement funds, college funds, Smith Barney statements. Everything seemed okay to her, but what did she really know? He had always been the money expert, even when they were students. "Let's buy a used car with your student loan. That way, we can live off what I'm making, and we're only paying three percent interest on the car," he'd told her. "Let's use the money your mother gave us for a wedding gift and invest it in the stock market. That's a real present," he'd said. "Let's use my benefits and take the money the university is giving you instead of benefits and put it in an annuity," he'd said. All these years she had nodded and turned back to her book or page, thankful that he could do this for her, that he was watching out for them, their future, their future together.

Flipping through the papers, Felice finally began to see that something didn't look right. The amounts for each—bank, annuities, stock market—were still the same, but they hadn't changed for months, no deposits for anything. She dug through to July, and the numbers were the same as in March. Where was the money going? She almost picked up James's phone to call him, but she put it down, not knowing how to tell him she'd broken into his office. *But it's my office, too*, she thought. *This is my house, half mine.* Felice pulled out July's and March's statements and tucked everything else back where it should be. *I'm planning for my divorce*, she thought and started to cry, bending down over his desk, breathing in the smell of wood and ink and cleaning fluid, nothing of her husband.

In the past few years, money had become everything to him. And he'd been taking some away from her and from the boys. He'd been doing something with thousands of dollars, and she didn't know what. In May he'd said, "Let's stay home this summer. The boys can really get into swim team."

"We could go to Hawaii for a week," Felice said. "That won't disrupt anything."

"When I was a kid, we just had all those long days of doing nothing. That's a real summer."

"I know. But maybe just a long weekend. The boys loved Pismo Beach."

"It's such a drive. And it's so grungy now. I felt like I had cotton candy on the bottom of my shoes the whole time we were there."

"What about Tahoe for the Fourth of July?"

"Well, let's think about it. But anyway, don't you want to stay home and keep an eye on Grace? You keep telling me how sick she is," James replied, but he never wanted to talk about it again, and Felice hadn't bothered to argue anymore. She'd just let him have his way. She'd just let him take and take and take. What an idiot! And where did that money go? What else was he doing? What was he doing about the Christmas fund? Was he siphoning off that, too?

Felice stood up, her legs shaky and nervous, like Brodie and Dylan when they started to walk for the first time, lurching for support as she moved toward the door. She turned to see the morning sun on San Francisco Bay, the light reflecting white off buildings, the sky a perfect baby blue. *I'll never come in here again*, she thought, clutching the statements in her hands. *I won't need to.*

In the afternoon, Helen dropped off the boys and Celia, all of them full of frozen yogurt. "Before I take Livie shopping, I'm going to go check in on Grace," Helen said from the driver's seat, Felice bending down by the passenger's side window.

"Is she okay today?"

Helen shrugged. "I think so, but since the mall's that way, I thought I would. Hey, are you all right? You look really tired."

Felice bit her lip, feeling another lie on her tongue. "Well . . . I cleaned all day. And then I worked on my office mess."

Helen laughed. "That explains it. I'll see you later at practice."

Felice watched her friend drive away and then went back to the kitchen, where she sat down numbly, surrounded by Tupperware and fruit, bags of pretzels, sandwich meat and sourdough rolls. A week ago, two days ago, even yesterday, she had been looking forward to this meet, imagining it was the perfect event before everyone went back to school. Grace was hanging in there despite Kathleen's abrupt abandonment, and they all would have had so much fun sitting by the edge of the pool, cheering the kids on. But now she felt like she was underwater, pressed away from oxygen by bank statements and betrayal, the very thought of packing up the first of many bags to take with her tomorrow to the Laney College swim complex impossible. But she had to make the weekend work; the boys were looking forward to huddling in sleeping bags with their friends on the cool pool deck, eating donuts and drinking soda, yelling to their teammates, all of them wanting to swim well and win for Tony.

She rubbed her face. Every time she was about to cry, she

imagined Celia. How could any of this compare to what that child was losing—her mother, her entire life? Days like this one would be rare, Felice knew, and she looked outside in the backyard, where Dylan, Brodie, and Celia were splashing water on the patio, crying out, "I see a dry spot. Kill it! Kill it!"

Celia took the hose and arced a fan of spray over the patio, Dylan and Brodie running underneath the drops. She pointed the hose, adjusted the nozzle, and squirted Brodie hard in the back. Felice gasped, watching a red blotch bloom, and was about to stick her head out the window, but Celia put the hose down and chased the boys around to the side of the house, the hose gurgling onto the patio.

She thought to run outside and say something to her, but every day, at least around the adults, the child seemed to grow quieter, her green eyes always watching, her mouth a stiff straight line. Maybe it was because Celia was handed between the three of them like baggage, each day a whirlwind of Helen, Stella, Felice, no time for her to be in her own house, in her own room, with her mother who had so little time left.

Next time, Felice thought, *I'll say something*, and she sat down again to her task, and sighed, wondering why she thought she had the skills to say anything to Celia when she didn't know how to manage her own life. But someone was going to have to do something soon.

"She's sullen," Helen had said just the day before as they watched Celia, Livie, and the other girls stand by the pool edge waiting for Tony to begin workout. They stood in a lean flesh circle, rearing back to laugh, stamping their feet, talking behind cupped hands.

"It's not 'sullen' really," Felice said. "It's more like a total lack of affect."

"Except when she's bothering Eric." Stella crossed her legs and rocked her foot nervously. "I asked her to stop bugging him at the beginning of the summer, but she gets her digs in when no one else is listening."

"What does she say?" Felice asked.

"She teases. Mean. Tells him he's a lousy swimmer, makes fun of his backstroke," Stella said. "She's nothing like she was before Grace got sick. She used to beg me to let Eric come over when he was little. She liked to pretend she was baby-sitting him."

Helen shook her head and flicked away a yellow jacket with her hand. "She has no reserves. Just like Grace. Neither of them has anything left."

"How could they have?" Felice dug through her bag for sunscreen and squeezed a white blob on her thigh. "How could Grace do anything for Celia right now? I blame Kathleen for so much of this."

"The poor kid. I wonder what she eats. Grace never cooks, does she?" Stella asked. "Once I went over to bake a birthday cake for Celia, and the oven didn't even work. It was either warm or broil. And I think two of the burners were out."

"We should bring meals over every day," Felice said. "We need to make sure Celia is better taken care of."

The women were silent, breathing in the hot August air crackling under their feet. No one saying, Felice thought then, what they were all thinking—that Grace was unable to take care of her own daughter, the girl she'd loved and protected almost solely, the girl she'd breast-fed until Celia was four. First her ex-husband and now Kathleen, one betrayal after another.

"Celia needs help," Helen said finally. "Someone needs to do something."

"I thought Doris would be up here by now. I can't even imagine what her and Grace's phone calls are like. Grace must be lying through her teeth," Stella said. "I think I'll call her again. Someone has to fix this mess."

But how? Felice thought now as she leaned against the kitchen counter, wondering how she could possibly be arranging grapes and melon chunks in Tupperware bowls. *We only have time for Grace, and we're not doing such a hot job with that. Maybe*, she thought, *maybe . . .* Then the phone rang and she pushed Grace and Celia aside, just for a moment, thinking, *It's James. What will I say? How will I tell him what I found?* Wiping her hands on the towel tucked in her pant waist, she picked up the phone on the second ring.

"I thought I was going to get your boring message." It was Sean, laughing, music in the background. "I'm back! I'm in love!"

Felice thought to laugh but could only twitch her lips and went back to her chore, tucking pretzels into a canvas L.L. Bean bag. "Big surprise, Sean," she said, tears licking down her face. "Okay. Let me guess her name. Finola? Raven? Genevieve? Siobhan?"

"Wow, you're in a mood. You're awful. Her name is Susan. She's from the University of Houston. I met her when I was in London. I went to the British Museum, and there she was sitting by the Elgin Marbles. She was writing a poem."

Without making a sound, she closed her eyes and shook her head. It was so typical of Sean. She could picture this Susan, a perfectly metered sonnet on her lap, her long blond hair pulled back with a silky ribbon, her body swathed in a delicate rose-patterned dress, a wicker bag by her side. She imagined Sean moving ever so subtly toward Susan, looking over her shoulder at the poem, a verse on stolen treasures, the lives of heroes, pain. Almost ready to laugh, Felice saw Sean's bright eyes, heard his first tentative question: "Are you a writer?" Felice breathed in, trying to swallow down her sarcasm, and said, "Are you going to see her again soon?"

"But she's already here! She has a sabbatical this year, and she can write anywhere."

"Oh. She's staying with you?"

"Of course. We're . . . we're going to live together. And if it works, well, we're going to get married."

"What? Are you kidding? Isn't this a little quick? You're pulling my leg, aren't you?"

"No, I'm not," he said, his voice tight.

"You're serious."

"It can happen that fast, Felice. It is possible. You of all people should know that."

She nodded without saying anything, knowing that Sean had been the one who waited with her at the door of her Western Civ class, pretending to talk with her as she watched James with shy eyes. He was the one who listened to a recounting of every ordinary conversation she and James had about homework and the professor and tests. Sean heard all the details of their first kiss, first sex, first declarations of love. And how could she warn him now if she hadn't been able to warn herself then?

"I guess you're right. I just want to make sure you know what you're doing."

"Don't you think I'd have to know? She's here, Felice." He laughed and began talking about Susan's research on feminist perspectives in the *Odyssey*, what ensued after the Elgin Marbles, the lavender smell of Susan's hair, and how lucky he was this time, really and truly.

Felice listened, asked questions, but felt the tiny little balloon she'd carried for twenty years in her chest wither and collapse. What would she do now? Now that she needed him? Even though she told Sean over and over that they were never meant to be together and meant it absolutely, she always imagined that if worse came to worst, he'd be there for her.

But now it had all changed. The worst was happening, and he had left her just as James seemed to be. Just as Kathleen had left Grace. A hot season of broken hearts. And she knew that now Susan would come first with Sean, as she should. Felice was truly on her own.

"Well, anyway," Sean said, breathing out his last detail about Susan, "how's your friend Grace doing? Is her cancer in remission?"

Felice closed her eyes, still surprised by the word cancer. "It's not good. The doctors told her it was only a matter of months. Her daughter's here right now playing with the boys so Grace can get some rest. She's on a major round of chemotherapy."

"Still? Wasn't she doing that last time we talked?"

"It's some kind of experimental chemo. A secret protocol at Stanford. We're not allowed to know all the details. But it's amazing! Her hair hasn't fallen out. She isn't even that nauseated. She manages to come up to the club every afternoon to watch her daughter swim. Sometimes she works out. It's like a miracle drug or something."

"That sounds a little weird. I wonder what Artie would say about that," he said, referring to a doctor friend of his she had met several times. "I should ask him. Do you want me to?"

"It's okay. She's got a SWAT team of doctors on her case. She's on the phone with them all the time. They all care about her so much. One doctor even calls her at home to check on her after a round of chemo."

"That poor woman."

"I know."

"That poor little girl. I bet that she can't even imagine what's coming."

Felice thought of the look on Celia's face as she squirted the hose on Brodie's back, calm and sure and completely radiant. "I think she does know, even though no one has told her. Kids are so smart."

Sean paused. "They are. . . . But what about you? What's going on with you? You sound . . . different."

"I don't think I know how to talk about it yet." Her tears appeared out of nowhere again, dripping on the counter. She dropped a package of peanuts on the floor and began to sob, realizing how she'd almost managed to hold back everything, to keep James at the far side of the room as she was talking. "Do you really want to know?" But how could she pour this ugliness out on him? For the first time, he was happy in a way that didn't involve her, and yet he wanted to listen. She was so selfish. She'd only cared about her career, her publications and tenure and honors, so busy with her own life that she hadn't seen James waving from another shore and then finally turning away, making fast tracks in the sand. So she'd gotten it all, hadn't she? But here she was, crying into the phone.

"Yes. Of course I do, love. Tell me."

So she did.

Felice sat at the dining room table, a glass of cabernet in front of her. She'd brought in *The New York Times Book Review* and submissions to *The Mediaevalist* to read, but she hadn't picked up anything, staring instead out the window, watching the horizon blacken and then shine with reflected light, the Bay Bridge loops of light in the distance. Brodie and Dylan had just gone to bed, but they'd seen something was wrong, Dylan throwing his arms around her neck. "I love you, Mom," he'd said, squeezing hard, and she'd held him, feeling his skinny ribs and flat hard back. It was already starting, Felice could see that. Here he was, comforting her, taking care of her, when that was her job. There would only be more hurt and more compensating, each of them trying to do more for one another, when inside, they'd all be in pain.

"I love you, too, Dyl." She looked over his shoulder to see Brodie in the doorway, his eyes watchful and dark. "Good night, sweetie," she'd called to him.

"Where's Dad?" Brodie asked.

"He'll be home soon. Don't worry." She hoped she wasn't lying. She wasn't, was she? He would come home, at least tonight, because all his precious, secret papers and plans were still locked in his office.

"Will he come to the swim meet tomorrow?" Brodie asked, his face still and white.

Felice swallowed, knowing that she had no truth to turn into voice now, knowing that James could very easily say he had work or a client in town or a golf game to talk business, anything to avoid her. "He said he would. I hope so."

Brodie had stared at her, and she wondered if she imagined anger on his face. She picked up Dylan and began to move toward Brodie, but he turned and walked to his bedroom alone. Already, he was moving away from her, like James, like her own father, everyone too far away to touch. But Dylan was still here, and she hugged him as he curled into her shoulder. Felice knew that, if she confronted James, finally, if she made him change, if she made him stay or go, there was time to pull them all back from the point of despair. But she had to do it now, tonight, or she would lose them all.

Felice almost jumped when she heard the garage door rumble, her heart beating fast, her breath coming short into her lungs and throat. What was she going to do? Admit her crime right away? Say, "I busted into your office and found out what you've been doing?" Or would she manipulate him into telling her the truth? She'd never been good at either approach, too scared to confront or hold a secret, each impossible.

James opened the door that led from kitchen to garage and almost flinched when he saw her sitting there in the darkened room. "What are you doing?" He put his keys on the counter and opening the cupboard for a glass.

"I'm waiting, James. For you to come home." Her tongue was thick with fear and cabernet. What was she going to say next? "We have to talk about what I found in your office."

He didn't flinch this time. Instead, he turned on the faucet and filled his glass to the top, drinking down every bit of water before turning back to her. "Why did you go in the office? I locked it."

"I knew you were up to something, hiding something. You haven't been honest for months," Felice said, amazed at how clear her marriage was now that she said these things aloud. And she knew it was over because he hadn't even tried to apologize.

"I can't believe you just went in there and snooped around. It's so typical of you these days, not saying shit and then doing something like this. Couldn't you have left it alone? Couldn't you have just stayed out? Christ."

"It's my house, too. It's my room to go in if I want. And I did say shit. I begged you to tell me what you were hiding. You just wouldn't, so don't lay this at my feet. It's not mine."

"Oh. So I can go through your office and dig around? Push through all that journal crap and student papers?"

"I don't have anything to hide. Nothing. You've been taking our money. You've been doing something with it." She picked up the papers she'd taken earlier and held them up for him to see. "I've got the proof right here."

James put down the glass and walked toward her. For a second she stopped breathing, almost glancing around for a weapon, as if he were a shadowy stranger she'd come across in the faculty parking lot late at night. But then she remembered it was just James, even if it was a James she didn't know anymore. Even if he were a different man, he would never hurt her. He wouldn't.

He walked to the table and then stopped, holding on to the top of a chair. She looked down at his hands curled over wood, his skin dusky in the living room light, a few fine red hairs shimmering on his wrists. She could see his veins under the skin, could almost feel the soft valleys between his fingers, the smooth pads of the tips, the curved moons of his nails. There was a rough spot just under the mounds of his palms where his laptop computer rubbed calluses, and a triangle scar on his left-hand pinkie finger, a Boy Scout knife incident. She had seen these hands cupped, full of a child's newborn body or her breasts or her hips. They had held the scissors that had snipped umbilical cords, baby wipes, bottles full of expressed milk, and diapers. He had taken these hands and rubbed them over her entire life, and she didn't understand how they could be the same hands that had hidden papers, filed away secrets, taken what was important from her and her children. Their children.

And here he was staring at her as she held the evidence of his deceit. Here he was, a man who no longer loved her or their family, who must have a mistress and a bank account in her name, money he took from this household, their household. He was running away, and Felice knew it, and she knew he knew it, too.

"It's all legal. No one will prove otherwise."

Felice stood up and moved toward the family room. As she headed away from him, she wished she could call Helen, Stella, or even poor, tired Grace, letting someone else witness this conversation. With her head buzzing, her limbs full of nerves, she wasn't sure she'd remember any of this exactly. "Who cares about legal, James? What are you doing?"

"I'm done. I can't live here anymore. With you. You've changed. You don't care about anything but your work and your projects and your university. I told you this last night. What I do seems irrelevant to you, doesn't it? Admit it!"

Felice gasped. "That's not true! But even if it were, does it mean it's okay to steal from me? From the boys? Because we don't get along anymore? Have you heard about marriage counseling? Wouldn't that be a likely first step, for Christ's sake?"

"I asked you about that three years ago, and you were too fucking busy with whatever committee it was. 'Later,' you promised. You even had Sean talk to me. So I kept waiting, and then, after a while, I stopped caring. You haven't cared. You don't care now really. It's something old, something I don't want to think about anymore."

"But can't we try again? For the boys?" In her sad question, she heard her voice, the voices of so many women in all of literature, the sound they made when a man walked away.

He waved his hand at her and closed his eyes. "It's too late for that. I've . . . I've met someone else. I'm in love with someone else."

Felice breathed in, hard, but her lungs wouldn't take in breath anymore, so she found herself panting. "I knew it. I knew that was it. This is nothing about me or what or who I am. It's about another woman."

James snorted. "Yeah, go ahead and think that, Felice, if it makes you feel better. You know, there was a time, not so long ago, when I really felt everything was going to be great. But what you said to Brant at the Christmas party? That was only the beginning. The way you look at me. The way you never ask about how my work is going. The way you feel so much smarter than me or anyone I know."

Felice began pacing, wondering how it was possible that the lights outside stayed on. How the world wasn't falling apart all over as it was in this house right now. "Again, does that mean you should be stealing? Aren't there other ways to get around this? Can't we work on it? Don't you care about the boys?"

"Don't even say that. They'll always be my boys, no matter what!"

"That's why you've been around so much for them lately, huh? Brodie asked me tonight if you were going to come to the swim meet tomorrow. And then what about Sunday? The banquet? If you were such a good father, you'd have been around all summer for all the meets. If they were really *your* boys, you would know as much about them as I do. If it was really just about me and how I felt, you'd have asked me to change. You could always talk to me. You could always tell me how you felt." Felice was crying now, imagining Brodie's face as he asked her about his father, feeling Dylan's arms still around her neck.

"I could? When was that? About ten years ago, before you became whiz professor and medieval goddess, off to conferences and meetings. And before you became the know-it-all mother, sure about everything for the boys. Whenever I wanted to do something with them, you had another better idea. Something you wanted to do."

"Why didn't you say something then? I would have changed. I know it. We were just so busy, I wanted to make sure things were—"

"Perfect," James slung in. "And I wasn't."

"But the boys don't care if you're perfect. I don't either. Things are different now. They need you."

"Don't pull that manipulative shit with me." He yanked on his tie. "And don't ever say I was stealing. It will all come out in court."

"So it's over? You're not even going to give me a chance? Us a chance?"

"I waited a long time before doing anything. But now it's over. I'll be there all this weekend, for the meet and the banquet. But Sunday night I'm moving out. You'll get the papers next week. It's over."

James looked at her, his eyes shiny in the darkness. She wondered if he'd ever cried about what he saw happening. She wondered if this was just some bluff, a plan to make her come crawling to him. But as she watched her husband stare at her from across the room, she knew it wasn't a bluff. It was real, and he meant it, and he'd stolen from her to make his life happen. Despite her. Despite the boys.

"Who is she?" Felice asked quietly. "Who is it?"

James turned back toward her and shook his head. "Amy," he said and walked out of the room. Felice heard him open his office door and then close it.

So it was Amy, the crisp blond woman in beautiful suits, her hair a blunt swing under her cheek, her lips a perfect bowed brown, her shoes small and polished. Amy, someone completely different from her and her cotton skirts and sweaters, her ink-stained fingers, her messy hair. She looked down at the papers in her hand, wishing they were rocks she could throw down the hallway. She thought briefly about the ice pick, wondering if she could use it again to open the door and then again on James's heart, stabbing away until she found a place in him that still loved her.

Felice sighed and sat down on a chair, the papers crackling as she shook, and she realized that the next person who would be touching them would be her lawyer, Mitch Gonzales. He would find out everything. He would find out how much money James had stolen. Felice would have to call him Monday. And her life would be over. *No*, she thought, wiping tears from her face, *it can't be over because I've still got the boys. But it will be different and sad. And alone.*

SIX

❦

IT WAS SEVEN O'CLOCK ON THE FIRST DAY of the Alameda swim meet. Stella, Helen, and Felice stood together drinking Peet's coffee on the almost deserted Laney College pool deck, guarding the damp square of concrete they'd staked out for the team. All the kids huddled under a sleeping bag tent they'd made, giggling and asking Helen to pass them doughnuts under the flap, small brown hands reaching out for more.

Stella could barely drink her coffee because her stomach was sour. She was nervous about Eric's event, the individual medley, a lap each of butterfly, backstroke, breaststroke, and freestyle. Tony had made the decision to put him in the race, and Stella had encouraged Eric all week, but in her head she could still hear Celia's bitchy chant, "Eric the Floppy Backstroke King." Now, though, they were all laughing together, and she hoped this meet would be something he pinned up in his memory, like a first-place ribbon on a wall.

She tried to sip her coffee while Helen passed out doughnuts. Felice yawned over her cup. Something seemed wrong; Felice was pale, her face almost translucent, her eyes and nose red. *Maybe it's allergies*, thought Stella. *Maybe meeting at six-fifteen was a bit of overkill.*

"You know," Stella said, "when I picked up Celia this morning, Grace seemed really good. The chemo must be shrinking those tumors like mad. She was going to go on a long run and then come here afterward."

"How can she run?" Felice shook her head. "I had Celia yesterday because Grace was *doing* a round."

Helen stood up and dusted the sugar off her hands. "And yesterday morning she was flat on her back. She wasn't sure she'd make it here at all."

"So much up and down. It's like she feels better finally, and then the next round throws her under. I don't know how she manages," Stella said.

"There's more," Helen said. "She told me she was thinking of running a marathon."

"How could she possibly?" Stella asked. "It's got to be just a fantasy."

"Maybe. She might be trying to think of something to keep herself going," Helen said.

"Well, really, something is going to have to change," Felice said. "School starts, and we aren't going to be able to have Celia all the time. I go back to work in a couple of weeks myself, and, Helen, you start school. We're all going to be driving kids around and whatnot."

Stella nodded, even though she would have no work or school, just the one kid to drive around. She didn't think Felice was suggesting that she take over Celia completely, but there was the assumption that if anyone could, only she would have the time. Stella thought about the Laney course catalogue she'd brought home earlier in the week, the classes she'd circled in red pen. "Yeah. I should call Doris again."

"Great idea," Helen said, putting her hands on her hips. "I still don't know why that woman hasn't come up yet. You called her months ago."

"She won't have any choice if things go along the same way," Felice added.

They were silent, listening to the noises of the pool, the lifeguards and maintenance crew pulling off pool covers and dragging chairs across the cement. In a few minutes, parents from other teams started to straggle in, carrying folding chairs and Igloo coolers, eyeing Stella, Helen, and Felice and their prime spot warily. Stella took off her scarf. Even though a thin layer of fog was spread over the Oakland sky, she could tell it was going to be hot. The air was already warming, the rising sun a muted yellow disk coming over the wall. She wondered if Grace was already on her way to the meet, her thin body in nylon shorts and shirt, her arms prickling against the cold. It seemed that what Grace was always working for—moving toward—was Celia.

"She wants to see Celia grown," Stella said. "She wants to see that girl grown up and in her own life."

"Isn't that what we all want?" Helen put on her Chevy's hat, Felice pulling on a ratty tail of straw that curled by Helen's cheek.

Stella turned to Felice, but her friend's eyes, usually so full of ideas, usually so alert and smart, seemed almost vacant. Stella wanted her to make some declaration, some pronouncement that would clear up this Grace mystery and tell them how to deal with Celia. But Felice shook her head, scuffing one tennis shoe on the ground.

"Here's Tony," Helen said.

"Good morning. Too early, I think," Tony said, putting down his bag, clipboard, and coffee, looking up at them, the whites of his eyes bright against his dark summer skin. "You have a great spot here."

Eric stuck his head out of the tent and poked it back in, and then they all pushed out, birthed from the tent like a litter of creatures, all scrambling to Tony. "Do we warm up now? Where's our lane?" Eric asked.

"We're going to win," Dylan said, long since brought up from the bottom of the pool, almost a freestyle expert at this point. "This is going to be the greatest."

Tony rubbed Dylan's head and smiled and looked at Felice, trying to catch her eye. Stella looked at her friend, seeing that Felice wasn't noticing anything, much less Tony. What did he want? she wondered, suddenly feeling protective, almost moving into his gaze herself.

Tony dropped his eyes. "Let me go find out what lane they've assigned us for warm-up. Get ready, okay?" Tony looked once more at Felice and then walked toward the officials' tent. The kids threw themselves on the pile of goggles, towels, and swim caps, jostling and pushing, excited to start the long day.

"He's a cute kid," Helen said. "Well, not a kid. I hate to say man. Too much baggage."

"He's still in graduate school," Stella said. "He was telling me about it. He's in your field, Felice. Whatever that field is. You know, important books only a select few understand."

Felice seemed to try to smile. "He looks young to me. It's been a long, long time since graduate school."

"What is he? Twenty-four?" Helen asked. "Well, I was working for Traveler Nine, flying all over the world at that age. I had so much fun back then."

"And then you met Darryl," Felice said flatly. "And then nothing was the same."

Stella turned to Felice, pushing a strand of hair off her friend's face. "What is it? What's happening?"

Felice rubbed her temple and closed her eyes. "If I start talking about it now, I don't think I could stay here. There's no safe place to talk about it at all."

Stella and Helen pressed closer. "Come on," Stella said. "The kids will be warming up for at least a half hour. Let's sit over here and you can tell us everything."

Stella put her arm around Felice and looked out toward the pool. Coaches and parents from at least ten teams were lined up around the edge, watching swimmers jump into the water and splash dry swimmers still on the deck who shivered in their Speedos. The snack bar opened, and a waft of coffee moved over the crowd. Parent volunteers grouped around officials, listening to the timing and judging rules. Stella sighed, wondering how they were going to get through the day, Felice's news so heavy. Helen was silent, leaning her elbows on her knees, pushing tears away with her fingers.

"I'm so sorry." Felice rubbed her forehead with her palm. "But you were right. I couldn't keep that in."

"Of course not," Stella said. "I feel so awful. I want to do something. I want to help."

"That asshole. That complete asshole." Helen stayed bent over. "Doesn't he know that he was doing more than stealing money from you? He was stealing himself away. I can't stand it!"

Stella dug through her jean pocket for a tissue. She pulled one out, shaking it gently, and handed it to Felice, who blew her nose.

"It seems crazy to be at a swim meet. I should probably call my lawyer this minute. God knows what James could be up to," Felice said.

"I don't know how he could show his face here." Helen put her arm around Felice's other shoulder, her hand touching Stella's.

"I don't know how he couldn't. The meet! The boys!" Felice cried out, putting her face in her hands.

"You have to call now. Right away," Helen said.

"Are you sure?" Felice looked up. "He won't be in his office."

"If he's not there, he'll have a machine. And it's a he? Shouldn't you get a woman?" Helen asked.

"He was my father's lawyer. He loves me. This is going to kill him." Felice wadded up the tissue and threw it into a trash can.

Helen pulled her phone from her purse. "Go out somewhere quiet and call him. Now. Before James sells all your assets, that jerk. Christ! First Kathleen, then James, and . . . well, it's too much."

Felice hugged Helen and Stella and stood up. "Thank you both. I wanted to call you after James locked himself in his office, but I could barely move. I stayed in the living room until three, thinking about nothing. Everything was dark, everything I could imagine."

She walked away, and Stella breathed out through her nose, feeling all her air escape her. She turned to Helen. "I don't believe it."

"I do."

"Why? Did she say something to you before?"

"No," Helen said. "I just knew something was up the last time I saw James. And . . . it's guilt. I can see it in everyone because it lives inside me."

"What do you mean, Helen?"

"It's a long story."

"It's going to be a long day." As Stella moved closer to Helen, putting a hand on her arm, Eric and Livie ran toward them, towels wrapped around their shoulders, their hair slicked to their faces.

"It's going to start, Mom!" Eric cried. "Come listen to the cheer."

"Hurry up!" Livie said, pulling Helen. They both stood up and followed their children.

"Come on," Helen said, and Stella trailed after. She wanted to stop Helen, pull her back before anything else could happen, before any more time could slip by, and say, "Tell me now." But Helen walked faster, pressing herself into the group of giggling children, and after a while, Stella couldn't find any trace of guilt in her friend's face, not one shadow of a sad story.

"If we don't leave soon, I swear Eric's going to jump in the car and drive himself up to the club," Aaron said, buttoning his shirt. "Are you almost ready?"

Stella sat on the bed, pulling up her nylons. "Yeah. Almost. I want to make one phone call, though."

"Well, God forbid we miss one minute of the banquet. I'll go out and calm him down, but I'm giving you no guarantees on how long it will last."

He smiled and left the room. Stella slipped on her dress, walking toward her desk as she zipped herself up. After watching Grace all weekend, her slow movements, her unfocused gaze, the puffiness of her jaw and eyes, she knew she had to call Doris. All of this had gone on for too long.

"Doris?" Stella said quietly, as if she was trying not to startle her, even though she had clearly answered the phone.

"Stella? I'm so glad you called. I talked to Grace not more than an hour ago. She told me—she finally told me," she said in a swirl, her voice full of tears. "Grace didn't say anything before because she didn't want to scare me. But I guess . . . I suppose it's really bad now."

"I'm so glad she told you. We've been so worried." Stella exhaled loudly, thinking that finally something would happen.

"And she told me more. I've been so wrong about so much of her illness. The one before, too. There were things I didn't know. Or I forgot. Grace tells me I don't remember so much about the first cancer. But I'm coming up. First thing tomorrow morning. Grace told me not to worry about tonight. I've already made my plane reservation."

Stella sat back in her chair. "What else did she tell you?"

Doris made sipping sounds, and Stella could almost hear the tea in a china cup. "I'm trying to calm down. I was so upset earlier. Anyway, she said she'd been going into the hospital at night for chemo, around one a.m., because of some special protocol."

Stella sucked in air, thinking about Celia. "One a.m.? I didn't know that. Even with Kathleen gone?"

"I know. That's why Grace called me. She felt so bad. She needs someone in the house. She also said the chemo is making her so sick, well, she's had accidents. You know, in bed, at night."

Stella shook her head, thinking about Grace this whole week leading up to the big swim meet, swimming laps during the adult swim time despite her treatments, helping to plan the rides and food and seating arrangements. Stella didn't know how this could be the same woman who was peeing or worse in her bed. "No." Her stomach pulsed and burned at the edges, as it had all weekend. "I don't believe it! She looks tired and sick, but sick enough to have accidents? Oh, it's worse than I thought."

"I know," Doris said, her voice strong again. "I just can't believe it happened like this. After what I always thought—that the cancer was gone. I just don't understand."

"Neither do I. I really don't."

*   *   *

At the banquet in the club's gym, Stella sat with Aaron, Grace, James, Felice, Helen, and Darryl. During the meal the younger kids made crazy figure eights around the tables, excited about being in their dress-up clothes and having won the first-place trophy, the large golden cup that showed they were the best team in Alameda County. Brodie, Dylan, Eric, Celia, and Livie ran up and down the corridor outside, their squeals echoing into the room. Other children sat at round tables, drinking sodas and eating cookies. Groups of parents sat in folding chairs around crowded tables or stood against the wall, sunburned and shiny, laughing with glasses of wine in their hands. The teenagers pretended to ignore the whole party, hanging out on the balcony, slipping in for food, then exiting altogether to go to the pool and gossip.

Stella had had one too many glasses of wine and was leaning on Aaron's shoulder, hot and tired. Everything felt somehow off-kilter, unbalanced, the world slightly foggy. And it wasn't the wine or the long day, the screaming and yelling as the kids swam, the uncomfortable wait on rickety chairs. There was something in her body, a movement of blood and worry, a tenseness in her abdomen and throat.

Stella looked over at Grace, who had dressed up for the evening, ditching her shorts and Jogbra for a deep blue cotton jumper that hung on her bones like a pretty sack. Grace's face looked tan, almost orange, but her skin was stretched taut, her hair was clean but dry and flat and almost crispy, and her eyes looked blank, with dark puffy purple welts under each. Kathleen hadn't shown up for any of Celia's races. Grace had looked back toward the pool entrance each time Celia stood up on the diving blocks, hoping, Stella assumed, that Kathleen had changed her mind about everything. And now, even though she was dressed up, Grace finally looked as sick as her mother said she was. Stella hadn't had the courage to mention her phone call with Doris, much less to tell Grace to go home and sleep and let the rest of them take care of Celia as they had all summer.

Stella caught her sigh before it left her throat. *It's Grace,* thought Stella. *That's what's bothering me. Of course. How did I imagine I'd forget, even today?*

Aaron moved slightly, lifting his glass to the table. "Well, folks, another year gone by. Here's to a successful parenting summer. All is well in the kid universe."

Darryl raised his glass and Stella followed him, clinking with him and Aaron and then Helen, Felice, and James, who barely seemed to be listening, plotting his next life, she imagined, preparing to simply disappear. Grace raised her hand to simulate a wineglass, even pretending to take a sip. Stella looked down at the table and saw Grace's plate was empty, as was the water glass in front of her. *She just can't eat,* thought Stella. *She can't even drink. Nothing can go in or it comes up or out at night, in her bed, like a baby.*

"All is well as far as we know," Darryl said. "Who knows what's going on in their universe?"

"That's optimistic." Helen frowned.

"Who knows anything?" James added, shaking his head. He looked into Stella's eyes, and she tried to tell him how much she despised him with a glance, but he wasn't seeing anything there, not the party, his wife, or his boys. All he could see was tomorrow and everything after.

"Don't say that! Look how happy they all are!" Felice said too loudly, her face flushed as she turned to watch the kids race past the door. "Dylan told me this was the best day of his life. His best day ever."

Grace smiled. "Wait until they get Tony in the water. It'll get even better. They love throwing him in and mobbing him."

"It gets a bit crazy. I think they asked the lifeguard to stay late and get everyone out of the pool by eight. That way Tony might just survive all the excitement." Helen looked at her watch. "They'd rather do that than eat."

"They deserve to have fun. Look at all the records the kids broke. Especially Celia," Aaron said.

"Here's to Celia." Stella raised her glass unsteadily. "What a swimmer."

"To Celia," everyone murmured.

Stella drank down another sip, the world whooshing around her, the sounds of the kids and the voices of all the parents like a giant macaw in her head. She looked at Grace, whose face seemed to be getting tauter by the minute, as if her cheekbones were just seconds from popping through. If she kept staring, Stella knew that she would see a skeleton sitting at the table, dressed up for a party. Felice was depressed, her eyes full of tears, the back of her neck red and tender. James had pushed his chair back from the table as if he were ready to bolt, throwing aside chairs and children as he made his way to the door and his new woman. *Just go*, Stella thought. *Why cause Felice pain any longer?* And Helen was bent forward over the table as if trying to avoid touching Darryl. Everyone looked awful, bizarre, cartoonish, and suddenly it was so hot, just like the entire day at the swim meet, and her face was burning, and then she saw nothing at all.

"Stella. Stella?" She heard Aaron's voice from the mouth of a dark tunnel.

Stella looked up through the darkness, pulling up into the sound and light, and opened her eyes. Her husband was above her, blinding white and encircled by black. As she blinked, Stella saw the rest of him, his arm fanning her with the banquet program. She wasn't in the gym anymore; she knew that, because it was quiet and cooler. She looked up again and saw Helen, Felice, and Grace all above her, too, their mouths pulled straight and slim in concern. For a second she wished for her mother.

"I'm . . . fine," Stella said slowly. "What happened?"

"You fainted," Aaron said. "You've never done that before."

Helen laughed. "Well, maybe it's the wine and song. This weekend was too damn much."

Stella clung to Aaron and sat up, her brain seeming to lag behind her. "Wow. That was weird."

Grace stood straight above her, her arms crossed over her chest. "You need to go to the doctor. Tomorrow if not sooner. Fainting is no joke."

"You've got to take care of yourself," Helen said.

"Health isn't a joke." Grace knelt down and gently stroked Stella's hair. "You know how I feel about that. You know how important it is to me. And where would I be without doctors?"

"I know." Stella leaned into Grace's touch for a moment, imagining how her friend must be with Celia, and then slowly sat up and placed a hand on Grace's bony knee. "I promise you. I'll go tomorrow. Really."

Stella sat in the Kaiser Permanente office in a plasticky, papery gown, her legs dangling off the side of the examination table. Her feet looked odd to her, white and thin, her Glory Be red toenail polish glaring against the greenish glow of the linoleum. The nurse had taken her blood pressure, temperature, and asked her a series of questions, some of which Stella couldn't even answer, only remembering the date of her last Pap smear.

"Your last menstrual cycle?" the nurse asked, bending over Stella's chart.

"Um . . . you know. I don't remember. My period's been off this year. I think I'm going through that premenopause thing."

"Perimenopause."

"Yeah. Whatever."

"Okay." The nurse put down her pen. "The doctor will be with you shortly."

As Stella waited, she imagined having to be in a room like this often, its cold white walls and racks of *Chlamydia*, *Panic Attacks and Phobias*, and *Penile Dysfunction* pamphlets the only decoration. *What must it be like*, she wondered, *to be here all the time like Grace?* How could Grace handle the smell and taste and sounds of a place like this night after night, the sickly ammonia bleached-out tang, the *shif-shif* of the nurses' clothes, everything so ugly green. Like wearing old pea soup, she thought, feeling ill again, her stomach pulsing dully. If she worked here, she'd have to do something: flowers in a vase on the metal cabinet, a poster of Italy, at least one newly painted wall, umber or yellow or clay. Anything, she knew, to make it seem alive.

After fifteen minutes, Stella's feet were purple with cold. Then Dr. Herrera knocked and walked in, smiling. "Hello, Mrs. Steinberg. How are you?"

Stella wondered if he were kidding about the question, knowing that few if any people would say, sitting naked under an ugly gown on a table like this in a place like this, *Oh, I'm just great.*

"Well, I'm okay. I guess. Now. I fainted last night at a banquet. It was hot and everything, but I felt queasy. Kind of sick."

Dr. Herrera nodded and wrote down a few notes on the chart. "Let's take a look. I probably will want to run a few tests, so if you have things to do in the next couple hours, you might want to cancel them. That way we can get the results and go from there."

Stella nodded and turned her face to the doctor's, lifting her head to the pinpoint light he shined in her eyes.

As she waited in the reception area, running through diseases known to her as well as new ones she'd found on the walls of the lab, nurses' station, and examination room, Stella decided she had tumors just like Grace or, at least, a serious blood disorder. Both could cause fainting—she knew that. And she knew her life would never be the same, filled with weeks and, if she was lucky, if you could call it that, months and years of endless tests and procedures. She wondered if she could somehow get Grace's doctors to look at her case, arrange to add her to the secret protocol. Maybe she and Grace would carpool to Stanford together, both their lives saved by miraculous drugs and hope.

Stella almost laughed, but then she thought of Eric and Aaron, and she closed her eyes, trying to disbelieve the idea away. *Anywhere*, Stella thought, *anywhere but here, now, with bad news.* She swallowed and wished for her mother, imagining Joyce's arms around her neck and shoulders.

"Mrs. Steinberg?" The nurse stood in front of the open door. "The doctor is ready for you now."

Dr. Herrera was smiling as Stella walked into his office. He took off his glasses and wiped them on the edge of his white coat. "Something interesting," he said.

"Yeah?" Stella squinted and tilted her head, as if she could duck his words.

"What I mean is that nothing adverse showed up on any of the tests."

"Oh, thank God," Stella said, interrupting him. "That whole fainting thing was really too weird."

Dr. Herrera coughed. "Your test came back positive. You're pregnant."

Stella stared at him for a long while before she realized she must look like some kind of paralyzed frog, her mouth hanging open in midcroak. "But . . . the doctors said after Eric that . . . well, it would be unlikely."

"Likely or unlikely, you're pregnant. How long has it been since your last menstrual cycle?" He flipped backward through her chart.

"I'm not really sure." Stella closed her eyes and tried to envision her box of tampons and how many were left. "Maybe two months. Three?"

Dr. Herrera made some notes. "Obviously, this is not really my expertise, and we didn't do a vaginal. I'm going to prescribe some prenatal vitamins, and then I want you to ask my nurse to get you an OB appointment for early next week. We want to get you set up in case you are more pregnant than you think. All right?"

"Okay." She numbly took the prescription from him. "So I'm not going into menopause?"

"It certainly doesn't appear that way, does it?"

"I'm forty," she said limply.

Dr. Herrera laughed. "My wife didn't have our first until she was forty-two. You're ahead of us!"

She tried to smile and then focused on the floor ahead of her as she moved toward the nurses' station. As she waited to schedule her appointment, Stella put her hand on her belly and wondered why she forgot to think about a baby, why this small creature inside her had hidden so long.

"Aaron! I've been paging you for an hour."

"I'm sorry. We were in the middle of something with the owner. There's a huge problem with the window orders. Damn double-hung shit. Anyway, are you all right? What did the doctor say?"

"The doctor said I'm pregnant." Stella heard her voice echo in the tin of the bad connection. The word *pregnant* bounced back into her ear. Here she was unfolding the sound of that forbidden topic all these years and hundreds of periods later. Another baby. She would be able to look at another woman's rounded belly without a slice of anger between her teeth. She wouldn't close her eyes when two young mothers stopped before her chair on the pool deck, chatting about breast-feeding and new teeth. Finally, the world she gave up when the surgeons sewed her belly tight was hers again.

Between the awful static and her own thoughts, Stella couldn't hear anything at the other end but some dim noise from electric tools in the background. "Aaron?" Stella said, sudden flickers of flame under her heart. "Aaron?"

Then she knew he wasn't talking because he was crying, and the whole nine years since Eric was born were busting open for him, too. He'd never said a word, holding her at night when Eric was a baby, saying, "He's healthy. He's beautiful." When people asked how many children they had, Aaron simply said, "The right amount." So all this time Stella had thought she'd been grieving alone. "Aaron!"

"Oh, my God!" Aaron breathed in wet breaths. "I can't believe it."

"Neither can I. Except I should have known. I hadn't been feeling well for a while."

"How far along are you? God! This is so amazing!"

"I don't know. Maybe three months. But I have an OB appointment set up for next week."

Aaron took his mouth away from the receiver and whooped. "I can't wait to tell the guys. But listen." He was suddenly serious. "You take it easy. Remember you just fainted. You might do it again. Call your mom and have her come over."

"I'll be just fine. Don't worry. I've never been better."

As she drove down High Street, Stella imagined herself with a girl. She knew she was moving too far ahead, an amniocentesis was still a couple months away, but she had the feeling this baby, this girl baby, would be exactly what she and Aaron and even her friends, especially Grace, needed. But she did have a squirm of nerves in her throat, thinking about all the girl issues she'd avoided by having Eric—the sullen spells, the princess routine, the furious streams of anger, the despair. Thinking about her own girlhood still made her cringe, even though that very childhood was what made her feel she'd be a good mother of a girl.

Idling at a stoplight, Stella imagined her girl would grow into a Celia or Livie, bloom with breast buds and attitude, challenge her about makeup and dating and life, moving out of the house because she was *sick to death, sick forever* of her. Stella wouldn't be able, as her own mother had been, to sit at her vanity table and brush her long blond hair because it would be gray. And she wouldn't be able to share Noxzema because she'd be using Retin-A or having glycolic acid treatments each week to get rid of all her wrinkles.

Maybe by then she wouldn't be able to tap back into the discomfort of her twelve-year-old body, fit back into her fear of her own flesh. The day her second period had started—the first had been almost nothing, a swirl of blood on her cotton panties—she'd felt bloody and awful and stupid, unable to get the junior-sized tampon in her so-tight vagina, despite Joyce's help from the other side of the bathroom door.

"Just relax, honey," her mother had said, her voice soothing even with the wood between them. "Put your foot on the bathtub rim and relax."

Stella was sobbing by this point, her stomach in her way, the tampon rough on her soft dry skin. Finally she threw the battered tampon in the trash and grabbed the maxipad belt her mother had given her the month before.

"It'll be all right next time," Joyce had said, but Stella didn't believe her. Stella knew she was the dumbest girl in the world—not even able to figure out a tampon—and fat and no one ever would love her.

Later, in her bedroom as she changed out of her bloody underwear, she chanced to look up, and there she was: large, rolling stomach, double chin, no breasts but a roll of flesh, all on top of her skinny legs. She sank to the floor, crying, taking brief glimpses at herself through her wet fingers, realizing that she had to change herself. It was almost too late. She was, as her mother said, a woman now, and was this the way she wanted to look as a woman? Who would ever marry her? Want her? Need her, if she looked like this, this stuffed sausage on sticks?

From then on, she'd thought about her twelve-year-old self every single day, carried that image to the grocery store to buy food, to the gym to work out, to Macy's to buy clothes. No one knew how much work it took to look this way, even if her long legs were a gift from her paternal grandmother. Stella exercised at least four times a week at the club, often more, dripping with so much sweat it seemed she'd been caught in a sudden, unexpected rainstorm. And then there was her hair, layered and long and now streaked every four weeks by Gino at his Grand Avenue salon. Sometimes, in the dead of winter, Stella went to the tanning place on Mountain Boulevard, lying on the tanning bed like a blind fish. She realized she'd become accustomed to her appearance, even if she didn't completely believe the reaction in others' eyes. *Is it true?* she wondered. *Do I really look that good?*

Her twelve-year-old self would have never imagined that she

could slim down to this size four. Stella knew that at twelve, she would never have imagined herself in this life, with Aaron and Eric, and another baby on the way. Stella tried to ignore the glances and comments from men and even women as she walked around the pool. Part of her thought they must be looking at the backs of her thighs or butt or flesh hanging on her arms. But then Stella would turn, and the people would smile, avert their eyes quickly, and as she walked on, she could feel their admiration.

The twelve-year-old Stella made this Stella keep the promise, even though her life had happened just as she feared it wouldn't. But she never, ever wanted to let that twelve-year-old down.

But what if she let her own daughter down? How could she possibly know what a child born forty years after her would need? What would she be able to show her? *There I'll be,* thought Stella, pressing down on the gas as the light turned green, *fifty-two or fifty-three years old and forced to remember my own adolescence, the shifts and lumps and movements of body and life and time, wanting nothing but to* get out, get out.

At the club, Stella slipped away from the pool deck and headed into the locker room, desperate just to start moving and push all of her tangled thoughts away. As she turned the corner in the locker room and saw Felice pulling on her workout clothes, Stella had half a mind to stop and slide backward, scooting down the inside hallway to the front door and then her car. She leaned against the wall, holding her hands to her stomach. It wasn't fair. Good news for her, and rotten news for Felice. By now James might already be gone, packed up, leaving only Felice's broken heart. Stella knew she couldn't hide her news, her happiness showing even if her stomach didn't. This baby glow shot straight out to the surface of Stella's skin, and Felice would recognize it when she saw it.

"Stella? What are you doing?"

"Oh. Nothing." She moved into the locker room, reaching out for Felice's elbow. "What happened?"

Felice sighed and they both sat down on the bench. Stella watched her friend's sadness as if it were squeezed between them, a dark shadow with crossed legs and a know-it-all look.

Felice rubbed her eyebrows. "He left. This morning."

Stella closed her eyes and leaned against Felice. "I'm so sorry. How do you feel?"

"Like a fool. Stupid. Sad. A loser. Like no one will ever love me again. Like I was never loved in the first place. Like it was a lie from the start. Maybe I didn't even know him at all. Twenty years. A joke." Felice leaned against her.

"No. That's not it, hon. There are those boys. Your two beautiful boys. That's what makes your marriage real. How it was supposed to be."

"Maybe."

"No. Really." Stella put her arms around Felice, who began to cry. At that moment Stella wondered if she could birth more than just a baby. It felt like there was more in her, a way to pull her friends together and save them all. But that was silly, ridiculous.

"Felice?"

"What?" She pulled away from Stella and looked at her, the story of her marriage in her eyes.

"I'm pregnant."

"Oh!" Felice cried. "Oh, my God! You've wanted this for so long. I know you have. That's wonderful."

"I was really surprised. But, Felice?"

"What, sweetie?"

"This baby. I feel like this baby is for us. That's weird, I know. But I feel like the baby is about this summer. How she—"

"She?"

"I don't know that. From the moment I found out, I've thought of her as she. But she was here all summer, hiding. She was with us when we found out about Grace. She was with us when you told us about James. She's here now. I feel like she's . . ."

"She's special." Felice wiped her eyes. "God, I've been crying so much. But, Stella, I believe you."

They both fell silent, the sounds of the gym echoing into the locker room, clanks of weights and machines. The steam slipped out from under the heavy glass door of the steam room, the air humid and close. Stella held on to Felice, seeing that it didn't matter if she had sold all her baby equipment. It didn't matter that she hadn't known that she was pregnant, drinking a few glasses of wine and sitting in the hot tub with her friends, bubbling in water over one hundred degrees. It didn't matter that she didn't understand everything at twelve. Maybe Grace was sick and James and Kathleen were gone and Helen was pulling away into something mysterious. Somehow, with this girl, her life and everyone else's would make sense.

"Felice?"

"Yeah?"

"If she truly is a girl, I'm going to name her Grace."

SEVEN
&

H E PULLED HER INSIDE HIS SMALL, CLEAN APARTMENT. She
closed her eyes, not wanting to see but feel this, him, his
soft, baggy pajama bottoms, his skin still new from sleep, his hair
a wild spring of curl under her hands.

"You've been gone too long. I've missed you," he said. "You
smell so good."

Helen didn't argue, didn't think how corny his words
sounded, like lines out of a high school romance movie. She believed him, saying, "So do you," meaning every syllable, meaning
the messages in her hands as they both fell on his bed and she
shuffled off his loose clothing. Helen believed in the rise of
Pablo's flesh as he bent over her, the pulse of blood just under his
skin, the arc of yellow light coming in through the window.

Later, Pablo asleep, Helen lay in his bed, her arms crossed over
her chest, and stared at his body. She knew that love and lust were
not the same—she'd talked about this enough with her friends to
see the difference. She'd felt the shift between the two with Darryl, the week early in their relationship when the smoothness of
his shoulders, the roundness of his calves weren't enough to keep
her from being pissed off that he didn't clean the counters or
flush the toilet. But here the feeling was again, in the shape of
Pablo's ass, the way his back muscles connected to his spine, the
hard roundness of his biceps, the curve of neck into shoulder. She
couldn't see what she knew was there, the ingrown hairs and
blemishes and imperfections, all the spots she would find on Darryl in a minute. And she liked this amnesia of being too specific.

She wanted to stay here, in this room that let her forget the particulars of a man, that let her move into this perfect body and forget. And as she brought a hand to Pablo's back, ran her palm down to the warm bowl above his butt, she imagined she could.

Before she had to rush home over the Bay Bridge to pick up Livie and take her to swim team practice, Helen and Pablo went to Maria's Taqueria in the Mission District for bean-and-cheese burritos. It was as hot as it had been on the weekend, and even in the city, people in shorts and T-shirts spilled over the sidewalks, almost ignoring the drivers, as if heat were a reason to break all the rules. Yet even though she knew Darryl was at a business meeting in San Leandro and Livie was at a play date with a school friend, Helen looked over her shoulder every now and again, blushing when Pablo saw her movements, unable to convert her glance into an appreciation of the bright day or the interesting pedestrians outside the window. He would catch her and shake his head. She bit her lip, wanting to press down hard, the pain driving out her fear, her worry, her own need to be here with him.

He pushed his plate away and leaned back in his chair. "So how's Grace?"

She closed her eyes and breathed in salsa and his smells, patchouli and warm skin. Here she was, living wrongly, while at home, back in Oakland, Grace was fighting for her life, Celia was closing down in preparation for being motherless, Darryl was giving a presentation about product inventory for her, for Livie, for them, and Felice was probably being abandoned by her husband of twenty years. But she needed this, despite all that, and it made her sick.

She started to cry. Quietly at first. So quietly that her napkin hid the first evidence, but then she burst into sobs, laying her head on her plate, her forehead sticky with leftover rice.

"What?" Pablo grabbed her arm. "What?" He slid his chair over to hers, pushing his body as close as he could. "Is it that bad?"

Helen nodded, her face still on her plate.

"What's going on now?"

Helen nodded again and then lifted her head up, wiping rice from her face and ignoring the woman at the next table who was staring. "Grace is the same," she said between breaths. "But the doctors say she has only months. It's in her lungs and maybe in other places. I don't know everything. But it's really bad."

Pablo was silent. He held on to her shoulder, pulling her toward him. "I'm sorry."

She shook her head. "You're going to think I'm a really bad person, but that wasn't the only reason I was crying."

"I don't think that." He didn't move, and Helen could feel the strength in his arm and the heat from his leg pressing against hers. She remembered his bed earlier, the blankets thrown on the floor, his dark skin on hers, her arms around his waist. In fact, she could remember all the times since that first day she nervously rang his doorbell, each and every time lifting her body back to life.

"What else, then?"

"It's us. I'm sorry. I just think about what I'm doing. I'm here with you while my friend is home sick. My good friend. And then there's her daughter. And my own daughter. What am I doing?"

At these words, he pulled back a little. She could feel his heat leave her. He sighed. "I know. You're right. I try not to think about your family. Your husband. What I'm doing, you know. I mean, I'm here doing all this, too. But, Helen, it's what you want, isn't it? It's what you've chosen. Me. At least for now."

She looked at him, this beautiful young man with life already under his skin and in his heart. "I have. And when I'm with you, I'm glad."

Pablo pushed her dark bangs back from her face and rubbed a thumb under her eyes. "Let's just be with each other. Now, okay?"

"Now," she said, wondering if Pablo would ever be able to teach her what that word meant, because all through the summer when Livie was at class or with friends, if Helen wasn't in Pablo's bed, she was thinking about it, imagining his young body under her hands. She was either kissing him, loving how it felt to touch someone new, different, the wetness that flowed and pulsed from her mouth down through her body, or conjuring up his kisses. She wasn't in the *now* but in a bubble of skin and juice and heat that couldn't compare to her real life.

And when she was in the Pablo bubble, she forgot to worry about Darryl and Livie and Grace and Felice, her own stretch marks, her household responsibilities, her studies. Nothing at all mattered in the dark. Every time, like today, Pablo would murmur into her ear, tell her how wonderful she felt, breathe in sharply when she touched him.

Before picking Livie up at her friend's house, Helen drove home for a quick shower. She rushed into the house, pressing off the burglar alarm, and went into the bathroom, turning on the water as she pulled off her clothes. As she slid her underwear off, a hot burst of Pablo and their morning pulsed up and into her nose. She closed her eyes, feeling sick, knowing that this smell, of him and not Darryl, was wrong here in her house. For the first time she could almost taste her betrayal, a slice of steel on her tongue, metal and impossible to swallow. She balled up her underwear and buried it in the hamper underneath a pair of pants, trying to remind herself to take all the clothes into the laundry room before she left, imagining how she could pour Clorox on her sin and sterilize it.

After showering and dressing, the washing machine now full and chugging away, Helen packed up the swimming gear. She held Livie's suit up to the light and noticed that chlorine and time had rendered the fabric almost see-through. Helen considered buying Livie a new Speedo, but it seemed silly with only a few more weeks of fall swim team left. And she knew that by next season Livie would need another size. This would be the year she sprouted breasts and hips, the winter not keeping her from growing. Helen brought the girl-sized suit to her nose, breathing in the tang of pool and Livie's childhood, all of it already fading away.

*   *   *

Up at the pool, almost breathless with rushing and guilt, Helen flopped in the chaise next to Grace, who was pulling Baggies out of her gym bag.

"What are those?" she asked as Grace poured small silvery wafers into her palms and tossed them into her mouth. Grace, in a Speedo and swim cap, was sitting on the edge of her chair, her goggles locked between her knees, eating wafer after wafer. Despite Grace's tan, Helen noticed the crosshatch of large blue veins just under her skin.

"Calcium tablets."

"Oh. Don't they make you nauseated? Or give you, you know, the runs?"

"No, these don't. It must be the high level of calcium, you know. It probably is absorbed right away, before it gets too far."

"Really? You don't have to eat something with them?" Helen asked.

Grace looked at her from the corner of her eye and laughed. "Don't worry. It's not my only meal. This isn't like a calcium sandwich. It's the chemo. It just wipes out everything in my body. I'm also taking megadoses of vitamin E and C."

"Do your doctors know about all the supplements?" Helen knew there were vitamin reactions with all sorts of drugs. To this day, she was forever scared of taking too much vitamin A because of Babe's early admonition: "Never, ever take too much vitamin A. You'll go blind!"

"Oh, Karl is all for it. He told me that most cancer patients take supplements. He said not to worry if people thought it was odd. He said that cancer was odd enough." Grace smoothed her cap over her perfectly round head.

Helen swallowed and then forced a question past her lips. "Have you talked to Celia about the cancer yet?"

Grace shook her head. "Karl says I don't have to. There's not a whole lot of great news, but he says I might just surprise everyone. There's always a chance. And I don't want to tell her that, well, you know, things are terrible and then have nothing happen. It's kind of optimistic, but I think it helps me."

"Whatever works, is my motto," Helen said as Grace stood up and adjusted her suit.

"That's right! That's what I've been living by." Grace tightened her goggles and adjusted them over her eyes and nose and looked up. Helen took a small suck of air, frightened by this insect version of Grace, her cheeks pushed out almost to the bone by the goggles, her eyes large green fly circles under her smooth yellow head, her body a knobby stick.

Helen breathed out and looked down for a second, conjuring up Grace as she had been two years ago, a bit of fat on her face, the smooth slope of temple to jaw. "Um, have you talked to Felice?" She wondered if Felice had decided to tell Grace about James, even though she'd said she would wait until she was calmer, until she wouldn't upset Grace quite so much.

"Not yet. She's working out with Stella, I think."

"Hey, is your mom here yet?" Helen asked. "I really want to meet her."

Grace shook her head. "She wanted to stay at the house and clean. It's her thing. I'll get her up here later in the week. I'm off."

Helen watched the thin flex of Grace's hamstrings as she dove in and began gliding across the pool in a perfect freestyle, her arms slim and free in the water. Sitting back in her chaise, Helen wondered how she would tell Livie she was sick, maybe even dying. She didn't know what it would be like to die in front of Livie, knowing that no matter what Helen said to her, no matter what special times they planned during the illness, Livie would eventually have to deal with death. There had to be things to make it better, words and walks and movies, but strangely, Grace seemed to be spending less and less time with Celia, dropping her off at the club in the morning, showing up in time for workout in the afternoon. Celia had befriended Felipe, the young man who worked behind the front desk, and she was signing members into the club, gossiping with him all day long, eating Snickers bars and Cheetos for lunch.

"My mom had to take medicine today," is what Celia often said when Helen asked where Grace was. "She had to stay in bed."

Instead of sleeping with Pablo, lolling in his bed on warm summer mornings, Helen knew she should have stayed home, picked Celia up, taken her on walks with Livie, driven to the Ocean Beach, the San Francisco Zoo, Half Moon Bay. Although she, Felice, and Stella had been with Celia every day this summer, the child had been crammed into their daily lives, stuck in cars while they shopped or dropped off kids or went to the bank. None of them had done enough.

She looked up and saw Felice and Stella walk onto the pool deck. Felice stayed down at the end with Tony, but Stella walked toward Helen, her eyes alive.

"What's up with you?" Helen stood up and pulled another chaise toward her own.

"Oh, you'll never believe it."

For once Helen didn't suck in her breath, as she had all summer when someone said, "You'll never believe it." After Grace's problems and then Felice's news, she knew she'd believe anything. But Stella was too shiny, almost shimmering, to worry Helen.

"Yes, I will."

Stella sat down and arranged her towel. "Okay, then. I'm pregnant."

"No way!"

"I told you it was hard to believe."

"It *is*. This is wonderful!" Helen reached over and hugged Stella, pressed into the coconut in her lotion, the melon of her perfume. She could only imagine how Stella would glow as she ripened, swinging a perfect round belly into next spring.

"Congratulations." She loosened her grip, yet kept a hand on her friend's shoulder, shaking her head. "That explains the fainting, at least."

Stella shrugged. "I guess, though it felt like something else. As we were sitting there, everything felt so wrong to me."

They both looked up as Felice pulled a chaise next to them. "So you've heard the great news?"

Helen nodded. "We're going to be aunts."

"Are you going to tell Grace?" Felice asked, and Helen looked at the pool, following the triangle of Grace's push through the water.

"Is she having a good day today?" Stella said.

"Yeah. Look at her. In fact, I think she was up here a couple of hours ago." In the pool, Grace did a flip turn, her spindly legs flashing out of the water and then disappearing as she pushed off the wall.

"Maybe later. I want it to be right."

"She'll love *your* news," Felice said.

Helen leaned forward to see Felice. "Oh. So, did he . . . did he . . ."

"He left."

"What did the lawyer say?" Helen felt an old business urge to move on, consolidate efforts, tie up loose ends. The sooner Felice put this behind her, the better.

"He's going to get a court order, an injunction—I don't know the word, though I bet James does—to freeze our assets until we can go through some kind of mediation."

"Oh." Helen closed her eyes, knowing that, like business, this was what everything came down to: money and who owed what to whom.

"Mitch said it wouldn't be right away, so I had to go to the bank and pull out money before James did. Just to live on. I knew I should have taught summer school."

Helen leaned over and grabbed Felice's forearm. "Listen, if you need anything. Anything. Please. I'm serious."

"That's right," Stella said. "Whatever you need."

Felice wiped her eyes and looked up at them and tried to smile. Helen was always surprised by the color of Felice's eyes, almost yellow, especially in the sun. But today, just as during the weekend, they were so full of grief. If they weren't at the pool, she imagined she'd push next to Felice, hold her in her arms, and let her rest. But they were here, everyone and everything out in the open, and besides, she would almost be lying, trying to say she was completely on Felice's side, when she understood the dark need James must have felt for this other woman.

"I'm so worried about the boys. They were both upset, but Brodie is really having a hard time."

Helen sighed. "They'll be okay, Felice. This fall workout and school will keep them occupied."

"I know. It should help. But I feel I've really betrayed them. I've made their good life shit."

"No! No! You haven't done anything, dammit!" Helen hit the arm of the chaise. "It's not you at all! It's James's choice, his unhappiness, his need that's made it happen. You can only blame him!"

She leaned back, trying to calm down, and closed her eyes again. She heard the sounds of water, the filter surging under them, kids splashing, Tony telling a child to keep going. Here was the normal world, and she was an unusual cog trying to fit in, make it look like everything was round and smooth and easy. But nothing was fine. Grace seemed to be dying bit by bit in front of their very eyes, Celia was growing silent and still, even though Grace imagined her child didn't know what was happening, and Felice was full of guilt she didn't deserve. *And I'm screwing around*, Helen thought. *I've been lying to everyone.*

"Helen," Stella said, "what is it? What's going on with you?"

"I've got to tell both of you something. And, Felice, you're going to hate me."

"No, I'm not," Felice said. "How could I hate you?"

"You will. I promise. Just wait." Helen reached out for Felice's arm and began her story.

By the time Helen and Livie made it home from the pool, Livie was cranky and feverish, a sunburn in full bloom on her shoulders.

"I didn't see this yesterday," Helen said, rubbing aloe vera on her daughter's shoulders.

"It wasn't there until night. And I wore the dress with sleeves to the banquet," Livie whined. "It hurts. Ow!"

"I hate to say it . . ." She lightened her touch, her fingertips barely skimming the fragile rose of Livie's skin.

"I know. You told me to keep my T-shirt on." Livie was near tears.

"Okay. Why don't you watch television until dinner? I'll go get some Tylenol." Helen rested her palm on Livie's forehead, dry from chlorine and sun. Livie shrugged her off, her mouth and nose wrinkled in grumpiness, her body stiff as she held herself still. Helen couldn't believe how beautiful she was. She would never understand how this child came from her body. Never before and never since had she felt as if she'd done anything admirable or charming or gracious. When she watched Livie swim or dance or read over her homework assignments, she knew that everything that was good in her, diffused and erratic, was rolled up and packaged in this girl who was now whining on the couch, still so beautiful despite her irritation.

"Sit tight for a minute," Helen said, swallowing down the memory of how Livie, bloody and covered with milky vernix and amniotic fluid, snapped her head toward Helen when she said, "Hi, Olivia," as they lay together on the delivery room bed. To Helen, it seemed as if Livie knew all along where she should be. As if she knew her place in the world, something her mother had never figured out herself.

Livie didn't look up as Helen stood up, but she nodded to her words, focusing on the TV show. In the kitchen, Helen was searching for the Tylenol bottle in the cabinet when the phone rang.

"It's me," Pablo said. "I miss you already."

She felt her body take in his voice as she had taken in his flesh that morning. His sounds slid into her ear and down her spine. She wanted to sigh, sink to the floor, welcome the release that came when she touched him. But Livie was in the living room, and Helen was a mom, looking for medicine for her daughter.

"You just saw me," she whispered.

"You can't talk."

"Livie's in the living room." Helen fumbled through the all-spice and coriander before finding the bottle of children's Tylenol.

"Okay. Class starts next week. Do I have to wait that long to see you? I need to see you again."

As she held the bottle in her hands, she looked out the window toward downtown Oakland, her bones so firmly here, in this place. She imagined seeing herself through Felice's eyes, a woman whispering into a phone to her lover, and all she and Pablo boiled down to were two people who were fucking. He didn't care about Livie or the fact that she was sunburned and listless. He didn't care about Helen's guilt, the fear she had of Darryl answering a phone call just like this. Pablo couldn't know how she was pulled by her body and then her mind, needing him, his flesh, his touch, the relieving disorder of time when they were together. Then she hated it, hated her embarrassment, her shame, the dead feeling inside her chest as she told her story, the stunned look today on her friends' faces even as they tried to soothe her. She hated the lies, the betrayal, his plain youngness, his belief in the present moment. Right now, as often happened in small sudden swift bursts as she drove Livie to a class or sat with her friends on the pool deck, she wanted no part of him and no part of herself that needed him.

"Look," she said, closing the cabinet. "I've got to go. I'll call you later." She hung up the phone and leaned against the counter, pressing the medicine against her cheek.

"Mom!" Livie called. "Where are you?"

"I'm coming, sweetie." But she realized she didn't have one clear idea where she was at all.

That night Helen had a dream she was shopping with Pablo at a department store. They were looking through towering piles of loose linens and bedding, the plastic squares of folded, packaged sheets and pillowcases scattered at the sides of the room. The store was almost empty, the lights above flickering off and on, when Pablo pulled her down onto the soft down of the floor model bed. She wrapped her arms around him, feeling his smooth shoulders. *He's so warm*, she thought, and then she realized she was touching Darryl, feeling his shoulders, not Pablo's. Darryl turned toward her and pulled her close, and she realized she couldn't stop him. After all, she had begun it, but as her husband moved over and in her, she wished she could fall asleep again. Why couldn't she go back to the dream bed and the fluffy bedspread? Why couldn't she go back to Pablo?

Afterward, Darryl lay on his back, staring up at the ceiling, a hand under his head. Helen lay in the pocket of his armpit, a hand on his chest. She used to be here all the time, this spot, the warm smell of his body in her nose, his hair against her temple. She wanted to sit up, to ask how it changed. Where had her soft heart gone?

Darryl's arm tightened around her. "What are you thinking about? You're so far away. And not just now, Helen. I feel like you're falling away from me."

"Stella's pregnant," she said suddenly into the dark room, cutting away his question with this clear fact.

"Really? Is that what the fainting was all about?"

"That's what the doctor said. Stella had no idea." She shifted on her pillow. "She might even be three months along already."

Darryl spun toward her, punching his pillow under his head. His eyes shone from light Helen couldn't see, deep pools that she imagined reflected all her lies. She wanted to turn away from him, but she didn't, hoping the darkness would keep her secrets. "Stella is so excited. She's, well, she's radiant."

"What would we do if that happened?" asked Darryl. "We don't have a thing left, do we? Didn't we get rid of it all at the Children's Hospital swap meet?"

Helen swallowed, wondering if he was really asking, *What would we do with our marriage if you were pregnant?* "I think so."

"You ever think about it? A baby?" he asked quietly.

"No. Not anymore. Not with school." But she was lying. She didn't want to tell him how every month her period reminded her of that first month pregnant with Livie, how that cessation of blood was a surprise, a damn miracle. A child! Her child. From the first second after she read the pregnancy test, everything, every single thing, was about being a mother, a good mother. She read all the books she could find, desperate to make this baby's life perfect. Just like now, every day was about giving Livie what she needed to survive and succeed. But what she was doing with Pablo wasn't helping her child, and the idea of bringing forth another human whose life she could ruin with her own awful needs made her almost nauseous.

"What do you want then, Helen?"

Here was the space, she thought, where it could all be said, but the truth was too heavy and she closed her eyes against the shadows of the room. "I don't know."

"I want you to know it would be okay with me." Darryl ran a hand up her belly and let it rest on her right breast. "I wouldn't mind another child at all. In a way, I think it would be wonderful."

Helen thought of Darryl and Livie sitting at the dining room table earlier that evening, Darryl aiming his fork toward Livie's ear, saying, "I know what I'm doing."

"Dad!" Livie said, pretending disdain but leaving her ear available for potential operations.

"I see it! It's becoming clearer. Oh, my goodness! It's a lizard!"

Darryl made a swift motion with his fork and then brought it to his mouth, swallowing the lizard, feet and all. "All gone."

"Was it good? Did you like it?"

"Of course," he said, smiling at Livie and then Helen. "Even a Gila monster from your ear would be sweet."

Helen sighed, thinking about Livie's smile, the way she bent into Darryl's body as he talked and laughed with her, the way Livie's and Darryl's mouths were exactly the same, thin lips that smiled without effort, little licks of grin at the corners. She thought of Darryl at swim meets, wrapping his arms around Livie and laughing, picking her up into a warm hug, turning to the other parents with pride, as if to say, "Look at my girl!" He would be good with another baby, but she couldn't even think about it, so she turned and pressed a bit closer to him, murmuring, "Hmmm," letting out long, deep breaths until she felt him lighten and settle into sleep.

Helen pulled away from him gently and looked at her alarm clock. It was four a.m., and there were hours more until she had to get up. She knew her dream about Pablo had long evaporated, and she couldn't go back to it even if she wanted to. As she lay there, her eyes burning, she wished for another dream to fix it, everything, so she could wake up and life would go on as it had for years. In this new, old life, she wouldn't have had to watch Felice's face as Helen unfolded the Pablo story.

"I just felt so alone. Like Darryl wasn't really there for me anymore," Helen had said.

"That's what James said," Felice had wailed. "That's what he told me! Oh, Helen, give Darryl a chance. Let him know how you feel."

She rubbed her forehead. "I . . . I can't. I don't know how."

Felice hugged herself, and Helen knew she was thinking about the hundred ways James could have told her about what he was doing. Helen, like James, was weak, a coward, unable to tell the truth while all the while taking and taking what she shouldn't have.

"I'm sorry, Felice," Helen said, touching her friend. Felice looked at her, and Helen glanced down, scared to see Darryl in her friend's eyes. Stella had smiled and nodded, but hadn't said a thing.

Now, in her imagination, she thought about waking Darryl, saying, "I've been having an affair. I'm lonely. I don't know what to do," and things would change, and her life would slip back into something similar but better, something she could hold on to.

EIGHT

ᐃᔥ

I N THE MORNING, GRACE WAS ABLE to pull herself awake to the
sound of the alarm, drag her body out of bed, and move down
the hall to Celia's room. Like every morning since school had
started, Celia was already up and dressed, her clothes neat and
pressed, Doris ironing everything before going home for the
weekend to pay her bills and make arrangements to stay with
Grace until she didn't have to anymore.

Celia's hair was brushed and tied back in a tight ponytail, and
Grace blinked her eyes, wanting to see her child, but the air
around Celia was whitish, painful as a migraine, and she squinted
away the brightness. Only later would she see that Celia had eaten
breakfast, a box of Hostess powdered doughnuts on the table,
two left, each sticky with sugar.

"Mom! I'm going to be late." Celia picked up her backpack
and bag lunch and walked out to the car. Grace followed her, slipping on a pair of sports sandals, realizing only after she'd locked
the door behind her that she was in a T-shirt and underwear. *Who
cares?* she thought. *I'm only driving.*

When they pulled up at the school, Celia turned to her and
shook her head. "Don't get out." Grace recognized Celia's look,
remembered how it felt under the cheekbones, knew she'd lived
in that same face her entire childhood. Celia's eyes were steady
but empty, all the feelings, the disgust, the embarrassment, the
fear, deep inside her like a stone.

Grace felt words on her tongue, apologies and promises, but
she remained silent and watched as Celia closed the car door and

ran into the building, not even looking back once. And Grace was glad her daughter was away from her, safe. It would be hours now until she had to worry again. Helen was picking Celia up and taking her to fall swim team practice. There would be lots of sleep and then a long, solitary run. No one asking her questions. No one reminding her of the past. Nothing the whole day but silence.

Late in the afternoon, Grace was running slowly on the Wildcrest trail above her house, wending her way through summer-bleached Johnson grass and Scotch broom, dust, and dandelion-seed fairies floating in the air she breathed in shallow swallows. Her eyes half closed to keep out the dirt and light, she took an awkward step and skidded on a patch of gravel and fell hard on her side. For a few seconds after the fall, Grace wondered if she would ever get up again, remembering the cruel jokes her ex used to make about the commercial where the old woman cried, "I've fallen, and I can't get up." *I'm finally like the old woman*, she thought, *and I'll never stand again.*

Jimmy whimpered near her face, licking her cheek in pink strokes, and Grace pushed herself up, screaming when she moved her leg. She knew something was terribly wrong inside, but she carefully moved to standing and limped back home through the dust. *I'll call Kathleen*, she thought. *Kathleen will have to come over and help me. She can't ignore me now. She won't leave me alone with this.*

"You've probably broken your pelvis," Kathleen said grimly an hour later, when she picked Grace up to take her to the hospital. "You shouldn't have waited for me. I couldn't leave the clinic right away. I told you that. You should have called an ambulance."

"I'm sorry, Kat. But you know how good you make me feel," Grace said, holding her hands against her hips, trying not to move. "I really needed you. Just you."

Kathleen whistled air between her lips. "Where is your mother anyway? You said she was here looking after you. Finally. God, I don't know why she put it off so long."

Grace closed her eyes. "She had to leave for a few days to take care of some business."

Kathleen held Grace's foot, gently slipping on a shoe. "My friends have been saying you need hospice. Obviously, you're not . . . you need help here, Grace. If your mom leaves, someone else needs to come in and help out."

"What friends?"

"Ruth mainly. She says all you need is Dr. Karl's signature. She could sign, too. He just has to write up the diagnosis and your . . . the prognosis."

"Karl says I'm not there yet! Why is Ruth telling you all this? It's none of her business."

"She's worried about you, that's all." Kathleen tied Grace's shoe and put her foot on the ground.

"Worried about me! Yeah, right. She's not thinking about me."

"What does that mean?" Kathleen stood up and dug through a drawer for a sweatshirt. Grace felt herself move into the look Celia gave her this morning, cool and calm and unaffected by anything. "Nothing. Forget it."

"Well, let's go. Christ, Grace! You should have called the ambulance. You can't depend on me. I'm working." Kathleen tucked herself under Grace's shoulder and arm, almost carrying her to the car, sliding her into the seat.

"I'm tired of going alone to the hospital. I've been so scared. I needed you to take me," Grace said.

"What about Felice or Stella or Helen? I know they'd go with you no matter what time. Why aren't you asking them?"

"They've got their own lives. Things are happening with them, too," Grace said, holding her leg still as Kathleen merged onto Highway 580, heading toward Kaiser.

"And why aren't we going to Stanford? Shouldn't your Dr. Karl know about this?"

"It's so much closer, and I'm sure the doctors at Kaiser will send the records. Professional courtesy." Grace turned her head away from Kathleen, unable to stop the tears.

"Where's Celia? Should I call someone?"

"Helen's picking her up from school. Maybe you could call over there from the hospital."

"I'll call her. But I'm not going to stay at the hospital. I can't . . . I just can't. Call me when they discharge you."

"You can't stay?" whispered Grace.

"Do you want me to call Stella or Felice to come stay with you?"

Grace was silent, holding her palm to her thigh. She almost imagined she could feel the crack in her bones. "No," she said. "I'll just do it alone."

Kathleen pulled off the freeway at Harrison, and soon she turned into and parked at Kaiser emergency, carrying Grace in her arms into admitting, where they waved them through, a nurse and orderly rolling up a gurney and rolling Grace away from Kathleen. As Kathleen took her hands away, Grace felt their absence, imprints of bone and blood, the love Kathleen once felt for her. As the gurney rumbled down the hall, she breathed in quickly, holding onto the remembered pressure and turned, angling her head for one last glimpse, but all she could see of Kathleen was her jacket and then the sole of her shoe.

"You've got a hairline fracture of your pelvic bone. Not bad. But see here, and here?" the doctor said, pointing to the X ray. "It looks like you've fractured this bone before. Have you had a bone scan recently?" The resident looked at Grace over his glasses, his brown eyes not letting her go.

Grace breathed in. "I don't think I've broken it before. And I haven't had a bone scan done. Not yet. I mean, well, I'm sure I have osteoporosis."

"You were running when this happened?"

"Yes. But, you know, it wasn't a long run. Just to stretch my legs."

The doctor didn't say anything, and she wanted to pull him to her and look in his eyes, press her nose against his and say, "Believe me. Believe everything." But she lay back against the examining table's small pillow. It didn't matter if he believed her. Not like it had mattered with her mother so many years ago. This guy, he was nothing. No one. He didn't matter. She just had to get out of here. Now. She had to get back to Kathleen, call her, make her come back to the hospital, take her home, sit on the edge of the bed, and listen.

"It doesn't even hurt that bad," Grace said finally. "I feel like I could walk out of here right now."

"What's the name of your regular doctor at Stanford?" the doctor asked, his head still bent to her file.

"Um . . ." Grace's whole body began to spin. "You know, I've only just begun to see him."

"That's all right. Well, there's not much we can do for the break but immobilize it and make sure you rest. It's not an area we can cast." The doctor stood up. "My nurse will be in with a brace that you need to wear and a sheet of instructions. Bed rest for at least two weeks. Then only minor activity. We'll X-ray again in four weeks. Oh . . . and here." He handed her a prescription. "Take one every four hours. If you need more, call in to the pharmacy. You should definitely take it with food or at least milk."

"What are they?"

"Percocet. You aren't on any other medications, are you?"

Grace shook her head. "Oh, no. I hate medicine. I never take a single thing."

Kathleen carried Grace into their bedroom and stood up to leave. Grace grabbed Kathleen's shirt, her pants, feeling as if her fingers would break from the force of her grip. "Don't go. You always leave. Stay for a little while."

Kathleen put on her sunglasses. "I can't. Let go, Grace. Just rest."

"Kathleen! Kat! You've got someone else. I know it! You're seeing someone else! That's why you won't stay. You don't care about me. You don't care that I'm dying and now I have a broken pelvis. I can't move from this bed! The doctor said it would be months and months before I was up and about."

Kathleen didn't say anything. She just stared out the window. *She's imagining her life without me*, Grace thought. "You're seeing someone else," Grace said, letting go. "You have a lover to go to. You've moved in with her already."

"You're exhausted. Go to sleep. Those pills should be making you drowsy. How many did you take?"

"I won't rest! I won't do anything until you tell me the truth. What's going on?" Grace cried, her head pounding, the Percocet churning around her stomach like acid.

"Fine. All right! Yes! I have a lover. A lover who will sit down and eat with me and go to the movies with me. She doesn't have to go out on a run for five hundred hours a day. She doesn't eat only green beans and rice cakes. She sleeps at night. She doesn't manipulate the shit out of me." Kathleen's face was covered with tears, her arms clamped over her chest.

"And she doesn't have cancer. She isn't going to die." Grace struggled to sit up.

"That's right! She's whole! She's normal. There's none of this shit going on."

"What? What shit?" Grace began to say, but then she felt herself pinned to the bed, her body convulsed in a grip from something outside her, a pulse of electricity twisting up her spine and out of her head. Inside her body, everything seemed almost pure and clear, but then there was pain, her eyes squeezing shut, her toes curling.

"Oh, my God! What . . . ? What . . . ? Grace!"

Kathleen rushed to the bed, putting her arms around Grace, holding her tight. Grace moved to the rock of seizures, feeling Kathleen's body. At last.

"Okay." Kathleen hung up the phone. "No more Percocet. The doctor you saw, Dr. Barat, is going to refer you to a neurologist. The nurse will call tomorrow with an appointment. If you didn't have the broken pelvis, you'd be in the emergency room right now. But I'll take you tomorrow, okay? I promise."

"Did you say anything about the cancer treatment? You know what will happen to Karl if you do. No one is supposed to be taking the drugs I'm on."

"No. I told you I wouldn't." Kathleen sighed. "But I should call Karl. He needs to know about this."

"I'll call him tomorrow. I promise."

Kathleen didn't say anything, but she didn't look scared or angry anymore, her expression softening into the look Grace loved best, the gaze that had held her for all these years.

Grace lay on her side on the bed, clutching her comforter. The seizures had lasted for almost seven minutes, coming in waves, then slowly ebbing away like the tide, only ripples left in her body. Now she felt as if she'd run a marathon, her body hollow and full of jitters. "Stay with me," she said quietly.

Kathleen was silent, but she sat on the bed and then lay down next to Grace, on top of the comforter, and put her arm around her. Grace backed into Kathleen's body, remembering this was how they always slept. "Thank you, Kathleen. I'm sorry I went off on you. I've just been so sick, and I'm scared. I'm going to die, and I'm frustrated. I don't know what to do."

"Shhh," murmured Kathleen. "Stop." And for a few minutes, Grace forgot everything: her pelvis, her illness, the hunger that was determined to boil up and outside her, devouring everything.

The next morning at Kaiser, a grim Kathleen in the waiting room, Grace had a difficult time with the neurologist's questions, his determination to get to the bottom of her seizures, his need to consult with her doctor.

"It's just that I didn't eat much, and then I fell and went to the hospital and took Percocet on an empty stomach. I was in a lot of pain, you know. I swear, I won't do it again," Grace said, smiling up at this doctor, the same way she had smiled at Dr. Barat yesterday. "It was really, really stupid."

"Well, your EEG doesn't show anything out of the ordinary. I'll talk to Dr. Barat. But I want to see you in a week. I'm recommending the same bed rest that Dr. Barat did and food and water. Sugars and carbos. You don't want to upset your body's chemistry again," he said, writing black squiggles in her chart. Grace wondered what all the writing said, visits here and there from the last few years, headaches and stomach pains and a bleeding throat; gyn visits when her period stopped; the psychologist Kathleen insisted on last year after they'd had a huge fight.

"I'm recommending, of course, that you call your doctor."

"Okay. Of course I will."

The neurologist closed the file and looked up, searching for the clues Grace held inside. At his glance, she wished she could shut down her pores. *He wants too much*, she thought, still smiling. *They all want too much. All of them. Everyone. They always have and they always will.*

"See the nurse for an appointment," he said as he left. "Take care of yourself."

"Oh, thank you," Grace said. "Thank you so much."

Later, after Kathleen had driven away, finally turning her back and walking out the door despite Grace's pleas that she cancel her appointments and stay, just stay, Grace put on her running shoes and shorts, wincing when the waistband went up over her hip. She pulled her Jogbra on and called for Jimmy and headed back up to the trail, barely moving, but glad to see her flesh active, feeling the blood running through her body, eating up what she didn't want, eating up what no one cared for, especially not Kathleen, who left, who was always leaving, who would never come back. To the soft, slow beat of her shoes, Grace wondered what it would take now to bring Kathleen back for another night, and then another, keeping her so long she'd forget to leave and go back to her new lover and the life she wanted so much more than she wanted Grace.

Grace was relieved to see only Stella at the pool when she and Celia arrived. The pool was calm, a dozen or so children sitting at the edge waiting for workout to start, the fall group running just three days a week, Friday workout an hour of relays and water polo games. The older teens had left for their first year of college and adulthood, and Tony had returned to graduate school at Stanford. A skinny high school swimmer was now running the show.

Stella was leaning back against her chair, and Grace felt a pain of remembrance, her own body full of Celia, her breasts big and heavy and ready to take care of her baby. She gained nineteen pounds, the numbers sometimes keeping her up, the bathroom scale a vision behind her eyelids, but she didn't stop eating, and then Celia was born, all seven pounds, ten ounces, a big beautiful girl. For a second Grace wanted to stop and sob for that time, that healthy time. It was all so far away, Celia already turning into the girl that Grace had been before . . . before everything. At night she thought of creeping into Celia's room, pressing her body against her daughter's and whispering, "This is what happens. This is what happened to me. We can make it better. It can be different for you." But it was too late for that.

Grace breathed in and adjusted her gym bag, walking slowly, with just a trace of a limp, toward Stella. "Hey, pregnant one!" Grace sat down on an empty chair. "How are you feeling?"

"Oh," Stella said, slumping down in her chair. "Tired. Fat. Nauseous. The whole package. I've been living on saltines and soda water. But I was like this for five months with Eric and it passed eventually. . . . But more important, how are you?"

Grace sat down carefully on her chair, trying to avoid the position that made her yelp in pain. "Oh, I just have a broken pelvis. Helen must have called you."

"No, Felice did. She was over at Helen's when you called. Are you okay? Shouldn't you be at home in bed?"

Grace shook her head. "No. I really wanted to get out. The air and sun make me feel so much better. And the bone will heal. I need to feel better because I got some bad news this morning."

Stella's eyes grew bigger, and she reached a hand out toward Grace, grabbing her wrist. "What? What is it now, hon?"

"Well, when I went into the hospital for my pelvis they ran some tests. They did a CAT scan and found a lesion."

"A lesion? Like a sore? Where?" Stella asked, leaning closer to Grace. "I don't understand."

"In my brain. The cancer's moved up to the brain. It's what happens at the end. With melanoma patients." The truth of her words pushed feelings as round as tumors up from her lungs into her head. She imagined the whitish lesions lumped behind her eyes, gnawing at her frontal lobe, pulsing and growing. She saw the bigger one split almost like a dividing cell, and then there were two. "Another spot looks likely. They weren't sure. But they sent all the records to Karl. He's put me on a new drug. More powerful."

Stella's eyes filled and spilled over. Grace remembered the relief of hormones when she was pregnant, all the feeling that came from somewhere deep inside her, long ago memories that came unbidden but welcome as she tried to cry them away. But Stella was crying for her, not for a memory, and Grace thought to suck her story back inside her where it belonged. Stella tried to stop, but soon she had her head in her hands, sobbing.

"Don't feel sad," Grace said, smoothing Stella's fine, soft hair. "I'll be all right. Karl calls me his miracle patient. Look how long I've lived with cancer, Stella. Since Celia was a baby."

"It's just too much, hon. Don't you deserve a break?"

"Yeah, I'd sure like one. But I'll take it on. I'll just keep exercising and taking my meds, and I'll be fine. Really. Stop crying."

"What's Kathleen going to do?" Stella wiped her face with her towel.

"She's taking it really hard. She was so upset she couldn't stay at the hospital when I went in. I had to beg her to stay with me that first night when I had the seizure. She's just so emotional."

"So emotional? She's selfish! She's awful. How could she leave you like that? And what about Celia? You're going to need help now for sure."

Grace nodded, putting a hand on Stella's shoulder. "Kat's just going through so much with this. She's been talking about figuring hospice out for me. She has her friends looking into it. And don't worry. Celia will be fine."

Stella moved into Grace and hugged her. "You're a saint, Grace. You *are* a miracle straight from heaven."

NINE

❧

"SO YOU WANT THEM THIS WEEKEND BUT NOT THE NEXT. You've got tickets and I have to change my plans for a conference. That seems fair." Felice shook her head, the phone pressing into her cheek.

"It's the playoffs. A client gave me first-row tickets behind home plate. Don't you think the boys will like that? Hmm, let me see. Yes! Can't you find someone to watch them next weekend? It's not like you're going out of town. It's at Berkeley, for Christ's sake."

She snorted, listening to James, wondering if he could hear how he was not supporting her now, much in the way he'd claimed she'd ignored his work. She was presenting a paper to a group of medieval scholars, and yet it didn't matter. She didn't matter. It was about James and what would make him happy. "I was actually looking forward to some quiet time to organize. But just forget it. You're being so hypocritical I can barely stand talking to you. Fine. They can go. I'll figure it all out."

"Great. They will love—" Felice hung up the phone, knowing James was nowhere close to knowing what anyone would love, much less the boys. He'd taken his time calling to see them in the first place, the boys pale with questions Felice couldn't answer the first two weeks, but then he'd called, arranging for them to spend weekends with him. Felice would pull up to his building on Sunday evenings, ring the bell, and wait for the boys to appear in the lobby. In a way, she could almost imagine that he didn't exist anymore, except both Brodie and Dylan came home with stories of the cool apartment with the elevators and the view of the bay.

She sighed loudly, a habit of late, her cheeks puffed out with the force and sadness of what was inside her. She looked at her watch knowing she had to meet Sean at the Chez Panisse café, the first time they'd really have a chance to sit down and talk alone, what with school starting and Susan moving her poetry and art and love into his life, pushing Felice into the corners of their office. Grabbing her keys from the table and locking the house behind her, she wondered, now that James was gone and the house was soon to be put on the market and Susan had moved in with Sean, what else she could possibly lose. And as she drove down Highway 13 toward Berkeley, she played out the scenario that had been haunting her into sleep. She started with James's ordinary day, obsessing about what he and Amy were doing, what kind of food they were scraping off Amy's plates. Felice knew they could live very well off what Amy made alone while he waited for a settlement, and she laughed, realizing they probably weren't even eating at home, dining instead at some fancy restaurant in downtown San Francisco, talking with bankers and businesspeople, everyone wearing dark suits and shined black shoes.

Then she would settle on Amy's refrigerator, full of Evian and Calistoga waters, champagne, Moosehead beer, the kind James liked best. Maybe there was some leftover Brie, a few wilted strawberries, chocolate for dipping, whipped cream, French preserves, caviar, Kalamata olives. On the bedside reading table, *Forbes, Wired, The Wall Street Journal, BusinessWeek.* In the bathroom, Estée Lauder and Lancôme bath products, clay mud masks, scented milled soaps. James's clothes now hung straight and free in Amy's huge closet; his shoes aligned in neat, unencumbered rows. Together, they watched those tasteful sex movies on her wide-screen television, learning Tantric orgasm enhancers, and then had cosmic sex at night when they came home from work and dinner, positions with bendings and arcings and legs everywhere, and galactic sex in the morning before they went out for a run together around Lake Merritt. On the weekends they drove up to Napa Valley in Amy's car—a Miata, a Saab convertible, a shiny BMW—to taste the best wines, eating at the French Laundry before driving home; or they rented a cottage near Point Reyes, listening to seagulls in the morning as they snuggled under clean designer sheets.

Shit, thought Felice as she stopped at a red light at Shattuck Avenue, her Caravan rattling. *Why do I do this?* She knew she imagined James into everything perfect, so she would feel what? Better? Like the victim? Like the wronged one?

But she did feel wrong, more and more incorrect every day, fighting with her slow, tired body in the mornings, forcing herself up out of the bed, into the kitchen where the normal mom routine took over. The boys made it to school, she made it to her classes, but her body was insistent on stillness, on the word *no*, on not moving at all. And there was no one to notice this, Sean preoccupied, James gone, her friends in their own turmoil, Grace sicker than ever. She didn't want to call her mother too often, scared Sofia would show up unannounced, ready to fix Felice's every problem, not that Sofia had been successful with that task historically. It was too much, she thought, pulling into the Andronico's parking lot, ignoring the Patrons Only sign. It was a miracle she'd made it this far at all.

Sean pushed back his black hair and shook his head. "I still can't get over it. I knew you two were having some problems, but this? Didn't this seem to come out of left field?"

Felice nodded numbly at Sean's baseball metaphor, thinking how Brodie and Dylan would love sitting behind home plate, laughing, the A's fans cheering wildly. She looked down at the sand dab on her plate, its perfectly articulated bones pulling right off the flesh as if they had never belonged there at all. Like James.

She heaved another sigh out into the space between her and Sean, picking at her fish. "I know. I knew something was really wrong for a while, but I just didn't think it was this bad. I imagined I could fix it. Cure it. Make everything better. You saw him last spring. Did he seem that unhappy?"

He shook his head. "He seemed just like regular James to me, but you know . . ." She knew that he was holding back, trying not to launch into the same argument he gave her back in college. "He's too ordinary, Felice," Sean had said then. "Too practical. How will you live like that?"

Sean ate a few bites of salad. "I never thought he was exactly right for you, and you know that already. But I didn't imagine he'd do something with money. That doesn't seem like James at all. Who is this woman he's with, anyway?"

Felice sat back against the uncomfortable wooden bench, shifting her thighs. "She worked in his office for a couple years. She's younger, prettier, makes more money. She must make as much as James does. Obviously, he won't be feeling the pinch like we are while our assets are frozen."

Sean put down his fork. "Don't even say that. If you need any money, anything, just say the word."

Felice looked at Sean and wanted to cry, wondering how she'd been so lucky to have Sean as well as Helen, Stella, and Grace in her life, especially now. "That's so nice," she said softly. "But we'll be okay. We've just got to get through these first months, I know. These will be the worst."

"And any help with the boys. I think I should take you all out to dinner tomorrow night. With Susan. Okay?" Sean smiled at her. "I want you all to meet her."

She nodded and ate a last bite of fish, moving back as the server brought her plate of risotto and Sean's steak and took away the appetizer dishes. "That sounds great. I might have Celia with me, though, Grace's daughter."

"Fine. It's probably good for her to get out. How is Grace doing?"

"Not good, Sean. She's just wasting away. I don't know how she can take all that medicine and still exercise so much. But I guess it keeps her going. It's just so awful to watch. Her mother finally came up to stay. Maybe . . . maybe till the end."

"Think how it must be affecting Celia. How horrible! Talk about future therapy bills."

"She is really getting depressed. She used to be so happy," Felice said, feeling suddenly like she was talking about herself.

"Have you thought about what you're going to do for her?"

"What do you mean?"

He salted his rare steak. "Well, obviously Grace is not taking care of her like she should right now. What about talking to her grandmother about putting her into some kind of therapy now? Better now than later, don't you think?"

She flushed, knowing that Sean was right. Since James had dumped his unhappiness on her, she'd moved as if covered in tar. If it weren't for the boys, she might not even move at all. And even though she worried and thought about Grace each day, Felice had hoped Doris would have fixed things, taken Grace to one of the melanoma treatment centers Helen had discovered in Holland or New York, or found a way to admit Grace to Stanford for constant care. After so many months of tests and drugs and rounds of chemo, Grace seemed to be just as ill, maybe a bit worse, but how long could her body hold on? "I think you're right. We haven't done anything, though. I guess we hoped Grace would pull out of it like she did before."

They both stopped talking and began eating, as they had for so many years. Felice felt like she was at her own table with Sean, knowing when to stop and when to talk, understanding the lengths of chews and types of swallows, the way he'd cut around all the fat on his steak and avoid parsley or spinach. He endured her stages, how she ordered a dish she liked over and over again until she was sick to death of it, risotto her current favorite. She wondered how it would be now that Susan was here, if they'd be able to go out like before, if she'd mind that Sean wanted to lend her money.

"It seems kind of ironic, doesn't it?" Sean said after minutes of chewing.

"What?"

"This. How you're free and now I'm not." He put down his fork and knife. "For all these years you've been with James and I've not really ever had anyone. And now I'm with Susan, and James is gone."

"Oh. Yeah." Felice said, flustered, hoping he wasn't saying what she thought he was, remembering their one awkward kiss.

"I love Susan. But you know I'll always love you, too. I mean . . . I don't know what I mean."

She looked at him, wanting to push his hair back, loving how it always fell in front of his eyes. She knew exactly what it would feel like under her hands, soft and thick and warm. And it would be almost as easy to slide next to him now, say yes to what he seemed to be offering, though both of them would later resent it, even as they tried to make it work because they were friends, because they loved each other. For the first time she imagined what life would be like with Sean, years of talks and books and travel, conferences and workshops, cocktail parties with the same crowd she'd been with for years. Nothing would change except it would be him she slipped next to at night, and she knew that while that part would be acceptable, she was not pulled to her friend in that way, and eventually she wouldn't be able to bear the silence between them.

"It's okay."

"Just remember what I said."

"Thank you." She reached for him, feeling his smooth Irish skin, squeezing his hand in thanks for all the years of love and all the years to come.

"Look! Oh, my God! Look!" Sean threw open the office door the next morning, waving a slim white wand in front of Felice's face so quickly that she could barely spot the pink stripe in the center. Felice stood up from her office desk, grabbing Sean's wrist and staring at the stick.

"She's pregnant?"

"Yes!

"Congratulations. You deserve this, Sean. It's your time now."

Sean leaned into her, and she could feel his heart under his button-down shirt, all of him beating into the future. "I can't believe it. How did it finally happen?"

"You chose love," she said simply, her hand on his shoulder. "You met Susan and you chose. You said yes. You let it happen instead of pushing it away."

He looked up at her and nodded. "Yeah. Yes. This time. I've got to call her and tell her what you said."

Felice sat back down at her desk and watched him dial, then turned to look out over the campus below, the air and trees and earth so October—dry and red and orange. As Sean began to whisper into the phone, Felice thought she should probably leave. Maybe it was finally time for them to ask for separate offices. She knew she couldn't rely on him forever and knew that if she stayed, she would have to endure the way he and Susan communicated a quiet, singsong baby talk. Even though the sound made Felice grit her teeth, she couldn't move, stuck to her desk by her elbows. Felice remembered how it had been for her when she first met James. When they kissed for the first time by her apartment door after a study date, she pulled him close and held on for the next twenty years without noticing that both of them had changed during that long kiss, without noticing neither one of them was enjoying it much.

Shifting her elbows off her papers, Felice knew her time had passed. She'd had the early marriage, the two babies, and now the divorce. She had already done the falling in love, the courtship, and the breathless, needful sex. She'd been left and passed over for a younger, better version of herself. It just wasn't her turn anymore. She was tired of thinking about her life, feeling like she'd been chasing the same dogs around the same park the entire time, never catching up to one. Felice pushed away from her desk, packed up some essays, and left for home, closing the office door quietly behind her.

* * *

As she sat in front of the boys' school waiting for the bell to ring, she felt guilt break free and rise in her body. At night, after she'd imagined James and Amy in joyful cohabitation, she'd run through the past months of the boys' lives and their lives to come, everything infected by the divorce. The worst scene, the one she played over in her head like a top forty single, was that of the first morning James was gone.

"Where did Dad go?" Dylan had asked as Felice moved behind the kitchen counter to make him breakfast.

"What do you mean?" she had said, an egg in each hand.

"His stuff is gone. His shaving stuff. I wanted to watch him shave this morning."

"His stuff is gone? Why would his stuff be gone, stupid? He would have told us last night if he was going on a trip," Brodie said from behind the couch where he lay, watching television.

"Not a trip, stupid. His stuff. Mom! Tell him. Tell him Dad's stuff is gone." Dylan was on the edge of tears already, his brother always pushing him to prove a truth.

Brodie stuck his head up over the couch. "Mom. What's he talking about?"

Felice held the eggs. They were so smooth and just barely cold, their shells so strong, and yet underneath, nothing but fluid.

"Mom!" Brodie said.

She put down the eggs and stared at the counter. Her eyes felt gritty, as if she could feel each vein during every blink. "Okay. Let's sit down on the couch."

"What is it?" Dylan said, tears dripping off the tips of his eyelashes. "I knew it!"

"Shut up!" said Brodie.

"Okay. Stop it. I'll tell you." Felice sat between them and grabbed a hand of each.

"No," Dylan said.

Felice held him against her chest. "Your father told me last week that he wasn't happy here with me anymore. He wanted to move out. He didn't tell you himself because . . ." Felice stopped, knowing that she had to be careful. She knew she couldn't say what she wanted to, tell her boys their father was an asshole, a thief, and a fucking cheater. What they heard now was what would last forever. "Because he didn't want to wake you up. And he knew I would tell you. He wants to see you soon, and he will call when he gets moved in to his new place."

"But why is he leaving?" Brodie asked. "What did you do?"

Felice swallowed. "It wasn't one thing that anyone did. He just wasn't . . . happy."

Dylan was silent, but his chest contracted with sobs. "But, Mom," he said finally, "he didn't say goodbye!"

"No, he didn't. But he gave me these special cards for you both. It has his direct line at work and his e-mail address so you can write to him whenever you want. And look, he's handwritten his new home number. He's going to call you really soon."

"But I want to talk to him," Dylan wailed. "It's not fair!"

Felice began to weep, the long night and the longer weekend hanging dark under her eyes and in her throat. "I'm sorry. I am so sorry. I wish it wasn't like this. I don't want it like this. But for now, it is."

Brodie looked up at her. "He might come back? You said 'for now.' "

Felice had bent down and kissed him on the head. "No. He won't come back. It won't ever be like it was. It will be different and we'll have to figure it out together."

Now she breathed out into the hot, stale car air and tried to shake the scene out of her head, knowing it would come back again soon enough. In some ways, though, the boys seemed to be doing better than she could have ever expected, arriving home from James's almost happy. Well, truly happy, she had to admit. *Everyone is adjusting,* she thought. *Everyone but me.*

The bell rang and Felice turned to watch the kids pour from the school, a few wild boys throwing their backpacks off the second-floor steps to the ground below. And then she laughed when she realized one of the wild boys was Dylan, who came charging toward the car. Brodie was running behind him, his hair swinging from side to side.

"Mom!" Dylan slammed the door behind him. "Cassidy Elders had a dead beetle in his desk. It looked like a monster!"

"What kind of beetle?" Felice asked, looking at Brodie in the rearview mirror with a smile as she pulled into traffic.

"A bad-ass nasty beetle. It was black with a horn on each end. I bet it stinks," Dylan said.

"Dylan!"

"Yeah, just like you," Brodie said.

"Shut up!"

"You shut up! I'm sick of your baby stuff!"

Felice banged her hand on the steering wheel. "Brodie!"

"Yeah, anyway, Mom," Brodie continued, ignoring her outburst as well as his own, "I need five dollars for the November dance in a couple weeks, and we need to get a present for our secret pal."

"Secret pal, secret pal," Dylan hummed. "It's a girl!"

Brodie flung himself around and punched his brother in the shoulder. "How do you know? I don't even know! Don't be stupid."

"Both of you! Stop it!" Felice's hands shook as she held onto the steering wheel. "Do you hear me? Do you? Why do you treat each other like this? Don't you see we're all we have?" Tears slid down her face and collected in the corners of her mouth. She sucked them in and licked the salt off her lips.

"Mom," Brodie said. "Sorry."

"Yeah, Mom," Dylan said. "Me, too. Sorry."

She nodded and put out a hand to pat Brodie, felt two hands on her arm, one from each boy. "I'm just tired. This hasn't been easy. I'm sorry."

"Maybe you need to have a boyfriend. Like Dad has Amy," Dylan said. "Maybe you wouldn't be so sad all the time."

Felice swallowed down and then pulled over to the curb. "What, Dylan?"

"Dad seems okay," Brodie said. "He's not sad."

She wiped her face. "Of course he's not. He's the . . . He's the one . . . He's just not sad."

"I bet you could meet one of the dads from school. Lots of kids' parents are divorced, you know," Dylan said. "I counted ten in my class."

"Oh, Dyl," she said quietly, closing her eyes, imagining his eyes scanning his classmates, looking for pain. Her face flushed with shame that she'd led her children into this new world. She rubbed her forehead and pushed her hair out of her eyes. "Oh," she said again limply.

"It's okay, Mom," Brodie said.

She looked over at Brodie, who looked at her, his blue eyes steady. And for a second, she thought he was right. "Let's go home," she said, pulling back onto Moraga Avenue. As she drove toward Alice Street and their house, she looked across at Dylan and in the rearview mirror at Brodie. She remembered the theory of reincarnation and the idea that we choose our own parents, the life we will lead, the people we will know. Felice couldn't understand why they would have ever picked her, chosen to fall into her belly, allowed themselves to come into this particular life, a life where they would support and take care of her. Felice thought of one of the pictures James used to have on his office wall at work. In the picture, Brodie and Dylan sat at a picnic table in front of Felice, who leaned back in a chair. They each held glasses of Coke in their chubby hands and smiled fully into the camera as Felice laughed, her face to the camera, caught between her boys' heads where they seemed to hold her up.

Helen's voice on the answering machine was cracked and desperate, full of anger or tears. "Call me. Right away. I've got to talk to you. It's important."

Felice erased the message, the only one, no lawyer, no James, no hang-ups, and looked into the dining room, where Brodie and Dylan sat at the table eating Mother's Cookies and drinking milk.

Praying that it wasn't some trouble with Grace or now Stella, she took the phone into the living room, sat on the couch, and called Helen, who answered after one ring.

"Yes," she said, her voice strangely flat.

"It's me. What in the hell is going on?"

"You are not going to believe it." Helen sounded like a voice mail system voice, staccato and inflexible. "I don't even know how to start."

"What is it?" Felice said, birds of anxiety flying in her throat. "Tell me! It's not Grace, is it?"

"Yes, it is. But not the way you think."

Felice felt another wave of the same tears she had shed in the car pulse into her eyes. She imagined Celia all alone, her mother so ill she'd been forced by relatives to say goodbye, to kiss Grace's cool dry cheek, to watch the last beat of her mother's tired heart. "Oh, my God. What?"

Helen's voice stumbled and faltered, the clipped irritation gone. "I don't know how to tell you but to just tell you. It doesn't make any sense."

"Just tell me!"

There was a second of silence, the gray of phone space between them, and Helen said, "Grace probably doesn't have . . . she doesn't have cancer."

Felice froze, her mouth still. She heard Dylan telling Brodie another story about the beetle, felt the puff of the heater vent near her feet, and smelled the basil she'd bought at Safeway on her fingertips. She wondered when her lungs would force her to breathe again, and then she did. "Helen! What are you talking about? What do you mean?"

"Yesterday, Grace's mom, Doris, called me and asked me to meet her at Rostier's Coffee. She'd tried calling Stella, but Stella was at the doctor's. Anyway, after I dropped off Livie, I met her there, and she told me that two of Kathleen's friends—both in health professions of some kind—came to Kathleen to tell her they didn't think Grace had cancer. I guess they all had been talk-

ing about it for a while and were really worried and finally confronted Kathleen. Kathleen didn't know what else to do but call
Doris, and then Doris called me."

"How could they know she doesn't have it? Why would anyone do something like that? And Grace! Our Grace?"

She could hear Helen swallow. "I guess she's been using the
cancer excuse for a lot of reasons. To keep Kathleen with her, for
one."

"But I don't understand. Doris called you and Stella first instead of family?"

"Yeah, it's weird. She told me that Grace has always said we're
her real family, aside from Doris. That we are the ones who really
care about her, who know her," Helen said, her shocked voice
even and quiet.

"What about her brothers?" Already, a part of her wanted to
shake this news off her and press back into yesterday, the day before, when Grace was still a blessing in all their lives.

Helen sighed. "There've been some problems in the family.
Big-time. I really don't know what, but once in the sauna Grace
said something about troubles with her dad and her older
brother, Miller. I got the feeling, the idea from what she said . . .
well, it was something awful. Something really bad. Abuse maybe.
But Doris didn't mention either one of the brothers. Or any family. She didn't say anything about them helping out at all, actually."

"Wait a minute. Just wait," Felice interrupted. "This is too
much. I don't get any of this. If she doesn't have cancer, what
does she have? What's making her so sick? What about all the
doctors and pills and hospital stays? That Dr. Karl? What is that?
How can anyone make something like that up?"

She was almost panting, her eyes focused on the red and purple squares in her Oriental carpet. The yellow lamp fanned out
bitter light into the room. It reminded Felice of the hallway light
her mother, Sofia, flicked on when Felice began to whimper and
cry during a nightmare. Felice would see the light and hear her

mother's calls even as the nightmare played on—the light, the voice all part of one terrible scene.

"They think she has anorexia. And everything else has all been a lie."

Felice, Helen, Stella, and Doris sat at a back table in the club's café. It was ten in the morning on a crisp October day, and bundled tennis players passed by, headed toward the courts. A stagnant pot of coffee burned darkly on a corner table, and in the next room a child watched *Sesame Street*, the puppet voices and songs an annoying but safe static in the background.

"How did this all start, Doris?" Felice asked, her arms folded across her body. "Why did these women suddenly come to you with this idea?"

As Doris cleared her throat and looked up, Felice saw what Grace would look like if she stayed healthy and lived. Here was an older, well-fed Grace, the same hair, though thinner and now dyed red, and the same green eyes, except in a finely wrinkled face. "Well, as I was telling Helen, this friend of Kathleen's, this Ruth . . . you know she's a doctor . . . apparently saw Grace at the club a few weeks back, and something just clicked for her. She's worked with girls with eating disorders, and she told me it was like a curtain pulled up and she finally saw what was going on. So later, she called over to Stanford and found out that the study Grace says she's in doesn't exist. And she did an Internet search or something and came up with detailed information on metastasized melanoma, and Grace isn't showing any of the particular symptoms. In fact, nothing added up. The treatment, the protocol. There also isn't an oncologist with the first or last name Karl at Stanford. She checked that, too. Then she called Madeline, Kathleen's other friend, and then Kathleen."

Helen slapped her hand down on the table. "Why would this Ruth person want to do all that? What's her motivation? She's not Grace's friend. From what I heard, I don't think many of Kathleen's friends even like Grace."

"Grace told you that," Felice said. "I mean, remember the story she told us that night at the movies? The whole radiation thing? From what we know now, that was all a lie."

Stella shook her head. "It's probably all about the house. This Ruth wants Grace out so Kathleen can move back. This probably isn't about Grace at all."

Doris put a hand on Stella's arm. "Trust me, I thought about all of this. Do you think I want to believe my own daughter could make up such a story? But I truly think Ruth was motivated first by concern for Grace. And then for Kathleen. Ruth told me that Grace needs to get help. And if she does, she could live. She wouldn't be . . ." Doris stopped, touching the corners of her eyes with a carefully folded Kleenex. "She wouldn't have to die. Anorexia doesn't have to be a death sentence. Not like cancer."

"You're right." Felice gently squeezed Doris's hand. "We can do something. We can help her. We can help Celia, too."

"What can *we* do, exactly?" Helen asked. "If this is all true, we need professionals. I'm not trained for . . . what? An intervention?"

"I think we have to be sure," Stella said. "How can we know this isn't about Kathleen's friends trying to get Kathleen's house back? What if this is just something cruel and awful? We can't believe this Ruth. I don't even know her."

Felice looked around the table. When Helen first told her the story, she'd felt like Stella, full of disbelief and anger. But once she'd hung up with Helen and begun making dinner for the boys, the pieces of the last year began to fall into place, the strange one a.m. hospital visits, the secret protocol, Grace's self-enforced starvation, her excessive exercise regime. "But anorexia makes sense, Stella. Now that I really think about it, there was always something off about the cancer story. I never, ever doubted her. I thought she was amazing. But think about it. People don't drive to the hospital at any old time of night. People don't live very long with melanoma all over their bodies, especially the brain. When you break it down, it doesn't add up."

Stella put her hands on her stomach, her belly round under her shirt. "There *was* that weird story, the one I asked you about, Doris. Grace told me that she'd had cancer in her liver the first time and that's why it came back. You said she'd had it on her skin."

"It was bad, but it never went to her liver," Doris said.

"So why would she say all that other stuff?" Helen asked.

"So she could get it to come back. So she could have a recurrence," Felice said quietly. "In a way, it's like she's been planning this for years. The stories started long before this summer. Think how long we've heard about Dr. Karl and her liver and all the treatments."

"It was her last resort," Helen said.

They were all silent. Outside, California towhees hopped on the rails and the wind pushed sycamore leaves through the air like magic cups. For an instant Felice had the urge to turn to Grace and say, "Can you believe this?" knowing Grace would snort and shake her head, her eyes brilliant with the terrible secret. But the secret was about Grace, and Grace was at home, flat on her bed, full of an imaginary disease.

"So there's no doctor?" Stella asked.

"Not according to any of Stanford's records, for as long as ten years back," Doris said.

"But I feel like I know Dr. Karl," Stella said. "Grace talks to him all the time, twice or three times a day."

"She must not be talking to a doctor, then," Felice said. "It's somebody else. There's somebody else in on this."

"Who could it be?" Stella asked.

Felice shrugged, imagining this shadow friend, someone who'd been there all along, who knew more about Grace than they ever would.

"But what about those drugs she's been taking for the pain?" Helen asked. "She told me this whole story about the pain-management clinic at Stanford. When I was picking up Celia once, I saw this vial by her bed. She had this huge syringe next to it, and she told me that Karl had prescribed morphine."

Doris rubbed her forehead. "I asked Ruth the same thing. She thinks it might be Demerol. She says morphine comes to patients at home in either little white pills or an elixir to take by the drop. She wouldn't have been given a large vial to take home. Ruth wants me to take some out of the vial and bring it to her so she can have it tested."

"So even if 'Karl' is a doctor, he wouldn't have given her that?" Stella asked.

Doris dropped her chin. "It's a highly controlled substance."

"Have you or Kathleen talked to a doctor at any time in the past few months?" Helen asked Doris.

"I've never met any of her doctors this time. When she had the cancer before, when Celia was a baby, I went to the hospital and stayed in her room. I took care of her during her treatments. I never met a Karl, though. I'd remember that. But this time she told me that I'd ruin the protocol. If anyone knew she was participating in the study, hundreds of people would be affected, all the melanoma patients. The whole study would be shut down. So I didn't press it."

As Doris spoke, Felice wondered why she hadn't forced Grace to give her a number, a name, a place to call in case Grace took a turn for the worse. Why hadn't she thought to question the strange night hospital visits and vial of liquid by Grace's bed? Didn't Doris, Grace's own mother, think that it was strange that her daughter was sick in bed all morning, but then managed to get up and work out for five hours? *What kind of mother is she?* Felice thought, and then she tried to take all her questions back, erase them from the cave of her own head, remembering that she had let a bad marriage simmer in her own house like poison.

"What is this going to do to Celia?" Stella asked.

"Oh," said Doris, closing her eyes. "It's terrible how she's changed. She never laughs anymore."

"What are we supposed to do now?" Helen asked.

Felice looked out the large window, wishing she could stand up and push her way out onto the deck. She needed to think. For about the hundredth time in the last two months, she had no idea what to do. Nothing made sense here. Nothing and no one seemed to make sense these days at all, not James, not Grace, maybe not even Helen. Not the fact that she was getting divorced and didn't know how to live. She looked up into the eyes of the women around her and shook her head.

"I know what," Helen said, clicking into her orderly mode. "I have a friend who's a therapist. She works with adolescents with eating disorders and addictions. I'll give her a call. I'll tell her what Ruth told you and all the facts we have. Maybe she could recommend some plan of action. There's got to be hundreds of clinics around."

"You know, Grace was just in the hospital with her broken pelvis. Couldn't Ruth get in touch with that doctor? Professional courtesy or something?" Stella asked. "What was his name? Does anyone remember? She told us after she hurt herself."

"Barnet? Barber? Barat? Something with a B sound," Felice said, remembering the way Grace unfolded that whole story, giving all the details of the accident, the emergency room, the X rays, more details than they'd ever had about her cancer.

"Barat," Helen said. "There was a neurologist involved, too. Remember those seizures she had?"

"She *said* she had seizures," Felice added.

"No, Kathleen told me all about it one day at the club," said Stella. "It was something about a reaction to a drug. Kathleen said it scared her silly."

"No one really knew she was on Demerol, or whatever it is," Helen said.

"And what about Kathleen?" Felice asked, wondering why Grace's supposed soul mate wasn't here sitting with them, desperate to save Grace from whatever this actually was. Kathleen should have come, bringing Ruth and the other friend who seemed to know so much. But, obviously, Kathleen didn't care that much anymore, and Felice wondered how it was possible to leave someone totally, despite illness and possible death. Then she thought of James, the sneer on his face as he left the house, his hair combed so perfectly over his awful head.

"She told me she was too upset to talk about it," Doris said.

"Great," Felice said. "So she just leaves it to us to pick up what she dropped."

Doris blushed, and Felice immediately felt bad. Doris was probably feeling like she'd ignored Grace's problems too, so she patted Doris's soft hand. And who was she to say anything, anyway? None of them, not she, not Helen, not Stella had ever taken even one of Grace's odd habits and held it to the light. All of them were responsible for this mess. "I'm sorry."

She smiled at Felice. "I know."

"It must be hard to live with something like this," Stella added. "I think people want to go into denial. It's so much easier."

That made them all fall silent, but Felice knew Stella was right. Just minutes ago, she'd mentally wandered away from the table and this problem because it was too complicated. How would it be, then, to stand inside Kathleen's shoes and watch Grace's life day in and day out? But at least they had all stayed alongside Grace, and Kathleen hadn't.

"All right, here's what I'll do." Doris carefully rolled up her tissue and then pulled a pad and pen from her purse. "I'll call Ruth back and see what she has to say. Here, let me write down all your phone numbers."

Doris passed around a piece of paper, and Felice scratched her number down, passing the pad along. She sat back, pressing her knee against Helen's, just to touch something that was real. She felt like, any moment, her heart would burst and she'd float away like a loose balloon, untethered as this story, as uncontrolled as Grace.

The room was full only of the sound of pen on paper, the passing of the list around the room, until Stella looked up and said, "How do we know any of this is true?"

Felice had no idea at all.

TEN

STELLA SAT UP LONG AFTER AARON AND ERIC HAD GONE TO BED, trying to read *Marie Claire*, desperate to keep her mind away from the terrible possibility that Grace had lied to them all. She'd left the club that afternoon, her head empty, but then something would bloom in color, a sentence Grace said—"I've been in the hospital all night" or "No one can know about this treatment or the doctors will lose their licenses." Then there would be nothing but fuzz until another idea flared up behind the one before it, the entire lie scenario suddenly making as much sense as Grace's truth once had. Maybe, she thought, this was what Kathleen had been trying to tell her that one day they'd had tea. But then if Kathleen had known, why would she wait for Ruth's push to say it out loud?

The phone rang, and Stella jumped up, feeling the pull in her abdomen, and answered it on the second ring.

"Stella," her father said. "It's me."

"What is it? Is it Mom?" she asked, her throat full of what she didn't know.

"No. No, nothing's wrong."

"Why aren't you asleep? This is long past your bedtime." Stella looked at the clock, knowing that at eleven, it was already past hers.

"It's just that I was thinking." Her father paused.

"About what?"

"Oh, this and that. But I was thinking."

"Dad."

"Okay. I was thinking about Eric's birth."

"What do you mean?" asked Stella, sitting down.

There was silence on the phone. Stella pressed her finger against her free ear and could vaguely hear the noises in her parents' house, the fish tank gurgling in the background, the quiet whine of the television. She imagined the yellow light in the family room where he must be calling from, saw the green carpet and the wood paneling Dave had put up when he built the addition. Joyce must be in bed because she heard no clacking of dishes or whir of sewing machine. "Dad?"

"Listen. What I'm saying is that I'd understand . . . I'd know why . . . Listen."

"I'm listening, Dad."

"If you didn't have the baby, I'd understand. I know it's late and all. I know you and Aaron have waited for this for a long time. But your condition . . . your health. It wouldn't be wrong to . . ." her father said in one stream of words, his voice trailing to a trickle at the end.

"I'm feeling great, Dad. Don't worry."

"I'm worried about later. About what happened before. How you almost . . . I don't want you to not do something because of anyone else. Of me. I don't want you to think of me at all."

Stella breathed in and put her hand to her belly. After all these Catholic years, all the comments about birth control and the sanctity of marriage and priestly devotion and the venal sin of homosexuality, she thought she was hearing her father say she could have an abortion for her own good, giving her permission to think of herself, for herself. She almost wanted to laugh, remembering how long she had waited for him to approve of Aaron and their courtship and engagement. Stella wanted to tell him how much easier he could have made things then by just saying, "If you marry Aaron, I will understand. It won't be wrong. You love him, after all."

"Dad," Stella began. "Dad."

"I'm serious," he said, interrupting her, full of conviction.

"You're not as young as you were with Eric, and look what went wrong then. Nine years have gone by. Your mother had both you and your sister by the time she was twenty-five."

Stella swallowed down the memories her father was dredging up: her first labor, the machines, the weak, woozy feeling she had as they put her under. And then she remembered how tired she'd been when she came home, could still feel in her bones, like cell memory, the anger she felt toward Eric, an infant, just because he wouldn't sleep. Stella brought the phone back to her chair and sat down, feeling the swell of this child, this person inside her, knowing that no matter what, she would have this baby, regardless of her health or anything else.

"Dad," she said finally, "I'll be fine. I promise. Nothing will happen to me this time. But, Dad?"

"What, slick?"

"Thanks."

"Who was that?" Aaron mumbled, pulling up the blankets to let her in, putting his hand on her five-month stomach, the baby beginning to flutter and kick as it did every night, all night, a sea creature practicing for land. "Was it Helen? Or Felice?"

"It was my dad."

"What's wrong?" Aaron lifted his head up over her shoulder.

"Nothing, hon. He's worried, that's all. He's scared . . . he's scared something will happen during the delivery. Like last time. I told him not to worry."

Aaron didn't move nor did he say anything, but Stella could feel his heart against her shoulder, the sound she'd listened to for years. "In fact," she went on, "I'm not worried at all. It's like I know everything will be okay. Maybe that's stupid."

"No. That's good. But . . . the doctors haven't said anything to you, have they? They haven't said it's dangerous? You didn't tell your mom something you haven't told me?" Aaron rubbed her arm.

"No. Really. He was up late worrying, that's all."

"What's keeping you up? This Grace thing?" Aaron lay back down.

Stella shook her head against the pillow, cotton rubbing her cheek. "I can't believe it, hon. But I've put together everything I know, and something doesn't make sense. Maybe it's anorexia. Who knows?"

"What are you going to do?" Aaron asked, yawning.

"We've got to research some of the things this woman Ruth found out, and we will have to confront Grace." Stella found the words hard to say, thinking that by even tossing them into the air, they would hit her friend, the doubt sharp as knives.

"Make sure you find out all you can before saying anything." Aaron pushed closer to her, putting his palm on her belly, and then she heard his sleeping breaths, one, two, and she closed her eyes, and breathed to his rhythms until she was asleep.

In the morning, after Aaron had left, Doris called, wondering if Stella could take Celia to dance class in the afternoon. "I need to do a little shopping. I want to get her some special things. It's going to be a hard few weeks around here."

"Of course. Is there anything else I can do?"

"No, that's it. Thanks."

"Listen, Doris. I'm having a hard time with this news. And I was wondering if you know how this all started with her."

Doris hesitated and then cleared her throat. "I don't know about anything until college. Maybe it was there before, but I had . . . I just didn't see it. Grace was going out for the basketball team as a walk-on. I guess she'd gained some weight during the summer. But, Stella, she was beautiful. You wouldn't even believe how wonderful she looked, her face, her hair." Stella could hear her trying to control her tears.

"Doris," she began.

"No, no. It's just that she was so stunning and so talented, and this coach said something to her like, 'If you want to start, you're going to have to lose some of that baby fat.' "

"Oh, no. She must have wanted to quit right then."

"I don't think so. It didn't seem to affect her, at least not right away," she said. "Or not outwardly. But she did lose the weight and then some more. By the time she'd graduated and started her MSW program, she looked just a little bit better than she does now. And then there was the cancer. She's never been the same."

Stella was quiet, remembering the high school graduation photograph Grace had once shown her. It was taken in the seventies, and Grace's straight red hair was parted down the middle, framing her face, neck, and shoulders. Her eyelids were colored with a thin whisk of green eyeshadow, her eyelashes heavy with mascara. But aside from the seventies style, Grace was lush, round almost. In fact, the photo reminded Stella of Celia, healthy, young, ready for life.

"This must be so hard to watch," Stella said finally.

"It is. It's awful. I just hope we can help her. I hope she can get well."

"And there was nothing else that could have started all this? Nothing in high school? Or maybe at home?"

Doris paused again, and Stella wondered what terrible history she might be trying to swallow down. "No," she said finally. "Not really. Nothing that we didn't talk about. We did have some family . . . issues, but the eating part must have started in college."

"Okay. Well, when do you think we are going to do this intervention thing?" She walked with the portable phone to a chair in the living room. "If we are going to do it, we shouldn't wait too long. Grace is just getting thinner and thinner by the day."

"We've got to meet another time at least. Helen's therapist friend is going to come."

Stella closed her eyes. "But, Doris, are you sure? Are you really sure about this? Have you looked through the whole house for any clues? Lab reports? Admission forms? Prescriptions?"

"I did! When Grace went on a run yesterday afternoon, I went through the whole house and the car. Even her drawers. And I didn't find one scrap of paper. All the bottles in the medicine cabinet are in Kathleen's name. The only drug I could find was that big vial by the bed. I couldn't even find a parking stub from the hospital garage."

"Were you able to take some of that medicine out of the vial so it can be tested?"

"I couldn't find another hypodermic needle. She has the one she's been using over and over, and I was scared I might break it, and then she'd know what I was doing."

Stella wondered why that would be so bad. Maybe Doris should confront Grace, let her know all of their fears, and tell her how much they wanted her to be well. *Who better than a mother?* Stella thought, imagining Joyce taking care of her when she was sick as a girl. Who better to comfort an ailing child? But maybe Doris was scared of the reaction. Maybe she knew a side to Grace none of them ever would.

"Why would she only have one needle? If she did get it from a doctor, they would have prescribed a box of them. My dad's a diabetic, and that's how he gets them."

"I don't know. I keep thinking she's getting it from another . . . well, a source. Whoever she's really been talking to."

Eric walked in the kitchen and opened the refrigerator, taking out the milk and pouring a glass. He looked up at Stella, and she smiled back as he went into the family room. "That's weird there isn't any clue in the house. There should be something. You just can't go to the hospital without a trace. Believe me, I know. Every time I go now, I come home with at least three pieces of paper."

"I know it. But I can't find a thing."

"Well, we should meet. And Kathleen should be there, too. Don't you think?"

"Oh, I do. I've left her a message."

"You haven't actually talked to her since we all got together?" she asked, feeling her breath catch at the back of her throat. She thought that if Kathleen weren't involved, this whole intervention would flop. And maybe Kathleen knew something none of them, not even Doris, knew.

"We've been playing phone tag. But she'll get back to me."

"And those doctor friends who started all this," added Stella. "They need to be involved after getting the ball rolling. They need to tell us what they know."

"Of course. Oh, you girls are so wonderful for doing this. Grace doesn't know how lucky she is to have friends like you."

Stella bit her lip, feeling not at all like a wonderful friend. In fact, she felt like she was betraying Grace in the worst way. Part of her still believed all the stories, the tales of hospital procedures and tumor sites and chemo reactions. She didn't care that Grace never lost her hair or that she probably wouldn't still be alive with multiple lesions in her brain and lungs. Stella just couldn't let go of the days at the pool, laughing, the smile on Grace's face telling her that yes, it would be okay.

"I don't know if we're really doing the right thing, Doris. But we'll do our best. And don't worry. I'll pick up Celia so you can go buy her something great. Maybe after everything is over, she and Grace will be able to celebrate the holidays together, well and happy."

"Maybe this *will* mean Grace will get better. Most of these treatment programs run one to two months, so we'll all have our New Year's wish, and she'll be home and healthy."

"We've got to hope," Stella said. She imagined that even with this ugly twist, Grace's story would still turn out all right.

By the time Stella arrived to pick up Celia, Doris had already left. She walked around back and tapped lightly on Grace's sliding glass door, squinting against the glare. Grace really didn't like surprise visitors. She'd told Stella once how horrified she'd been when a woman from the club showed up uninvited and unannounced at her back door, the same door she was tapping at. Now she wondered if Grace's fear was about what someone might come upon—Grace eating wildly or throwing up or injecting herself with . . . what? Once, when Stella had stopped by to drop off a book, Grace was out for a long run, and Kathleen had invited her in for tea. Kathleen was taking a week off from her veterinary practice for a deserved break, and as she poured the tea into Stella's cup, she burst into tears. Stella knew even then it wasn't a bursting into, rather a continuation, of tears, the kind that come and don't stop, no hysteria before or after, or puffy red eyes or ragged raw throat, just a constant wet sadness.

"What is it?" Stella asked, leaning over the table to put her hand on Kathleen's. "What's wrong?"

"I don't know . . . I can't . . ." Kathleen stopped talking, bringing her hands to her face, her shaking shoulders rattling the teacups.

Stella felt an old, odd thought flicker through her head, the one that said lesbians were men-women, tougher, stronger, braver. But here was Kathleen with all the same feelings she knew she would have if she were fighting with Aaron. It didn't matter that Kathleen had gone through eight years of college, started up her own business, and bought her own home. It didn't matter that she'd lived and grown strong in a world that thought she was different, weird, sick even. Despite everything, Kathleen was just like any woman Stella had ever met.

Kathleen sat up straight and wiped her eyes. "It's Grace. I want to eat together. You know? We don't have that!"

"You don't? Never?" Stella burst out, and then she tried to pull herself back in, feeling uncomfortable talking about Grace despite her curiosity about her friend's relationship. Grace always spoke so lovingly of Kathleen, but Stella always felt there was something underneath the talk, a darkness Grace would never reveal. "Why?"

Kathleen put down her teacup. "She doesn't eat until ten. By the time she gets home with Celia from the club and the grocery store, I'm almost ready for bed. I've begged her to try. To come home and eat, but she says . . . well, she says she's got to work out. Celia never gets a decent meal."

Stella nodded, imagining Grace's thin body on the StairMaster, the funny way her knee clicked because of a basketball injury years and years before. Stella knew when Grace was on the machine even as she walked down the hall that led to the workout room—her machine would be humming, her steps pushing the machine as fast as possible. "I know it must be so hard," Stella said, understanding Kathleen's need for the very things she herself wanted: a nightly meal, a time to settle into family flesh, the night wrapping warm and safe around the house. "It must be so hard, but she really feels that it's what keeps her alive. I don't think she'd be like this unless she was scared of the cancer coming back."

"I know! So how could I ever tell her to stop? It would be like a death sentence to Grace. But it's more than that, Stella. It's the food. It's the way she eats. It's what she doesn't eat. But I feel guilty about wanting to take her away from what's really working for her."

"Have you called Grace's mom?"

Kathleen snorted. "No one in that family really cares. Whenever I bring up Grace's health to Doris, she starts talking about how wonderfully she's done since the cancer. I called Grace's brother Frank to help me broach the subject with Grace, but he wouldn't. Said I needed to leave her alone. The other brother won't even return my phone calls. They both think we're sick. They think I've turned Grace into something evil. So if her own family says she's fine and wants to leave well enough alone, what can I do?"

"You've been so wonderful to her and Celia," Stella said. And it was true. Kathleen and Grace had traveled to Florida every year; Kathleen enrolled Celia in an all-girls private school and paid for the club; Kathleen encouraged Grace to quit working at social services so she could focus on Celia. Even though Kathleen was not much more than an acquaintance, much like James was and, to a lesser degree, Darryl, Stella appreciated how Kathleen loved Grace despite her problems. She admired their relationship, and the smooth way it seemed to work.

Kathleen nodded and wiped her face with her hands. "Oh, you

don't know. You don't know how hard it is sometimes. You've never seen Grace mad. You've never heard what she says to me."

Stella felt a defensive wall start to slide between her and Kathleen. "Every relationship is different at home. I know Aaron and I get into fights that would surprise people."

"No, that's not it. It's more than that." Kathleen shook her head. "No one knows her like I do. And I don't know how to take it anymore. Oh, Stella, I just can't do it. But how could I leave her?"

"Do you really want to?"

"No. But how can I keep living like this?"

"I don't know. I really don't." She put down her cup and squeezed Kathleen's strong hand, hoping that this spell of sadness would pass and Kathleen would go back to being the strong support at Grace's side.

But things had only become worse since then, Kathleen backing off so much Stella had begun to resent her silences and lack of action. And here Grace was now, in bed, flat on her back, her face so tan it almost looked orange, her stick arms flat on the white comforter.

"Hey, girl." She motioned for Stella to open the door and patted the bed next to her. "Celia's almost ready. Sit down for a second."

Stella felt the blood in her face and a rush of nerves like pins in her throat. "I've got Eric in the car," she said, but she sat down lightly on the edge of the bed. "How are you?"

"Oh, it's been bad. The chemo is really wiping me out. I had to rush in last night for a treatment."

Stella could imagine Helen next to her, whispering, "Find out what you can," nudging her along. "Really? Was it a late visit?"

"Like usual. But it was rough."

"I was wondering about that. Are there people ready to admit you at that time of night? Is that their shift?" Stella made sure to look at Grace, to watch her friend's face and eyes, making sure nothing seemed out of the ordinary.

"They love me there. I know all of them so well . . . you know, I had bad news last night."

"About the treatment? What is it?" Stella felt herself fall right back into belief, worried about Grace's veins and blood counts and tumor size.

"No. I wish. They found another lesion, right by the brain stem. I've had the worst migraine for days."

Stella nodded, her thoughts pulsing in her head. She didn't know what to do or say. Part of her wanted to ask, "Is this really cancer? Do you really have it?" But she also wanted to crawl up the bed and take Grace in her arms, holding her friend to her own growing body. "That's terrible. What are they going to do?"

"Karl found the lesion with a CAT scan. Here. Here it is." Grace pointed to the corner at a thick manila envelope. "Look at it. You can see all the lesions for yourself."

Stella stood up and walked over to the envelope, picking it up and holding it in both of her hands. On the label, printed neatly in ink, was the name Jennifer Schwartz and a long medical record number. "Who is Jennifer Schwartz?"

"That's who I was last night. Karl gave me that name. You know. It's all part of the protocol. I'm always somebody else because I'm not even supposed to be there."

"Is she a real person?"

Grace nodded, her mouth turned down at the corners. "She was. Once."

Stella slid the X rays into her palm. She held one up to the light, and there, in fact, was a head full of clotted white milky spheres in the front and one down at the base. Stella had only seen CAT scans in photographs or on television, not like this, not in her hands, but she could clearly see the orbs of disease in this particular brain, whoever it belonged to.

"Oh, my God, hon. This is terrible." She brushed her hair back with her free hand and wondered if this was how poor Jennifer Schwartz died, her brain taken over by cotton.

Grace nodded. "But there's still hope, right? Don't you think I've done great?"

Stella put the X ray back and coughed down her disbelief. "Well, for having this much cancer in you, Grace, you've done fabulous. You are a miracle." Stella looked at Grace and realized she still meant it.

When they all met at the Chinese restaurant Helen recommended on College Avenue the next day for their final preintervention meeting, Stella told Felice, Helen, Helen's therapist friend, Jean, Doris, and Grace's college friend Drew about the CAT scans. "It didn't have her name on it. It wasn't hers. I mean it was labeled 'Jennifer Schwartz.' "

"Where do you get CAT scans?" Felice asked. "You just can't take records home with you, especially if they aren't yours. Sometimes I think doctors would prefer you never saw your own chart."

"On eBay, maybe?" Drew asked.

"Oh," Stella said. "I hadn't thought about that. Maybe. But these seemed to have all the tumors she's been talking about."

"Maybe she's had them for a long time and used them for the diagnosis she gave herself." Helen put down her soup spoon. "Remember that research she asked me to do on the Internet? She asked me for malignant melanoma. I pulled up tons of information on what happened when it went to the brain. I spent about seven hours printing up everything. It wasn't too much later that she told us the new diagnosis."

The waitress brought over a plate of warm pot stickers and a cruet of chili-seasoned sesame oil. Stella looked around the table at all these women able to slip food onto their plates and eat it, ask for more, add a new entree onto the list, while at home, Grace starved herself to a fraction of herself. What, she wondered, made Grace so unable to feed herself?

"So what are we going to do?" Felice asked abruptly. "We

can't just talk about this for weeks. She's getting worse by the day."

Jean, Helen's friend, wiped her mouth. "I've called two treatment programs. Both have space. But she has to voluntarily admit. No one can force her. She has to walk in the door herself and sign on the dotted line."

"She won't go," Doris said. "She won't. I know it."

"We have to try," Felice said. "If we don't try, then we will have done nothing."

"We've been her friends," Stella said softly. "We *are* her friends."

"But if we don't at least say something, confront her, then we aren't really friends," Helen said. "This feels awful. I hate it, but we have to try to help her. She's killing herself, either way. If we find out she does have cancer, well, at least we can get her to take better care of herself. She *could* eat more and stop exercising so much. If she has anorexia, then she can live. She can pull through. She and Celia could have a normal life together."

"What about that stuff she's taking? What if what's in the vial is Demerol?" Stella asked. "Will the treatment centers be able to deal with that?"

Jean nodded. "If she does have a problem, both have a chemical-dependency counselor on staff. And twelve-step meetings."

"What about Kathleen?" Felice asked. "Why isn't she here? And what about those doctor friends of hers? That Ruth, the one who started all this?"

Doris sighed. "I called Kathleen from my cell phone last night when I went to Safeway. I didn't dare call from home. Grace won't even let me pick up the phone now."

"Why?" Drew asked. "Why would she keep you from doing that? That doesn't sound like her at all. Not the Grace I know." Stella realized that Drew knew a Grace none of them did: a college Grace, a Grace before cancer. Maybe she'd had anorexia, but she had never been ill, had never been with Kathleen when Drew met her. She wished Drew would tell them all what she'd been like, hoping the story would be full of roundness and food and laughter.

"I don't know. It's like she's afraid I'll say something wrong or that the wrong person will call." Doris looked down at her plate.

Stella wanted to say, "But you're her mother! You are in control! You are the one who can actually get up out of bed and answer the phone!" But she didn't, seeing the tender steps Doris was taking around Grace, trying, like any mother, not to hurt her young.

Doris looked around the table. "But anyway, I left a message for Kathleen about the meeting and asked her to bring her friend Ruth. I told her it was an emergency. But she never called me back."

"Oh, that's sweet," Helen said. "Is she expecting us to save Grace all by ourselves?"

"Maybe she's scared," Stella said. "Maybe it's too much for her. Aside from Doris, she's the closest to Grace."

Helen shook her head, and Stella could see all sorts of comments forming in her friend's mouth. Stella nodded over to Doris, and Helen sighed and let them go, twirling her fork in her hand and shaking her head.

"Well, I'll try Kathleen again tonight," Doris said. "I just don't know what she's thinking."

"Did you ever talk to her doctor? The one from the broken pelvis," Jean asked Helen.

"Well, yeah," Helen answered. "He couldn't really tell me much because of doctor-patient confidentiality, but he did refer me to a psychiatrist in the mental health clinic who gave me some information on interventions. I don't think the doctor would have done that if he didn't think something was up."

For a moment they were all silent, twisting noodles onto chopsticks. Stella thought of Grace on her bed, bony, wizened arms, pleading voice, just wanting to be seen as good, trying, winning. Stella looked over at Doris, who was crying, tears falling on her moo shu pork.

"So are we going to intervene?" Stella asked.

Helen looked at Felice and Drew. "Yeah. We should. Soon.

We should talk about what to say. Jean has some information, and I have what the psychiatrist said."

Stella took Doris's hand and squeezed it. "You're not going to go, are you?"

Doris shook her head, silent.

"It would really muck things up in this case," Jean said. "There's too much . . . history. I think if you all, the friends, go, and then I go as the 'authority,' then there should be some balance. Grace will feel like she can count on her mother."

Stella felt the slosh between her hips, almost as if the baby were trying to wake up her heart. She closed her eyes for a second, then turned to Doris. "Then I won't go either. I'll stay with you. Okay?"

"What?" Helen said. "Stella! We really need you. Grace trusts you more than any of us."

Stella shook her head. "I just can't. Not now. I'm all for it. But I can't go. I can't see her the way she is, and I can't see her trapped. I almost broke down when I saw her yesterday. You should see her, flat on the bed. Like a scarecrow. I just can't. Not now." Stella took her hand away from Doris's and began to cry.

Felice reached over and put her arm around Stella. "No. Stop. It's okay. Stop. You don't have to go. You stay with Doris and pick up Celia and Eric after school and go for ice cream or something. Maybe they can play at the house afterward."

Helen nodded. "I'm sorry, Stella. It's fine. We've got Drew here. I'm sorry."

Stella looked up. Everyone around the table looked at her kindly, bending toward her, offering Kleenex. Stella sniffed and stopped crying, putting a hand on her belly. Even though she knew she couldn't confront Grace, Stella thought that if she were ill, dying or killing herself, she would be blessed to have these friends around her, these friends trying to save her life.

"What are they going to do?" Aaron was rinsing off plates and stacking them in the dishwasher, while Stella sat at the table surrounded by Halloween candy, plastic Baggies, and black and orange ribbon.

"An intervention. Where everyone important to her gets in the same room and tells her, well, that it's got to stop." She took a sip of orange juice. "Of course, her brothers won't be there. Doris hasn't even told them."

"Why not?"

"There's some bad blood there. They can't accept Grace being a lesbian. And something else from a long time ago."

Aaron stood up straight and massaged the fleshy heel of his hand, always sore from work. "So then what? They go to her house, say everything, and then leave her there? You think she'll actually change after that?"

She counted out ten pieces of candy corn and five mini-Snickers bars. "No. Helen's friend Jean found a couple places that will take her. Grace has to want to go, of course."

"I don't know." Aaron closed the dishwasher. "Do you all know for sure? Did you ever get in contact with a doctor? What if . . . what if you're wrong?"

"It's a risk. But either way, we have to help her. We can't pretend we never heard any of this."

Stella looked at Aaron as he wiped the counters, his strong arms flexing, his body out of place in the kitchen, even though he was often there, cooking and cleaning. Sometimes, she imagined the differences in their worlds—hers full of Eric and all his toys, schoolwork, and clothes, the piles of laundry on the couch, her furniture, the kitchen, the bedroom. Aaron's world seemed so different, so male, his mind always on something she couldn't grasp. Once, she looked over his shoulder at a blueprint, and he took her movement as interest, saying, "See, here's where the old foundation ended," and she stopped listening, feeling only his arm, breathing in the sawdust and sweat and plaster in his hair. He kept talking, and Stella knew that what she loved about him had nothing to do with what he did.

Now Aaron blinked, but his gaze stayed straight ahead, waiting for her answer. His question was a good one, the one that bothered her. Despite the clues and details and Grace's own words, all of which contradicted the cancer, Stella felt her own indecision like a nightlight in her chest, faint but glowing. What would happen if Helen, Felice, Drew, and Jean stormed Grace's house only to find perfectly labeled bottles of chemotherapy treatments, pain pills, and syringes? What if Grace could produce hospital admission sheets, parking passes, lab results, everything Doris somehow missed during her sweep? What if Grace felt so betrayed and deserted by her friends that she did something awful to herself?

Eric walked into the living room, carrying the latest Harry Potter book, and sat down at the table with Stella. He didn't like to be too far from one or the other of them, Stella thought. She wondered if he would need them more or less once the baby came, or if he would become the baby's comfort, its shield against the real world.

"Hey, chief," Aaron said, walking out from the kitchen and running his hand over Eric's head.

"Let's play Nintendo," Eric said.

Aaron smiled. "Sure. Go get it started. I'll be right there."

As Eric slapped his book closed and headed down the hall, the noise of the television and then the video game echoing into the living room, Aaron turned to her. "I just don't want you to be wrong. And I know how much it will hurt you if you are."

Stella nodded and watched him disappear into Eric's noisy room, the male sounds something she was used to, the sounds that excluded her but made her know she was home. But all this might change. Her amnio was coming up, and the doctor would ask her if she wanted to know the sex of the baby. She wasn't sure she wanted to know, even though she was certain it was a girl. A girl she desperately wanted, despite her own girlhood, her own girl body, the body she was still recovering from. Even now, as hard as she worked on her body, she didn't believe it had all come true. Once at the pool, Helen had thrown her magazine down on her gym bag and shaken her head. "Christ, Stella. I don't know why I even bother to look at those magazines, when here you are with a perfect body. Can I have it? Please? Just give it to me."

"What are you talking about?" Stella cried.

Helen laughed, nudging Grace, who was listening. "She doesn't get it. You've just got that thing, that oomph, that sex deal going on. Once I saw some guy checking you out at a swim meet. I think you were wearing a sweatshirt and jeans and a visor, for Christ's sake. I wouldn't get that much attention if I were nude on a horse!"

Grace clapped her hands together, leaning back and nodding. "Even Kathleen's friends check you out! I had to tell them I knew you weren't a member of *our* club just from watching you walk."

"What does that mean?" Stella asked.

"Do I have to show you?" Grace pulled her red hair behind her head with a rubber band and prepared to stand up.

"No," Helen said. "You don't have to show her. Her walk has a sound. It goes, 'Boom, da, da, boom, da, da, boom.' "

"You guys," Stella said. "But really, how does a lesbian walk?"

"Like Grace," Felice said, smiling.

Stella thought about it, knowing she could pick Grace out in a crowd by her stiff, sure, forceful walk, the way her body didn't move save her legs. "So all lesbians walk like Grace?"

"Okay, we're getting into very dangerous ground here," Grace said. "Let's just say, you don't walk like a lesbian."

"And," Helen added, "lesbians usually don't wear bikinis with beads and tinkly goldie things on them. And no dangly ankle bracelets."

"Shut up," Stella said. "You are being bad."

"No," Grace said. "Listen. That's not it. They just *wish* they could wear a bikini and look like you, Stella. Really."

Stella had closed her eyes and leaned back against the chair, smiling, trying to believe that what her friends said was true. She was still trying to believe it, even now.

Maybe, Stella thought, turning off the lights and walking down the hall to her bedroom, it would be different for this baby, this girl in her body. And for the next four months, the baby was something Stella could simply imagine and dream about and hope for, while at the same time knowing that no matter what, her baby was solid and real and inside her, alive and moving. With Grace, though, there was nothing solid or real. Everything seemed like smoke and air, swirls of truths and lies so twined that Stella couldn't see a single thing.

ELEVEN

"I'M STILL KIND OF DISAPPOINTED IN STELLA," Helen said as Felice got into the car and closed the heavy door. "I mean, not really. But Grace trusts her so much it would be great if she were coming."

Felice sat back in the passenger's seat in Helen's Toyota 4Runner and put on her seat belt. "Well, think of it this way. We couldn't do it without her. She and Doris are watching all the kids."

"I wonder why she wouldn't come. Is it just the baby?" Helen started the car.

"No. I think it's more. I think it's her religion, the Catholic thing. The Jesus thing, forgiveness, compassion, and casting the first stone stuff."

"She's not that religious." Helen adjusted her rearview mirror. "It's not like she's hailing Mary all the time."

Felice laughed. "I know. But I've met people brought up in the church. It's not like you have a choice; the religion is in you like blood. There's nothing you can do about it."

Helen shifted into first and pulled onto Moraga Avenue behind a truck. Dead leaves spun out of its bed like lottery balls. "Well, okay. I just think Stella is nicer than anyone. Softer. Certainly softer than I am. And this might go better if she were with us. She might keep me . . ."

"Calm?"

Helen laughed. "That's a good choice of words," she said, looking quickly at herself in the mirror. She didn't know how she could be calm when she hadn't been so for months, the hair on her arms and neck standing on end every time the phone rang, when Darryl whispered her name softly and she imagined it was Pablo calling to her, when she turned down the hall at school the first day in September and saw Pablo, bending over a water fountain. As Helen walked closer to him, she felt her hands literally tingle as she reached for his waist, her fingers sliding across the smooth skin just under his shirt. He looked at her calmly, unstartled, and said, "Hey," his voice even, as if this was what he expected, as if what he wanted was exactly what he could have.

Helen knew she wasn't ready to forget the feel of his hands on her body, the soft mini-lectures he gave her in bed about following her bliss. "This is what you want," he'd say, telling her the story only a young person could believe. But with him, in his warm, worn, rumpled bed, Helen could believe. It was still possible to imagine she wasn't hurting anyone, even when Darryl looked at her sadly and pulled the covers up to his chin. Even when he said, "I feel like you're falling away," and she tried to laugh her husband's fears away, saying, "How could I fall any lower than this?"

Pablo gave Helen something she hadn't known she wanted, surrounded as she'd been by her plans and activities and daughter, and now she imagined she couldn't live without this discovery of her own flesh.

She looked over at Felice, who was studying a list of questions they'd brainstormed together with Jean, Stella, and Drew the night before. Felice looked pale and not just because her golden, beside-the-pool tan had worn off, or because she was tired from grading essays or lecturing to halls full of university students or working on her own writing. "How are you doing, Felice? With all that's going on with Grace, I keep forgetting to ask. What's up with James?" Helen asked as she stopped at a light.

Felice folded up the sheet of questions and put them back in her purse. "We're talking better finally. And the lawyers have ironed out some agreement. We're going to have to sell the house. Soon. And the market is hot. The realtor James and I agreed on called me yesterday to say he doesn't even have to hold an open house. He has buyers knee-deep. I don't know how I'm going to tell the boys. That's the only house they've ever lived in," Felice said all at once, breathing in sharply as she finished.

"Oh, God! What do you think you're going to do?"

Felice was silent as they drove toward the freeway. It looked so cold outside, even the houses were dark, muted, the sky falling down around them. "Well," she said finally, "a colleague of mine called yesterday to tell me a friend of hers in Piedmont was selling a two bedroom, one bath. I don't know, Helen. It's just too much to think about. And now Grace. Can this really be happening?"

"It's too weird," Helen agreed. "It's crazy. *I* can't believe sometimes that it's really happening. For God's sake, this is Grace we're talking about. Our Grace! She saved us all a hundred times or more, just by making us laugh, caring about us, remembering our birthdays every single year."

"I know. It just can't be true. She just couldn't have done this to—"

"To us. To her family. To Celia," Helen said sharply.

"But she did! How could she look us in the eye and tell us those stories, Helen? How could this be happening?"

"But it is."

"I know."

Helen was silent as she merged onto the freeway, staring into the side-view mirror as if expecting an answer. "Nothing seems normal these days," she said, flicking off her turn signal. "Not a damn thing."

"So what's happening with your . . . with Pablo?"

She glanced over at Felice, who had turned her body toward Helen, her hands between her thighs. "I know you think it's wrong."

"I'm mad at James, Helen. Not at you," Felice said softly.

Helen smiled and bit back tears. "It's just as crazy as Grace. I don't know what I'm doing. But I don't know what I'd do without him, either."

"And Darryl has no idea?"

"He knows something is up."

"What do you mean?"

"He's trying harder than usual to be . . . nice. Paying attention to me. But then he'll ask me a question like, 'What did you do today?' He's a lot like Stella, really. He can't believe the worst. I never deserved someone like that."

"Of course you do. Why wouldn't you? But what are you going to do?"

Helen pressed down on the gas, trying to pass a Ford Fiesta. She never knew what to do. She wasn't like Stella at home, Felice at the university, or Grace on the basketball court. She had never had a comfort zone, any time when things just clicked, when she felt sure and strong and even. Except recently, with Pablo, in his bed.

"It *can't* last, can it?" Felice asked, almost loudly. "He's not really what you want, is he? I mean, do you love him, Helen?"

"No. I don't know. What do I know? He's just . . . different. He's . . ."

"He's not Darryl," Felice said, her voice the sound of rust. "I wonder. I wonder if that's all it ever is. Is it really a new love or just change? Are we that fickle? Can't anyone just stay where they're supposed to be? But where is that? Where are we supposed to be?"

Helen took the High Street exit and stopped at the light at the bottom. "Where are we supposed to be? Who are we supposed to be with?"

Felice shrugged. "You're asking me? I thought I knew, but I was wrong, I guess. James seemed perfect, always, the man of my dreams, Helen. When I met him, I thought we'd die side by side in our retirement home bed. But look at my dreams now."

When Helen had been a teenager, she imagined her perfect match to be an older man in a business suit, one who made calls and told people what to do. He knew the answers to every question and could arrange anything with a single telephone call to the right person. In bed, he would sweep her into his arms and teach her things, show her the way to happiness. They would go to the symphony, opera, ballet—adult things. Helen realized her fantasy was conceived when she wanted to escape her family, especially her father, desperate for order, certainty, structure, peace. She'd never found that man, and what she was getting from Pablo was sensuality, passion, a ripe burst of warm skin, tender touches under a blanket. She knew she was still needy.

Helen took a left and then a right onto Grace's street. "No one knows a damn thing."

"Everything just seems so fucked up."

Helen looked around her, the eucalyptus trees hanging in heavy arcs over the house, sycamore leaves like yellow stars on the asphalt. "I think part of living is learning to be okay with the fucked-up parts. I don't know how to do the okay part, but I'm great with fucked-up."

She looked over at Felice and smiled as they pulled up in front of Grace's house. They were the first to arrive. Kathleen had refused to come, calling Doris late last night, suddenly imagining that her own doctor friends were completely wrong, wanting "no part of this abuse!" They had all been ready to pull out, but Doris stood firm, saying, "I know it's true. I've talked to so many people and looked through everything Grace has. Maybe she has something, some illness, but it's not cancer being treated at Stanford."

"So," Helen said, sighing. Outside, the wet October sky spread out dark gray, the edges of clouds rimmed in black. Helen imagined Grace inside the house, flat on her back in bed, her dreams full of Demerol. It would be easy, Helen knew, to start the car, U-turn, and drive away, forgetting about all of this, at least for now. After today, either Grace would be in a treatment program or she would hate them all forever. They were either saving her or losing her. Either way, it wasn't going to be easy. "God, I hope Drew and Jean get here soon before I chicken out and drive us home."

* * *

Grace stared at them like a caught and bloodied animal, its heart quickening for one last attempt at freedom. "We have to talk to you." Helen closed the sliding glass bedroom door behind the four of them.

"Just a minute," Grace said, bolting into the bathroom and slamming the door behind her. Sounds of retching echoed under the door and into the bedroom.

"It's fake. It's fake. She's not really throwing up," Helen whispered. "Remember that."

Drew nodded but closed her eyes and rubbed her forehead. Helen put her hand on Drew's back, feeling her heartbeat under her hand.

"How do you know?" Drew said. "Maybe she's nervous. Maybe she knows what we are going to say."

"If she does, she might try to leave through the front door," Felice said quietly. "I'm going to go into the living room and pretend to look at pictures or something."

Jean nodded, and Felice went down the hall. Helen felt like she wanted to bolt somewhere as well, but her knees were shaking so much, she knew she couldn't; so she sat on the edge of Grace's bed listening to the raspy retching in the bathroom. "What is she doing?" Drew asked. "What could she possibly be pretending to throw up?"

Helen shrugged nervously. "A chemo reaction? *Shh, shh . . . here she comes!*"

Felice scooted into the room just before Grace opened the bathroom door and walked noiselessly into the room. *She doesn't weigh enough to make a sound*, thought Helen. *It's as if she's made of air and nothing else at all.* Grace didn't look at them but moved closer and leaned against the wall. "What's up?" she asked.

Helen swallowed and said, "This is my friend Jean. We all came here because we're worried about you. We just think . . ."

"We think that you've got something else going on with you. Besides the . . . cancer," Felice added. "And we want to help you."

Grace glanced up, the trapped look still in her eyes, but Helen could see her trying to fight it, her jaw already beginning to work as she thought of a story. "What are you talking about?" she asked.

"It's this treatment you're going through. It's the not eating during the day. It's the going to Stanford at one in the morning. It's the morphine in the bottle and only one syringe. It doesn't add up, Grace. It doesn't make sense anymore," Helen said, her hands moving as she spoke. "It's what's happening to Celia."

Grace shook her head and then raised her chin. "You *know* about the treatment. I've told you about the protocol and why it has to be a secret. I've told you all about it from the very beginning. Karl would lose his job if people found out. So many other people are at stake here. I can't jeopardize their lives by telling everyone too much or going into the hospital during the day."

"We called the hospital," Felice said. "We know there isn't a Karl in oncology. We talked to some nurses, and there isn't any way you can be admitted into the hospital at one in the morning. You mom said she looked through the house, and she can't find any admission forms."

Grace stood up slowly, pressing against the wall with her palms. Helen could hear Grace's stomach growling as she slid upward. "My mom is losing it. I swear she's in the early stages of Alzheimer's. She doesn't remember a thing. I mean, she's seen me take my pills! Just last night! She's talked to Karl on the phone herself. Didn't she tell you all about this?"

No one said a word. Helen realized she had never seen Grace angry before. Jean cleared her throat. "I know you don't know me, Grace, but I work with people in trouble, all kinds. I think your friends want some kind of confirmation of your illness. I think they are worried you have an eating disorder. Maybe an eating disorder as well as the cancer, but the eating disorder is not helping you now as you try to fight the cancer."

Grace snorted. "I haven't had an eating disorder since college. How can that be the problem? Why is this coming out now?"

Helen closed her eyes and tried to remember the last time she saw Grace eat. Once, when she and Darryl threw a party, she saw Grace eat a spoonful of a green bean salad that her friend Judy had made. But aside from the glasses and glasses of ice water, nothing, ever, and Helen had always believed it was because of the radiation and the long-ago gastric scarring. How could it be that until now no one had done or said anything about Grace's patterns? How could Kathleen have stayed with Grace so long and not confronted her strange menu, nighttime meals, and the bathroom visits? Or maybe Kathleen did know and hadn't been able to face it. Maybe that's why she moved out rather than deal with Grace.

"You don't eat, Grace." Helen shook her head. "You should be able to eat something, bland foods. Not just at night. Your mom says you eat, but just cans of green beans and rice cakes and NutraSweet. Those aren't the easiest things to digest. There has to be other food you can take in."

Grace paled under her tan. "My mother's been going through the garbage? My mom? She told you what I eat?"

"She loves you, Grace. She's terrified of losing you. She thinks that if this is all an eating disorder, then you might get better," Drew said.

"Oh, I wish," Grace ran her fingers through her thin hair. "In my dreams it would be so easy. And it's not a disorder. You know what I went through in college, Drew. These are the leftover bad habits from back then."

"Aren't bad habits a disorder, Grace?" Felice said. "If you can't change bad habits then you are sick. Like an alcoholic can't stop his habit of drinking. Or a drug addict can't stop—"

"That's not the same thing at all! Maybe I do just eat at night. That doesn't mean I *don't* have cancer."

"Well, your friends were wondering if they could meet your doctor, this Dr. Karl. Could they come with you and talk to him? Or could they talk to him on the phone?" Jean asked.

"I can come to any appointment," Helen said. "You really shouldn't be driving anyway."

"I'll stay with Celia at night when the boys are with James," Felice added. "When your mom isn't here, she shouldn't be alone when you check in at one a.m."

Grace was silent, looking up at them with large eyes, the whites yellowed and bloodshot. For a sad second, Helen heard Grace's stomach growl again, and Helen knew the body never let go, even when you wanted it to.

"What about the pain-management clinic you work with?" Jean said. "Would you be willing to let your friends talk to them? They're worried about the drugs you're on."

"Remember that day I came by to bring you some books," Felice said, "and I banged on this door but you wouldn't wake up? I had to stand here for a few minutes just to make sure you were breathing."

"I made a mistake, that's all," Grace said. "I took too big a shot."

"That's not a small thing," Helen added. "That's called an overdose. The clinic wouldn't want you making that kind of mistake."

"The point is, your friends want you to be taken care of," Jean said. "If you let them talk to your doctors, they will feel you are getting the best help you can. Do you think you could let them do that?"

She watched Grace's face as Jean went on, adding details to the plan, Felice saying she could help out at the house, Drew assuring Grace that all they wanted was for her to get well. Helen imagined she could see Grace grasping at her story, hooking her hands on the edge of something they all would believe. Grace looked up at the ceiling, reeling out first names—Karl, Suzanne, Ralph—doctors who knew her story, doctors whose lives and careers would be ruined if they all flooded the hospital, asking questions. She talked about fellow patients—Lester, Annie, Maria—who could be kicked out of the protocol, too. Grace's face was pulled taut, her skull and jawbone as clear to Helen as if she were a Halloween costume sitting before her. Her arms were spread out and to her sides, her hands flared and pressed against the wall, each finger tense, long, and bony. If Grace could, Helen knew, she'd just fly away, arch her long arms up and over them all, disappearing into a place where no one asked questions or looked through garbage or called hospitals asking for doctors who didn't exist. It would be a place where no one asked her a single question and no one ate a damn thing.

Grace shook her head, crossing her arms over her thin chest. "You don't know what I've been through," she said. "You're doing it again."

"What, Grace?" Felice knelt down and put her hands on Grace's shoulders. "Tell us. Tell us what you've been through."

"Your friends care about you," Jean said. "They want to help you."

Grace shook off Felice's hands and put her own hands over her ears. She looked up at them and spun on, her words slick and fast and confused, all of them surrounding her, stunned by the verbal flume, the quickness of her stories, the fluidity of her lies. In the midst of Grace's wild story, Doris pushed open the sliding glass door so hard it hit with a bang, the doorframe clacking against wood. "Wait!" she said, her eyes riveted on Grace. Helen saw how horrifying the scene must look, Grace surrounded and pressed up against the wall, throwing words out into the room. Helen stood up and walked toward Doris, but Doris ignored her and all the other women, as if they hadn't met constantly during the past week, talking daily on the phone as they planned how to save Grace.

"Stop!" Doris bent down to her daughter.

"Mama," moaned Grace, leaning into her mother's side. "Mama."

Doris clutched Grace, holding her shriveled, emaciated daughter against her flesh, an instinct Helen knew from holding Livie. Doris turned and whispered, "Please leave. Now."

Jean looked at the women and raised her eyebrows. Felice, Drew, and Helen shook their heads and shrugged, suddenly not knowing how to proceed. Jean leaned tentatively over Doris. "Are you sure, Doris? We haven't finished. Grace was just going to tell us what she'd been through."

"Doris," Helen said, "what about all we talked about? What about Celia? We can't just leave here without doing something."

Doris turned to them again, and this time the woman Helen had known was entirely gone, something animal and vicious in her place, like a mother wolf guarding her dying pups. "You've done enough! Get out!" she hissed, and after a clean, silent second, they all walked out of the bedroom, and Helen closed the door behind them.

They sat around Stella's kitchen table while in the family room Eric, Brodie, Dylan, Livie, and Celia were playing Monopoly. "I'm the shoe, stupid." Celia's voice echoed into the kitchen. "Now give me my two hundred dollars for passing go."

Stella poured two cups of Peet's decaf and sat down. "I'm telling you, I was in the kitchen making coffee, and Doris stood up and walked out of the house. I thought maybe she went to her car for something, but when I looked outside after about five minutes, she was gone. I thought to call you, but I knew the answering machine would pick up."

"She didn't say anything before that?" Helen asked, pouring milk into her coffee.

"Not about going over to the house. I mean, we were talking about the kids, school, hairstyles. Nothing out of the ordinary."

Felice sighed. "It was so strange. I was actually scared. She reminded me of this character in a book I teach. Well, I don't know if she's a character; she's the mother of a monster named Grendel. There's this line I can't get out of my head now. Something like, 'Grief-racked and ravenous, desperate for revenge.' "

"I thought the same thing," Helen said. "Well, not about Grendel's mother, of course, but Doris reminded me of any creature saving her young. A wolf. She scared me."

"I just thought she was upset. I don't know about Grendel." Stella raised her eyebrows. "I haven't read it lately."

Helen put her hand on Stella's shoulder, thinking how her friend often tuned out when Grace began a conversation about society or the law or when Felice talked about literature and poetry and writing. But here was Stella, the only happily married one of the bunch, her perfect body carrying a child, Eric well-adjusted and thriving, her house full of careful decoration. "I think I read that once in college, but who really knows about Grendel other than Felice?" said Helen. "Who but Felice would say, 'Oh, yes. This is reminiscent of Grendel's mother?' "

Felice smiled. "Okay, fine. But I read it every year, so there it is. I'm a teacher. Give me a break, you two."

"I was just about to go back to school," Stella said. "Before the baby. I really had the Laney College catalogue on my dresser. But now . . ."

"You're *good* at what you do," Helen said quickly. "Don't feel bad about that. This baby will go to school, too, and then you can go. Hey, that's all of five years from now."

Stella nodded. "This is what I always wanted, though. A husband and kids and a home. It's what my mom did. I like it. Sometimes, though, I just feel like I'm doing nothing."

Helen finished her coffee and sat back in her chair. Wasn't that how she herself felt? Wasn't that why she was in school and still sleeping with Pablo despite knowing she shouldn't? Why she and Darryl slept on opposite sides of the bed, their skin never touching unless a dream intervened? It was all the nothing in her life. All the nothing but Livie, who had become everything. And that was wrong. But now there was too much, and she didn't know how to deal with that either.

"Well, I guess we're doing nothing about Grace now," Felice said. "What can we do after something like that? Now not even her mother or ex-lover want any part of an intervention."

"What are we going to do?" Stella asked. "Grace can't have that much more time, cancer or not. She's just so tiny. It's like she's shrunk."

"You should have seen her today, Stella. She was in her run-ning clothes, and I could see every single bone in her body."

"I know," Felice said. "I can't believe she's still alive as it is."

Helen shook her head, thinking about the eight or so years of summers, the kids growing up in front of them all, moving from the baby pool to swim lessons to workouts. All the great talks, Grace throwing her head back, laughing, the deep, throaty, full sound echoing around the pool, pulling them together. Grace would put hands on their thighs, say, "You won't believe this!" and tell them what she heard in the locker room, the sauna, the gym. Grace was the force that drew them together, year after year, arranged movies and parties, remembered Felice's first day back to work at Cal each semester, Helen's anniversary, Aaron's birth-day. *And now*, thought Helen, *she's on her bedroom floor, almost dead, sobbing in her mother's arms.*

"Maybe we didn't give her enough," Helen said. "Not like what she gave us. I know I never remembered her and Kathleen's anniversary."

"She called *my* mother on her birthday," Stella said, rubbing her belly. "That's just the way she was."

Helen heard the past tense in Stella's words and knew that it was the past, that those times were finished. Grace had been the glue and she'd unstuck herself from them and from life, not let-ting anything in: food, words, or love.

"What can we do now?" Felice asked.

"Well," Stella said, "I have an idea. Maybe you could do one of those swell interventions again."

Helen put down her cup and began to laugh. "Oh, we inter-vened, all right. What was that, anyway? I remember Felice say-ing, 'Just keep walking. Don't stop,' as we climbed up the back stairs toward Grace's room. Then we're in the room and Grace runs to the bathroom. After that, I forgot what we were sup-posed to do. Jean was the only one who asked normal questions. But our plan sucked. I think we all forgot what we were supposed to be doing. And then Doris barged in and the whole thing fell apart."

"I don't know," Stella said. "It sounds like you guys might want to print up a brochure or something. 'In trouble? Call us!' I bet you'll end up on *Oprah*."

"Maybe we can open up some franchises," said Felice. "Interventions-R-Us. We'll make a fortune."

"We'll get some hats and T-shirts printed up." Helen leaned over the table, looking into her friends' eyes. "We can just pass them out at the club."

Felice started giggling, and then so did Stella. Helen wanted to reach out around the table and take their hands, so she did, and they sat at the table laughing until the tears came again at their failure to save their friend.

A few days later, Helen sat with Pablo at Starbucks. As he stirred a lump of brown sugar into his herbal tea with a spoon, his head bent down, Helen thought she saw one gray hair curling up through his soft dreadlocks, but then he shifted and looked up, and she knew she was only imagining he was older.

She cleared her throat quietly, trying to find something to say, something other than: "Let's go to your place."

Helen sipped her decaf mocha. "I hate this class," she said finally.

"I *like* this one."

"Really?"

"Well, it's better than spring," Pablo said. "Except spring was when we hooked up."

"Right."

She could feel his eyes read her, and she tried to close herself so he wouldn't find out something she didn't even know. "Right. That's when we *hooked up*. Sounds like crocheting."

"What?"

"Never mind."

Outside, the street was wet, the slicing slash of tires on the street, the gurgle of the rain gutters. "But how's your friend Grace? Anything new?"

Helen sighed with relief, grateful that he'd found a topic, even though she didn't know if she could tell him what had happened since they last spoke. Would she have believed such a twisted story when she was twenty-seven? When she was that age, enchanted by foreign travel, colors, busy with numbers and projected sales, Helen would have snorted and said, "Christ, can't you just get her to eat? What's wrong with you people?"

She sat back in her chair. "I don't know how to start. It's been weird. We don't really know . . . I don't know . . ."

"What is it?"

"Well, we think . . . We're pretty sure now that Grace doesn't have cancer."

He put down his spoon. "How did you find that out?"

She reached for his arm, soft and dark, smooth black hair on his wrists just under his sleeves. "Her mother brought us all together to tell us. Some doctor friends of her lover's did some checking, and there was one lie after the other. When I found out, everything just started to make sense."

"What do you mean?"

"Well, there were these weird times. She'd tell us she was going to the hospital, and then her partner wouldn't know about it. She supposedly was admitted in the middle of the night, but no hospital does something like that. She could have eaten more than she did; she didn't have to exercise five hours a day. I thought it was weird, but I didn't want to believe my friend would lie to me. None of us thought she was so . . ."

"Mentally ill?"

"Yeah. I guess that's it."

Pablo looked at her the entire time, his eyes so tender, so different from Darryl's current anxiety and irritation. But then again, Pablo hadn't had to live with all the phone calls, the disturbance in the house, Celia with them when she wasn't with Stella or Felice. "What about her daughter? What's happening to her while all this is going on?"

"I think Grace's mother is still there, but I don't know, really. We were dismissed. About two hours after the intervention, Doris called us to say that she'd talked to all Grace's doctors and that Grace really, truly had cancer. She's stuck to the story, too."

"It's child abuse." Pablo sat back in his chair. "It's flat-out neglect. You can't leave Celia in that house with a mother like that. It's not right."

Helen ran her hand through her short hair, knowing that Pablo was right, that Celia was the ragged bone none of them had been able to swallow. They'd tried to help Grace, but they'd left the girl in a house with a bedridden mother who drugged herself, who couldn't shop for food, who only cared about something none of them could fathom. For all Helen knew, Doris could have already gone home, leaving Celia to fend for herself, eat Top Ramen or peanut butter for dinner, and stay by herself in the house when Grace went off for her one a.m. "treatments." And even if Doris was still there, what would happen to Celia as she grew up, watching her mother prone in bed, drugged and starving? What kind of woman would Celia grow into? What messages was she getting about flesh and love and life? Had they really imagined they could all turn away and walk out Grace's sliding glass door without looking back? "Oh, Pablo. You're right. But we feel stuck, what with her mother telling us to stop."

He tapped his fingers on the tabletop. "That kid deserves better. Couldn't you call Child Protective Services? I had to do that once. For a kid at a camp I was working at one summer." He touched his mug, his hands spinning it in the saucer.

He's so full of energy, thought Helen, *he can't keep it inside, just like when we're together, his hands all over me.* For a second, she forgot about Celia and traced his touch on her body with her memory, recalling his strokes, his pressure, the way he gripped her shoulders.

"Well? What do you think?"

She bit her lip hard, too hard, shocking herself back into the conversation. She hadn't imagined Pablo having to deal with anything like this before, and she knew that was just one of the ways she made him small, kept him a child, an underling, someone not her equal. "So you called the authorities?"

"Yeah," he said, putting down his mug. "It was awful, but the kid ended up in a better place. Safer."

"Grace can tell a story, though. When I was in the room with her, I could almost believe it all. And if I hadn't known her, hadn't done the research and called around, hadn't seen all the inconsistencies, I would have left thinking she was simply a survivor. I would be completely fooled." She felt a harsh laugh stick in her lungs, but as she tried to push it out, her throat stung, and she swallowed it down.

"Someone with a trained eye would see. You love her. That's why you didn't notice. Didn't want to notice."

But she knew Grace was powerful. After all, here she was, still worrying them all, her grasp so long, no one could forget her. Here Helen was with the man she thought about every night as she fell asleep, desperate for his touch, and they were talking about Grace. All she really wanted to do was reach her fingers to his face. She closed her eyes and saw the way his back suddenly arced into his ass, his biceps and stomach tense.

"What are we going to do?" she asked, wondering how many more days they would have like this, sitting in a coffee shop in San Francisco, far enough away from anyone she might know, her husband, her child, her friends. "How much longer can I do this?" she wanted to ask. "How much longer can you?"

"I don't know," he said, shaking his head. "I really don't."

Late that night, the sound of the flatland trains echoing up the hills, Helen lay in bed, her arms folded across her chest, Darryl asleep on his side of the bed. Unable to sleep, she started thinking about what Doris had told them about Grace and her college basketball coach. "She left home for her freshman year an angel and came back starving to death. She was never right again," Doris had said.

Maybe, thought Helen, *I won't let Livie go away.* That first year of spinning away from the family might be too hard for anyone to bear. It had been hell for her. That was for sure. For almost all of her childhood, her father had been a mystery, one wild emotion after another, until her freshman year when she found a part of him she'd never seen before.

She moved up to UC Berkeley from Los Gatos to stay in a dorm, rooming with two best friends from Pasadena, who spoke in a code Helen never could crack. Before she'd left home, her own best friend, Rita, kept saying, "Cal is so hard. You're going to have to study all the time. Day and night."

Helen had shrugged, thinking about all her high school A's in an orderly row on her transcript. "I'll be fine."

"I don't know," Rita said. "Just stay home and go to Foothill College with me. Come on. It will be so much fun. You won't just be studying all the time."

Despite Rita's pleading all summer, Helen had gone to Cal, but Rita was right. Her high school hadn't compared to Cal, and she felt lost in her own dorm room when she came home from class, her arms full of books, her head whirling with tests and assignments and deadlines, lost as she walked to class, looking for an answer, a reason for being there at all.

By the middle of November, Helen had stopped calling home or eating with other students in the cafeteria, just grabbing a banana and juice and heading to the library before class as well as after class, reading and reading and reading to find what she needed.

Finally, just before Thanksgiving break, Helen looked up from her history textbook, her eyes red, and there was her father, Jackson, standing by her table, dressed in his work suit, shadowed by the morning light. Helen wondered if he were a mirage, a hallucination, a bad dream.

"Let's go," he said gruffly, and she silently picked up her books and bag, her stomach a pulse of nerves as she thought about the classes she would miss, the pages of notes she would have to copy later from a classmate, how far behind this one morning would put her. But she couldn't say no. This was Jackson, her father, and she followed him to his car, and he started the engine and pulled into traffic, driving slowly down University Avenue.

"How is school?" he asked quietly.

She looked out the window, watching students head toward their classes, classes they wouldn't miss. They all looked so determined, ready, as if answers were just inside their mouths. How could she tell Jackson that she had no answers for anything, no clue at all?

Helen said nothing. Jackson slowed the car a bit and turned to look at her. "You're so thin," he said finally, making a left onto Shattuck Avenue. Helen bent to look at her thighs, feeling the hard bones under her palms.

She was about to say, "I'm not really thin," but she looked up instead and saw Jackson was crying. He wasn't making a sound, but his face was wet, his hands clutching the steering wheel. Helen almost gasped. If it weren't for his face, it would be impossible to know that he was any different from his going-to-the-office self, all business, ready to get cracking. But he was crying. Crying for *her*? Helen had no idea what to do. She'd never seen him do anything like this before, not once, not even when his own mother died. She was unsure how to move toward him or next to him. She was scared to put a hand on his jacket arm. And because she didn't know what else to do, she began crying herself, thinking, even though neither of them said anything else of importance the entire drive, that he loved her. He must.

After Jackson visited her in Berkeley, her mother insisted on weekend visits home, picking Helen up herself, packing bags of food for her to take back on Sunday nights. After Christmas break, Helen's roommates moved into a sorority house, and Lia moved in—smart Lia, who taught Helen how to make flashcards to study with and to drink a glass of beer without taking a breath.

By the end of her freshman year, Helen had regained the weight she'd lost, made more friends, received B's in all her classes, and even found a job in Berkeley for the summer. When she went home, Jackson was his same self, teasing her and yelling if the house was dirty, no sign that he thought about or even remembered what had happened between them in the car.

Back then it was Lia and her mother and father who showed her the way; next it had been Darryl; now it was Pablo. When would she learn to change without using someone else? And who had ever helped Grace? No one had been able to ease the pain that had made such a terrible ruse an option. Maybe people had tried to help before, and Grace turned them all away, just as she had done with them.

Helen spun toward her husband, his blanketed body a known landscape in the night bedroom. Before, she would have closed her eyes and reached her hands under the covers, feeling for his smooth body, knowing the curves of shoulder and hip and waist. Now she didn't know if she could find her way. And behind him, there was the shadow of her own need. She didn't know if she could reach out to either, satisfying him or herself, filling up the holes in her life with busyness or lists or order and, just recently, desire.

She stayed still, knowing she couldn't touch anything yet. Something would have to happen. Someone, she knew, would have to help her again before she was forced, like Felice, to live with someone else's choice. It would have to happen soon because Helen didn't know if, when she finally reached out to Darryl, he would still be there.

TWELVE

∾

"Do you have cancer?" her mother asked, sitting on the edge of the bed she'd just tucked Grace into.

She looked into her mother's eyes and saw the concern she'd always craved. But it was too late! Too late! Where had this look been before, back when she needed it, all those years of craziness, her father running mad through the house during the day, people tiptoeing around at night, everyone awake but Doris, the one who could have changed things.

"You can tell me," Doris crooned.

Grace sat up and pulled away from her mother's touch, suddenly feeling like she could throw up, even though she hadn't eaten a thing, her disgust so thick. "No, I can't. You won't care. Just like always."

"Wasn't I here for your last illness? Haven't I been here for weeks? What do you mean?" Doris sat up straight, the gauzy veil of denial tight around her shoulders. *It was useless*, thought Grace, knowing that this time she couldn't live through any more.

"I can't do this! I can't have everyone thinking this about me," she whispered, gasping for air. She felt pummeled by the afternoon, all her air and blood sucked dry.

"Are you dying?" Doris leaned over her again. Grace could smell the mints on her breath, the coffee she must have had at Stella's.

"Of course I'm dying," she said. "I've been dying for a long time. No one saw it though. No one could tell. And then Kathleen left, and now my best friends, and you won't even believe me. You don't care that I'm dying. I will die. Oh, Mom!" Grace began to cry, then keen, her heart beating faster again, so fast she tried to slow down her tears.

"What can I do?" Her mother was so calm. She'd never been like this when Grace was a child.

"They can't know! I can't live with that. I can't! I will . . . I'll have to kill myself." She imagined the knife, the full syringe of Demerol, the gun she knew she could find in West Oakland, where she found everything else. It would be so easy. So easy. But what about Celia? What about Celia?

"Stop it!" Doris pulled Grace up and to her. "Stop that!"

"I can't! I can't live with this. I'm sick. I'm really sick. But . . . I just can't . . . take the questions. But my friends wouldn't understand. They wouldn't . . . love me anymore," she sobbed.

"Hush, now," Doris soothed, the old lull something Grace imagined she'd heard before.

When Grace was little, she remembered her mother's silhouette at the kitchen window as she washed dishes, her apron crisp and tied in a bow behind her back, her skirt falling perfectly just below her knees. Grace would slowly sidle up to her mother, not close enough for Doris to notice, but enough so she could breathe in her mother's smells, the Jergens hand lotion, the Dial shampoo, the clean sting of Tide. At night, after tucking Grace into bed, Doris closed the bedroom door, as if making sure she wouldn't leave. Grace could see the handle turning, as if her mother were practicing opening and closing the door. Maybe, Grace now wondered, she was testing to see if it made a sound, something Doris must have known she should hear. The sounds she should have heard all along.

"All those years," she wailed suddenly, her chest full of coils. She breathed as if she had bronchitis, the words like coughs, mucousy and thick. "Why did you let it go on all those years?"

Doris held her tighter. "Hush, hush," she said, stroking Grace's head. "Don't talk. Just rest."

Grace shook her mother off, pushing at Doris with the heels of her palms. "You will listen to me! Finally, Mother! You will hear this story!"

"Don't. Don't say anything."

"You won't talk about that, but you will sic my friends on me! You'll go through my garbage! You'll tell them about my eating habits and my past! But you won't talk to me about Miller and what he did? Every night, in my room, touching and touching and using me like a toy! *That* you won't talk about?"

Doris pulled herself into almost the same position Grace had been in earlier, tight and flat against the wall. "Stop it. Don't say another word. Don't even talk about it."

"You won't even talk about it now! You're not even sorry?" Grace cried, the corners of her mouth white with spit. "You're a hypocrite! What a liar! Why didn't you ever come in to see what the noises were? How could you let Miller do that to me! Did you ever try to find out what Dad was doing in the boys' room? You just stopped looking and made *me* see everything! I had to see it all! I had to know it! I did! And I don't want to see anything anymore!"

"I told you, stop it!" Doris yanked on Grace's shirt. "Stop saying those words. I won't hear any of it! Why are you doing this?"

Doris began to sob, her head in her hands, her shoulders shaking with each deep inhale. Grace wiped away her own tears and looked at her mother, almost seventy-five years old, gray at the roots when once her hair had been thick and red, curling just under her chin. Doris's hands were spotted and the skin so thin, Grace could see the purply-blue veins, lumpy and almost painful looking, running to Doris's arthritic fingers.

"I can't talk about this," Doris finally said, her head still bowed. "Your father's illness . . ."

"Don't blame him for everything. You were there! You could have stopped it!" said Grace. "How can you blame him when you had two legs and you could walk and you had arms that could hold me and take me away? He was crazy, but you weren't. And instead of saving me, you kill me with this now, just as I'm trying so hard to stay alive. Do you know what this will do to me? I can't do it. I can't."

She slumped down against the pillow, exhausted, her head pounding, her stomach curled into an acid fist. She wanted to do nothing but sleep, but Grace knew she had to make her mother fix this one last important thing. "I'll get better. I promise. I will start to eat and I'll gain weight and I'll go to counseling. I'll even go get a job, and we can move out of this house. But you have to do what I say. You can't back out, or I won't do any of it. I know I'll die." As she spoke, she saw the force of her words on her mother's skin. She saw her mother's resolve split and crack wide open, and the place that had once held all the desire to see Grace in a treatment program filled with this new idea, the one that would really keep her alive.

"What? What do you want me to do?"

"You've got to tell them that it's not a lie. That it's all true. That you talked to the doctors and went to the hospital. You've got to tell them that you've seen the CAT scans and that you know everything. You've got to! I can't live with them thinking this about me. I won't! I won't do it!"

Doris wiped under her eyes with her crooked fingers, her mascara and eyeshadow a blue-and-black blur. She was breathing quickly, almost panting, and Grace could see the *tick-tick* beat of her mother's heart at the base of her wrinkled throat, the skin there smooth and soft as warm paper.

"Can't you take me with you to the hospital?" Doris asked quietly. "Can't you show me what is real?"

"No. It's mine. It's my illness, not yours. Not anyone else's. You don't deserve it."

"Why?"

"You've never cared enough."

"This can't be the only way, Grace. You don't know how much your friends love you."

"So why did you come barging in? Why did you interrupt them? If they love me that much, why didn't you trust them to take care of me?"

Her mother shook her head. "I was scared. I felt . . . I felt like you needed me. Like I'd made a mistake."

"You've made so many and that's why I'm like this. You owe it to me to fix this mess," Grace said. "You've owed it to me for years."

"How can I say I've gone to the hospital? They'll ask questions," Doris asked. "All they want to do is help you."

She was silent, thinking how Doris couldn't see how those words to Helen, Stella, Felice, and Drew would be the very thing that would save her, that would help her the most. "You just have to," she said finally. "It's your turn to help. Or else I'll die. It's that simple. And I told you that I'd get better. I'll start to eat more. I promise."

"Really? And the cancer? Is it . . . will it go away? What happens with that?"

"Don't worry about anything. If you do what I want, then it will be better."

Grace breathed in the truth of those words, imagining her red blood cells full of iron and nutrients, her stomach digesting vegetables and cheese and rice completely, her intestines sucking down nourishment. Just like the tumors she'd seen bloom in her lungs, she saw health spiral through her body with blood and nerves and fluid, her hair thick, her skin soft, just like she'd been before her father and before Miller and before her mother forgot about her altogether. Just like Celia was now. Maybe, without anyone bothering her, she could do this. She could really do this.

Grace felt herself puff with ripeness, could almost see the inches of fat under her skin. And she knew her mother saw it, too, the vision of how she used to be.

"All right," Doris said. "I will. I will tell them everything."

Grace sat on the edge of her bed as she listened to her mother run water in the bathroom for a long time. Her mother turned the faucet on, shut it off, turned it on again, trying, Grace imagined, to stop her tears, the ones she'd earned, the ones she deserved.

After she was done in the bathroom, Grace heard her mother walk to the kitchen and begin making calls, her voice the same one Grace knew from childhood, full of excited highs and sympathetic lows, commiserating and empathizing, so social and clever and charming that all the neighborhood mothers loved her, looked down at Grace and said, "Your mother is so wonderful." Grace would stare up at them, her eyes wide, and wonder what they were talking about. They didn't know, as she did, that it was all pretend, that late at night the house was home to monsters.

She stood up, feeling clear, feeling strong, her legs not as shaky as they had been when her friends showed up and she could see on their faces what they would later say. As they approached her, Grace saw through the glass door how they no longer believed her, how doubt was chipping away at their love for her. Helen's eyes looked black with certainty and disgust, Grace thought, as if walking in the door was painful, as if looking at her was a chore, a duty, a summons. And Drew and Felice moved toward her with the same pulled-away distance that someone might assume over a loved but highly contagious person. Grace knew, in that instant, that eventually they would all leave. And it would be like it always was, Grace deserted by brother and father and mother and husband and lover, people peeling off her tight grasp, saying, "No more," even as she gave them everything she had inside.

Outside, a fine fall rain had begun, the sky rippling with gray and orange. Grace pulled on a pair of sweatpants and a windbreaker, tying the hood under her chin. She put her wallet and car keys in her pocket and slipped out the door, closing it carefully behind her, hoping Doris would be worried, praying Doris would think that it was too late to make amends. She wanted her mother to pay for this and everything, and Grace wanted her to hurt, finally and now and forever.

"Where have you been?" Doris opened the sliding glass door and rushed to Grace, pulling her daughter into her arms. She felt her mother's heart against her chest, almost as if it were her own.

"For a treatment." Grace pulled out of the embrace and moved toward the bed. "Is Celia home?"

"I went and picked her up at Stella's and made her dinner. She's in bed now. But didn't you say . . . didn't you promise me the cancer would go away?"

"I didn't say when, did I?" Grace felt a crackle of excitement pulse through her chest, knowing that she was going to get everything that she wanted, for once. "What did you say to Celia?"

"I told her you went to the hospital. So . . . that's where you were, right?"

"What else did you do?"

Doris sat down on the edge of the bed, picking at specks of lint on the comforter. "I called them all. I told them you were sick and that I talked to the doctors on the phone. I even called Kathleen and told her to tell her friend Ruth to stop bothering us."

Grace slid into bed, pulling the comforter up to her chin. "Did they believe you? Is it over? Did you make it stop?"

Doris rubbed her hands on her thighs, her palms sliding up and down on her rayon pants. "Yes. I think so. Mostly. They all still have questions, but I told them I would find out more. I told them . . . I told them I was going to the hospital with you tomorrow," Doris said, her voice cracking. "But I'm worried now. You said the cancer was going away. That you would eat. That you would get better."

"Tomorrow. Tomorrow, I will start getting better."

"Okay. Tomorrow. I'll go to the store. I'll get some food. I'll make some meals. We've got to get the stove fixed."

"What did Kathleen say?" Grace asked, her voice ragged on her tongue.

"I don't know if she believed me."

"You've got to call her again! Call her again," Grace said, her neck tense on the pillow. "If she doesn't believe, I can't get better."

"I will. I promise."

Grace relaxed and as she settled into bed, her mother's voice was like a bad television show. The drug reached up a slickery hand and began to pull her down, and she slept like she only did when on it, a full and deep sleep that stopped everything.

In the kitchen at three a.m., Grace sat surrounded by rice cake bags and green bean cans, everything empty. Her mother hadn't awakened tonight, sliding into the kitchen in her slippers to watch Grace eat, so Grace had forgotten time, place, limits, pushing the cakes into her mouth, one after another, chewing in big crunching gulps, bits flying out of her mouth, saliva pooling under her tongue and dripping onto the table. After the rice cakes, she smashed eight beans into her mouth at once, glopping them down, taking a small sip of soy milk after chewing, just enough to help push the food down. Her fingers were sore from using the can opener. But she was still hungry. She stood up and opened the cabinets, pulling out food Doris had bought for Celia, Triskets, Wheat Thins, a boxed German chocolate cake mix. She cut open the cake mix, wet her finger, and dipped it in the brown powder, licking the sweet into her mouth, then tilting the bag to her mouth, pouring it in until she choked. Grace sipped soy milk and then poured down more, not tasting anything but already feeling the sugar in her blood. When the cake mix was gone, she ate the crackers, and then opened the refrigerator. In a cast-iron pot were leftovers, stroganoff, just like she remembered from her own childhood. Sitting on the floor by the open door, Grace scooped the cold beef and sauce into her mouth with her fingers, feeling the shock of protein on her stomach. Just as the stroganoff pot was empty, Grace felt ripples, minute muscle contractions then waves of nausea. Standing up and then tripping over the pot, she lurched to the sink and threw up, all of it in order, the paprika red of the stroganoff, the swirled browns of crackers and cake mix, the green mush of beans, the white bits of rice cake, soy milk curdling in silvery wisps.

After she cleaned the kitchen, running the garbage disposal and opening the window, scouring the sink with Comet, she went to the bathroom to brush her teeth. She opened her mouth in front of the mirror, the back of her throat red, her teeth yellow and stumpy, all the taste buds on her tongue white and enlarged. She closed her mouth and looked at her face, strangely dark, a pallor under her tan, her eyes ringed with black. When she was thirteen, she'd looked in the bathroom mirror of her mother's house and realized she was all wrong, she was fat, she was ugly, her skin not right, nothing fitting together as it should. And somehow, Grace learned to stick her finger down her throat, feeling the bumpy beginnings of her pharynx, and she felt the lump of dinner push up and through her mouth, into the toilet. It seemed so easy. And after she'd washed her face and stood looking at herself, Grace felt clean and real and true. And that feeling lasted, for a while.

Now, all these years later, no amount of throwing up or starving made her feel better. It was as if her bones were filled with sand, her head full of steel wool. There were no answers through emptiness any more. What would happen now? she wondered, washing her face. Where would she go from here? Would her mother be able to save her after all these years? And would anyone believe Doris after what happened here this afternoon, in her house, in her own room? Would her friends ever really believe her again?

And why should they? Even though all of them had listened to her stories and understood her answers, today had been completely different. Her own mother had turned her in, turned all of them against her, every friend she had counted on for years. And Doris didn't believe her about the cancer and hadn't believed her story about Miller, when she tried to tell her years ago.

Grace turned off the bathroom light and slipped into bed, looking up in the dark room, blackened tree branches swaying over the skylight, the flicker of bats and night birds, the sounds of a faraway siren. For years it had been her friends Helen, Stella, and Felice who had listened and believed her. How could she get them to come back and say everything was all right? But did she want them now that there was this stain of disbelief covering everything? She didn't know how to tell them that something dark and powerful was in her blood and body, creeping up her spine like a vine, pulling her down and back into a time she thought she'd forgotten.

And now her mother was finally here, with her, living in her house, having to deal with the minutes of Grace's life, as Doris never had had to before. *She owes me this time,* thought Grace, *every single minute Miller was on me, every hour and day and week my father raged insane. It's mine. It's all mine.* But did she want her mother with her forever? She didn't know what she wanted anymore except Kathleen. Kathleen's skin and Kathleen's voice and Kathleen's idea that Grace could live through anything. The only person who believed her was Kathleen. Kathleen didn't ask the wrong questions about her health and Kathleen didn't say she was crazy. Kathleen hated Miller because of what he'd done to her, writing him off completely. And Kathleen hadn't shown up here today, like everyone else. Grace knew she would die without being able to be back in her arms and this bed, right now. Only Kathleen could make all of this go away. But how could she get her to come home? How could all of this end as it was supposed to? Grace and Kathleen and Celia all here, in this house, in this safe, comfortable house.

She knew she would never sleep, and she begged the night gods, the ones who had abandoned her so many years ago, to come back, to tell her what to do, to show her what would happen next.

THIRTEEN
❧

Before Felice left for what she called "The Fall Tour of Baby Nurseries," she decided to call Doris. It had been almost two weeks since she had last spoken to her or Grace, both of them in seeming seclusion in Kathleen's house, licking their wounds and trying to determine their next move. It was a crisp mid-November day, the air full of water and sound, the creek by her house noisy with recent fall rains, a perfect day—she didn't teach on Tuesdays—to visit Stella and Sean and Susan and to call Doris, catching up on what work usually swallowed whole.

Felice expected the machine to pick up as it had the last time she'd tried to call, but after the third ring Doris answered.

"Hi. It's Felice. How are you?"

There was a pause, and she felt she could hear Doris walking, the phone pressed to her face, and then a door close. "Fine. Fine. Everything is much better. Much better."

Felice had to shrug away some anger, realizing she still couldn't understand why Doris had interrupted the intervention and sent them all away. Then again, she wanted to apologize, sorry for the pain she saw on both their faces as she left Grace's house. "I tried to call a few days ago. I wanted to see how things are going."

"Oh, Felice. It's such a relief to meet all these people. The doctors. The nurses. Even the lab technicians. They just love Grace. Love her. They all call her their miracle patient."

Felice felt something in her jaw, surprise or laughter or amazement or terror. Could any of what Doris said be true? What if they'd all made the biggest mistake of their lives, walking up the steps to Grace's house, pushing in, and demanding that she go to a treatment center. If it wasn't true, why would Doris, a mother, someone who cared more about Grace than they ever could, say all this? "So you've gone to the hospital?"

"Oh, yes. Whenever she needs a treatment."

"Chemo? She's still getting chemo?"

"It's the experimental drug. It's different than other drugs, you know."

"Wow." Felice rubbed her forehead. "Grace must be wiped out."

There was a pause. "Yes. She hasn't been up much except for those hospital visits."

"Can I talk to her? Is she awake?"

Felice heard the sound of more walking, another door closing. "She's still napping. But lately, she's really been feeling well in the afternoon. She might even be able to start working out at the club again. But I'll tell her you called."

"Oh. Okay. But, Doris?"

"What?"

"Do you need any help? Are you okay?"

"I don't know how anyone could be okay after something like this." When Felice later hung up the phone, she thought that was the only true thing Doris had said the entire conversation.

Her first stop was Sean and Susan's apartment. Susan opened the front door, a waft of lavender sailing out and around Felice. She was exactly as Felice had imagined her during that first phone call with Sean—pale blue eyes, long blond hair, a beautiful figure under flower-printed dresses. But after talking with her and eating out with her and Sean and the boys, Felice knew she liked Susan. A lot. She was perfect for Sean, the missing piece he'd been looking for all these years he thought he'd loved Felice. It made her wonder why, if there were, in fact, parted twins for everyone, soul mates desperate to connect, it took so long. And why were there fake soul mates, people who seemed right before the masks fell away? Like James, her perfect man, the love of her life. A mistake, all along.

After an inspection of the nursery—Sean's converted writer's study, sonnets and free verse mingling with diapers and Desitin—and a cup of jasmine tea, she was back in her car, driving to Stella's.

"I talked to Doris," Felice said as soon as Stella opened the door.

"No!" Stella pulled her into the warmth of her house.

"Yeah. She says she's met all the hospital staff. Everyone loves Grace, can't believe how long she's survived. A miracle. And Doris says Grace is still on chemo."

Stella shook her head. "Why would Doris say all that if it wasn't true?"

"I don't know. I even started to think maybe it was. I had to remind myself of what we knew all along, what we discovered before the intervention."

They both stood in Stella's dining room shaking their heads. "Well, forget it for now. Aaron just finished painting yesterday. Come see."

Unlike Sean and Susan's nursery, which was still a place for writing, Stella had no design for this room other than baby, the walls painted perfectly pink, fluffy latex clouds swirled on the ceiling, a soft cloth mobile hanging over the oak crib.

"It's beautiful," Felice said, touching the blankets, the folded sleepers, the tiny T-shirts.

Stella nodded. "Thanks. It's a dream I always had. I know it's kind of stupid, but I wanted a girl's room. Once the test results came in, I bought all the little soft, pretty things."

Felice laughed. "Well, I wanted that, too. But it's too late now. And it seemed silly to have another baby just to decorate the room. Though I thought about it, believe me. I dreamed of buying the most expensive crib and changing table I could. Solid oak or cherry. But James only wanted two. No more. And it was hard enough having two when we did. I can't believe we all made it through alive." She looked up at Stella, raising her eyebrows and shrugging slightly. "Actually, we didn't come through it alive, did we? There goes *that* family."

Stella put a hand on Felice's arm. Stella was so warm, as if her blood was rushing through her, on her, just barely under her skin. But she wasn't ill, Felice knew, just completely alive.

"You *are* a family. Just different than you were. And who's to say it isn't better? Who's to say it isn't exactly what you wanted?"

Felice fingered a soft bear, nodding as her friend spoke, her body warmed by Stella's touch and words. She never would have planned it this way, back when she was striving for everything, career, family, home, happy marriage. James had just become part of her striving, someone she wanted, something she wanted, the perfect husband, aware, astute, politically correct, financially adept, fascinated with what she did. What had she given to him? Maybe in the beginning she had given him her promise and body, her love of books and ideas, but she hadn't given him enough obviously, because he'd left. Plain and simple.

So maybe in the Piedmont house that would soon be theirs, Felice thought, she and Brodie and Dylan would be the family they were supposed to be. Within days of being put on the market, Felice and James's house had sold for sixty thousand over asking, and the next thing she knew, she and the boys were doing a walk-through in the Piedmont house with their realtor, Ricardo, both Brodie and Dylan sliding in their socks on the smooth, empty hardwood floors.

"I love this, Mom! Look at me," Brodie had said as he slipped by.

Dylan said nothing, and Ricardo patted his head. "This house is perfect for you."

It was possible that Stella and Ricardo were right. It might be better. It just might be perfect.

Stella moved over to the bureau lined with Winnie-the-Pooh books. "But sometimes people don't make it through," she said.

"I mean, look at Celia. Just think about what she's going to have to deal with." Stella rubbed her belly. Felice imagined she could see this new daughter stretching inside her friend's body. "Celia has to worry about Grace all day. And she probably thinks we are the worst people in the world after what we did to her mother."

"I wonder what Grace has said to her."

"She's probably told a million stories."

"Lies, you mean."

Stella nodded slightly. "Well, yeah. Lies."

"How could she tell her anything true? I don't know how Doris can ever leave now. Grace can't take care of Celia. There's no way Grace is doing any kind of decent parenting now."

Stella moved to the crib, smoothing a blanket that hung over the rail. "But I worry about Celia. It's so hard to grow up even if everything is going okay. And it's hard to be a parent! It's so hard and you think you're going to lose your mind, surrounded by nothing but baby food and diapers, and then, well, it's over. And here we are, our children busy at school, not thinking about us at all."

Stella was right. At this moment Brodie and Dylan had better things on their minds than Felice, both of them busy with words or crayons or computers. And she wasn't always thinking about them, either. She didn't have to stay up until three, writing articles or finishing student papers or editing submissions to the journal. She wasn't worried about tenure or job security or committee responsibilities as she had been when they were little and James was away on business. She used to cry each morning when the alarm went off, knowing the same kind of day was starting all over again. In a way, all of them were starting over: Stella with her baby, Felice with the boys, Helen with whatever would happen with Darryl. And Grace? Well, Felice knew that, one day, someone would call her to tell her that Grace was dead, her life disappearing into the next.

"Forget all this!" Stella rubbed her arm and pulled her close. "I'm so excited for you to move in to your new house. I can't wait to see it with all your furniture in it. This is so great, Felice. Your own house."

She hugged Stella back, feeling the girth of her formerly thin friend, loving the wide curves of her belly. Stella was right. The house would belong to her. Not James. Whatever happened there would belong to her and the boys. Just them.

"Let's eat," Stella said, turning off the nursery light. "I'm starving. And I better eat while I can."

Before picking up the boys, Felice stopped at the club for a quick workout, knowing that what kept her going sometimes was the fast flow of blood in her veins. Before she even made it into the gym, she heard the wild whirring push of Grace on a machine, the gears working faster than they did for anyone else. As she approached her friend, Felice had to shake herself free of all Doris's words, because Grace's eating disorder was so apparent now. There was the story: the smudges under her eyes, the swollen jaw, the broken blood vessels in her eyes, the strange hair growing on her body, soft as down.

She moved slowly toward her friend, unsure how to talk to her so that she didn't run away or become angry and leave. How would she herself feel, Felice wondered, if they had come over to her house for some reason, heaving ideas and plans on her? Even if they were right, she knew she would feel upset. "Grace?" She stepped onto the machine next to her, putting a hand softly on her friend's shoulder.

"Hey, girl!" Grace stepped down and moved to hug Felice. Felice leaned over, pressing Grace against her body. There was nothing but bone left, she thought, feeling the starved landscape of ribs, shoulders, spine.

"I talked to your mother today. I didn't know you'd be here."

Grace climbed back up and resumed her hard strides. "It was your call that got me going. My mom told me how worried you were, and I thought, well, I've got to get out of bed. I've got to get better. If I'm in this protocol, then I have to survive. And I had to show you all that I am really trying. After what we went through."

Felice punched in her workout and began to move. "Yeah. We were just so worried, Grace. We don't want you to be unwell."

"My mom's met everyone. She told you that, right?"

"She did. She said they all love you."

Grace nodded. "They do. And you know what else? Karl told me this happens."

Felice looked at Grace, her tiny legs moving fast to nowhere. Felice looked around at the other people on machines and wondered what they were all doing here. What was the point of all this futile movement, all this energy expended? Why were they doing this? The room was full of doctors and lawyers and retired businesspeople, each machine occupied all day long, and Felice imagined what they could do in the real world with the sweat they left here. *We could cure cancer*, thought Felice, *or maybe even save Grace.*

"What happens? What do you mean?"

"The whole thing that you guys did. Friends and family stop believing. They do interventions on cancer patients." Grace huffed up an imaginary hill.

"There's a history of *this* happening? What we did happened to another patient?"

"Oh, yeah. Tons. It's really common. The patients start looking like they've got other problems, you know. Eating disorders. Anorexia or maybe drug use. AIDS. And with protocols being so secret, people stop believing. So they intervene."

"Really?" Felice said, half expecting Grace to hand her an article on the topic. But then she looked at Grace, could see her friend covered in a sheen of hope that her story would become true, that she was a cancer patient with overconcerned friends.

Felice closed her eyes, wondering what they would do next. Or maybe, she thought, it was time to let it all go, let Grace whir herself bone thin, let Doris and Grace end this together.

* * *

Packing up her briefcase with essays and outgoing mail, Felice glanced over her shoulder. Sean was deep in conversation with Susan, using the same lulling voice that didn't grate on Felice's ears anymore. In fact, she smiled, remembering how calm the world became when she was pregnant, everything reduced to the life within her, the beating of that tiny heart, the flow of blood around and in her abdomen, the baby's movements. Sean seemed wrapped in his own cocoon, and she almost lunged at her phone when it rang, trying to keep his world safe.

"This is Professor Gaitreaux."

"It's me," James said.

"What? Is it the boys?"

"No. Nothing I know."

"What do you want?" She sat down, her briefcase in her lap. She glanced back at Sean, who was still talking quietly.

"It's about Friday."

"Great. What do you want now? I have to take them? You know I'm starting the move. You know I have people coming over to help. Your *own* movers will be there, too. I was counting on you, James."

"Could you give me a chance? Christ. I wanted to see if you could drop them off. I won't have time to get them at school."

"Oh." Felice pressed her briefcase against her chest, as if trying to flatten the tears that came so easily when she talked with James. Right away, no matter what, she assumed he wanted something else from her. An hour. A weekend. More money from the house. A piece of furniture that was given to both of them. Half the china her mother and father gave them at their wedding. Pictures of the boys that she had in frames in her office. Twenty years. Twenty of her best years.

"Fine. I'll bring them by after school. Don't worry. I won't come up."

"Felice . . . so when does your house close?"

She wanted to hang up, not wanting to talk to him about anything that mattered to her, her life no longer any of his concern.

But how could she, when for so many years, every piece of paper had two names on each line, his social security number in her head as clearly as her own, all the crucial documents in their lives—birth certificates, mortgages, life insurance, divorce papers—shared. "Anytime," she said finally. "Now maybe."

"Do you like it?"

"Yeah."

Phone static erupted between them, and then he was gone, his cell connection disappearing somewhere in the Bay. She looked at her phone and then hung it up, not surprised when it rang again immediately.

"You need a new service," she said.

"No, I don't," Ricardo said. "We've closed. Come on over and sign."

"Enjoy," Ricardo said as he dropped the keys in her hand. "It's all yours."

She closed her palm around the keys and looked up at him, wondering again how anything could be just hers and not James's as well. "Okay," she said. "Thanks."

"I told you it would be a snap. You know what they call me— 'the Closer!' " He turned away from her and slipped into the next deal and the next.

Felice walked out on the Montclair Village sidewalk, the day crisp and clear after weeks of off-and-on rain, yellow leaves pasted against windshields, her breath almost visible. She looked at her watch and decided to pick up the boys, buy some Chinese takeout, and go to the new house to eat their first meal, even though it would be early and they'd probably get hungry again by nine. But she didn't care. As she walked to her car, she felt okay for the first time since August, her steps swinging, her jacket flying behind her like wings.

"Is it really ours?" Brodie asked. "I mean, we could sleep there if we wanted to?"

"Yes, we could," Felice answered. "But we'd be pretty uncomfortable."

"When do we *have* to sleep there?" Dylan sat hunched in the back seat.

"We're going to live there, Dylan," Brodie said. "Where else are we going to sleep?"

Felice pulled into the driveway and turned off the car. "We'll start moving on Friday. Sean and Helen and Darryl and Aaron are going to come over and help me on Saturday morning with the big stuff. I even rented a U-Haul."

"You can't drive a truck," Dylan said.

"I know. That's what will make it exciting."

Brodie opened his door, and then they all stepped out, Felice clutching her white bags full of sweet-and-sour pork and lemon chicken. "Let's go in," Brodie said, and he held out his hand for the key. She handed it over, almost seeing the man he would become, hoping he wouldn't try to become that man too soon, feeling responsible, needing to take over where his father left off.

"Has Dad seen the house?" Dylan asked as they walked in and put down their jackets in the foyer.

"No," she said. "I didn't . . . No."

"Why not?"

"Dylan!" Brodie said. "*He's* not going to live here. He lives with Amy. Stop being so stupid."

"Okay. That's enough. Let's eat, all right? It's hot. The restaurant gave me extra napkins and forks and spoons. Let's just sit on the kitchen floor and gobble it all up."

She smiled at Dylan, and he shrugged but followed his brother through the empty house.

After dinner, the boys went outside in the darkening light, exclaiming over found treasures: an old picnic bench, a nozzle, a flip-flop, a butter knife. Felice pushed all the garbage back into the plastic bags from the restaurant and washed her hands in the empty sink. She turned around and looked at the kitchen, one that reminded her of the kitchen of the house she grew up in in Orinda, just over the hill. She remembered watching her mother in the kitchen as they all waited for her father, Lawrence, to come home from the insurance agency, the sharp light from the bulb over the sink, her mother's *clack-clack* walk on the tile floor, her voice as she called Felice and her brother, Gage, to the table for macaroni and cheese or hamburger patties and iceberg lettuce salad or Hungarian goulash made with canned tomatoes. After dinner, her father would be resting in the family room as he did each night, and Felice would go sit by him at the end of the couch and stare at his feet, his toes visible through the worn-out wool. Making sure neither her mother nor Gage were watching, she would lean forward and put her nose as close as she dared to his feet, breathing in the sticky sweat of his day, his fatigue, the old leather of his shoes. Sometimes, she ran a finger gently over the shiny fabric of his thin sock, terrified that he would wake and see how close she was to him.

Even as she was bent over him, seeing the fat pads of his toes, Felice wondered if it was really possible she was this close, had access to this private part of him he would never show her if he were awake.

"Mom?" Dylan said suddenly, standing on the stoop outside the kitchen door that led to the patio below.

She turned to him, wiping her hands on her pants. "What, sweetie? What did you find?"

"Mom." Dylan held a dirty spoon in his hand. "I'm still hungry."

"You just had a Chinese feast, Dyl," she said, putting a hand on her hip. "Can you hold on?"

"I'm hungry," he said, starting to whine.

She walked over to the door and bent down to her younger son, reaching out for his shoulders. At her touch, he began to cry, tears falling down his face and onto his dirty shirt. "I want Daddy." He wiped his face. "I want to go home."

Felice tried to swallow, anger and hurt and despair thick in her throat. She pulled Dylan to her and looked around the empty kitchen, the house a box, echoing with nothing, no evidence of the life they'd all had together. "I know. I want to go home, too, you know. But this is our home now, Dylan. This is where we are going to live."

"But it's not ours," he said, shaking. "It's not where we live."

She closed her eyes, wondering how children were always so right. No, this house wasn't where they lived . . . not yet. It was a place where they had landed abruptly. How could she tell Dylan that, in weeks or months, he would look around this kitchen, his room, and realize they were his. That eventually he would see this house was where he belonged. Maybe only time would help him and her, too, Felice realized, knowing that in the last few days she'd been desperate to get the keys to the house, start putting her life in order, making sure she had a place to come home to.

She clutched Dylan more tightly, feeling the dirt of school play and the new backyard on his shirt, breathing in his clean, still-baby skin, touching her lips to his neck. She hoped that he could one day see that she had chosen this house on purpose, for them, that she actually wanted the life she fiercely hoped they would one day have. It just had to be possible.

"Mom?" He sniffed into her ear.

Felice kissed him again and pulled back, holding his face in her hands. "You're right, Dylan. It's not our home yet. But it will be. I promise."

He pushed his face back against her neck, and here she was, with her boy, his hair in her mouth, his tears on her face, and she knew she'd gotten closer to him and Brodie than she'd ever gotten to her father or to James or anyone, ever. Maybe this was the reason she'd found herself with both James and Grace in her life at the same time. Maybe after having to let go of her old life, watching Grace let go of hers, Felice saw how important these boys were to her. It was here, in this house, that she would learn the rhythm of family she'd never known how to listen to.

By the time they were in the car on their way to the Montclair house, Dylan was talking about the fort he would make in the dense growth of ivy and thumbergia by the back fence. "It'll be like the Batcave," he said.

She looked in her rearview mirror and saw Brodie nodding. "Yeah. And we can put our bikes in there." Felice felt something solid and warm sink to her stomach, and she smiled, ducking her head, hoping Dylan and Brodie hadn't seen her spying.

Later that night, when the boys were reading in bed and she was opening and closing kitchen cupboards, imagining what she would pack first, Helen called. "We've got to meet. Thursday for lunch. Drew and Stella, too. I have an idea."

"I thought of doing something," Drew said, dipping a piece of French bread into olive oil. "I mean, I haven't been able to put it behind me. I keep thinking about how Grace was in college. How she could make these tremendous shots, the basketball just hanging there and then going in. I can still see her face, how she could concentrate, how proud. This whole thing has made me crazy." They were at Ghirabaldi's on College Avenue at a back table, rushing in from classes and work and the hospital.

"Me, too," Stella said, her stomach large and looming next to the table. "I can't sleep for thinking about it. I've been so tired Aaron's either calling me Sleeping Beauty or wondering if I have narco . . . narco . . ."

"Narcolepsy," Helen said. "Well, you're sleeping for two, that's all."

Felice put her hand on Stella's belly. "You don't need to do anything, but you needed to be here when we talked about it. I just can't put Celia out of my mind."

Drew nodded. "We just didn't finish."

"That's right," Helen said. "And we have to finish. We just have to find out the damn truth once and for all."

"Don't we know the truth?" Felice asked, thinking about Grace on the StairMaster, her almost invisible legs, her swollen jaw, her bloodshot eyes, her hair thin and brittle and dry. "It's so obvious. I just saw her, and the anorexia is so clear. At least now. I can't believe I fell for the story the whole time. I didn't even question her. I feel like an idiot."

Helen put her hand on the table, spreading her fingers. "Then we're all idiots. All of her friends, all her family. Kathleen. Doris. And no one, not her family, not her partner, tried to get Celia out of that house. It's up to us."

They were all silent as the waitress placed their meals before them, chicken in warm sauce, salad with walnuts, potatoes crackling with garlic.

"I've been living on restaurant food." Felice lifted her fork, wondering what to spear first.

"It's part of the moving diet," Helen said. "I didn't cook for two weeks when we first moved into our house."

Stella took a bite of chicken and then shook her head. "We can't do anything for the sole reason of finding out the truth. We have to do it for Celia, and for Grace."

Helen dropped her knife. "You're right. Part of this for me is about knowing the truth. It's like a puzzle where you lose the last few pieces. It sits on the table, and you keep imagining it whole, but it never is."

"So what are we going to do?" Felice asked, wondering for a second how Helen could be so in command here, but at home, her husband was surrounded by her confusion.

"Okay, so here's the plan." Helen tapped her fingers on the table. "We're going to follow her. We're going to find out what she does at night. We're going to video her whole trip, and we're going to call the authorities if something weird is going on. Which it is, I can tell you already."

Stella's hand was still on her belly. "But how will this help Celia? She'll go nuts. She doesn't do anything without Grace's approval. She'll be traumatized!"

Helen looked up from her plate. "But isn't she being traumatized now? Look what she's living through. How can that be good for her? I know it will hurt her, but we've got to do it."

Felice saw Stella's eyes were suddenly full of tears, and she remembered her own pregnancies, the weepy weeks before the birth, the weepy weeks afterward. She watched Stella sip her water, breathing in deeply after each swallow, struggling with the ugly ideas of both a neglected child and a betrayed Grace. Under the table, she patted Stella's knee, and Stella struggled into a smile.

"Should we tell Doris? Before we do it?" Helen asked. "Or before we call the authorities?"

"What authorities?" Stella said. "Not the police?"

"No. Child Protective Services. CPS," Felice said. She looked at Helen, who raised her eyebrows and shook her head slightly. "I don't think we should talk to Doris about this. We've already tried to help the reasonable way. We've tried to talk with her. And we heard nothing from any other family member. No one but us wants to help. No one else seems to care now. And Helen, your friend Jean always said Celia should be out of that house. There really isn't any other solution."

Stella sighed. "I guess you're right. It's awful, though. It's . . ."

"It's crazy, is what it is," Drew said.

"We have to do it," Felice said. She looked around the table at these women, again feeling how lucky Grace was, even if she didn't know it. She looked at her food and knew she'd wish for their help if anything should happen to her. "So when shall we do this?"

On Friday afternoon, Felice went to pick up the boys at school and then drop them off at James's apartment, waiting by the glass door for the buzzer to ring so she could let Brodie and Dylan slip by and run into the elevator that would bring them to their father. But when the door clicked open with the sound, Felice suddenly found herself in the lobby with them.

"What are you doing, Mom?" Brodie looked at her, his eyes wide and round. "Are you going up? Why?"

"I don't know." She shrugged and smiled despite the twirls of nerves in her belly. She had no idea what she was doing, but she had the notion she couldn't stand alone at the other side of the door her entire life, letting the past simmer like a bad soup on a back burner, something so easy to walk away from.

"I can show you my room!" Dylan said. "You've never even seen it!"

"Our room." Brodie punched the elevator buttons. "It's *our* room."

"I have my own Lego town," Dylan said, grabbing Felice's hand. "But it's not as big as our other one."

She smiled again and then swallowed down the air that threatened to leave her body altogether. Even though she'd had to break into James's office to discover he'd "misplaced" funds and lied, after the first few weeks the separation and then divorce became part of her routine. She would expect James's calls, brusque, "Be here at six," or "Where is Dylan's baseball glove?" or "We need to meet at my lawyer's office." The money was "refound," a symptom, James's lawyer said, "of a marriage gone sadly awry." They'd sold the house, splitting the proceeds just as they should have, worked through dividing their possessions without too many arguments, and the boys were adapting. In a way, the divorce was almost the same as the last couple years of their marriage had been, orderly but punctuated with moments of anger and rudeness. One day as she was driving to work, Felice realized she didn't actually miss James. What she did miss was love, and that she'd lost a long time ago.

James opened the door as the elevator opened, his eyes fixed on the level of the boys' heads. Then he saw Felice, and his mouth went slack with surprise.

"Oh," he said, stepping back.

She nodded and stared at this man she'd lived with for almost half her life, the boy she first met in college. Felice breathed out and knew whatever she saw in him at Stanford was still there in her heart, but it was contained and safe and didn't need one more thought.

"Come on, Mom. Come see my room!" Dylan said, and both the boys ran off the elevator and into the open apartment door.

"Hi, James," she said, stepping out, the doors closing behind her.

James moved back another step. "Why are you up here? What do you want?"

She was about to say something snide or cynical, answering maybe, "Everything," or "What do you have?" But she didn't, looking down at the carpet, a rich burgundy plush under her shoes. "I just wanted to . . . to see the boys' room."

"Oh. I don't know."

"Is Amy here?"

"No. She's still at work. I come home early on these Fridays, you know, for the boys."

Felice felt an evil smirk under her tongue, pressing to her lips. When was the last time he'd even tried to come home early before he left? Not for birthdays or holidays or special evenings out. All she'd had of him were late-night arrivals and his back as they slept. Had the divorce changed him? Had Amy? Felice felt old tears pulse in her throat, thinking that maybe, all along, this marriage was never supposed to have existed. That it was wrong from the very beginning, that she'd wasted the best years she had on this planet. Felice wanted to say something, something permanent and strong, but as she looked at him, she saw he was tired, lines under his eyes, his shirt untucked and wrinkled. A burned smell—something like frozen pizzas on an aluminum pan in a too-hot oven—slipped through the open door. Even though he had Amy and his apartment with a stunning view and was finally rid of her, Felice saw that his life wasn't perfect either. Despite all his careful, secretive planning, life hadn't turned out exactly as he'd wanted it to.

"So what's the problem?" she asked, her hand on her hip.

James cocked his head slightly to the side. "Nothing now," he said. "Really, nothing at all."

"Mom!" Dylan poked his head out from behind the apartment door. "My room!"

"Our room," Brodie said from inside the apartment. "Don't say it again!"

James smiled slightly, his body softening, moving back, letting her pass, and Felice knew that nothing had been wasted. There had been some good times, long over, and there were the boys, who had come from them both, no matter how they felt about each other now. They'd been lovers and partners and enemies, but they were still parents. No matter what.

"Come in," James said. "Come see *their* room."

After she left James's apartment, Felice drove to Diesel Books on College Avenue and slid into the big soft chair at the back of the store to finish reading the *Beowulf* translation she'd been picking up and putting down for months. As she opened the story, she felt a wave of relief sweep over her. She was hungry, but more than anything she was so tired, too tired to think about Grace or James or the boys or the new house and the move, and for the first time since the divorce, she was glad Brodie and Dylan were at James's. She couldn't even begin to think about the crazy scheme she and her friends were planning for tomorrow night. Right now, she needed this late afternoon, this chair, and this book. As she read, Felice let herself slip into another time so fully that when someone touched her shoulder and said, "Hi, Felice," she nearly bolted through the window before her.

"Oh. Tony," she said, breathing in, laying the book against her chest. "It's you."

"Who were you expecting? Grendel? You can't be that deep into the book," Tony said, smiling. He was still tan, his hair blond, glistening, and slightly green from the early-morning workouts he did with a USS team, a *master* swimmer even though he was only twenty-four.

"No. But I've read it before, you know," she said, laughing. "It's still the same old story."

"Sometimes the same old story is the best kind," he said, sitting on a bench beside her.

She smiled. "I always like knowing the ending. It's comforting. Don't tell anyone this, but I always read the last page of a book before I get to the end. Maybe not right away, but sometime before I actually get there."

"That's awful! That's cheating." Tony crossed his legs. "But how can Beowulf dying be comforting?"

"At least I know what's there. That's why I like teaching these books over and over again."

"I think I somehow got out of having to write about *Beowulf*. I don't know how I managed that."

"You sound like all my undergraduates. They try to wait until Chaucer before writing an essay. They love that Wife of Bath."

"I was in your class once. For about a week." Tony leaned closer to her. "You don't remember this face?" he said. "I was that completely brilliant student who sat in the back to the left."

Felice laughed and shook her head. "I thought you went to Stanford."

"It was a summer session. I was staying with my dad here in Rockridge. The class was an introduction to medieval literature."

She remembered that summer two years ago, the fights with James, the widening slit of separation in their bed at night, the large, almost wild class in the summer, her TA with a piercing on every facial orifice. "So what happened? Did I bore you to death?"

Tony sighed. "No. I just had to work more. I started coaching the USS team—the little kids—that summer. So there went my morning classes. But I liked it. You were funny."

"I was?"

"Yeah."

"I wish all of them thought that way." She realized she'd never really seen him as just a guy before, seeing him only as the young man who coached Brodie and Dylan. And then she thought of Helen and her young lover, and a strange thrum pulsed across her chest.

"Are you hungry?" she asked suddenly, standing up, tucking

Beowulf under her arm. "I really feel like something right now. Maybe a pastrami sandwich."

"Pastrami! You mean you aren't a vegetarian like everyone else around here these days?"

"Not me. I pretend in some circles, but I'm a carnivore through and through."

"Like Grendel," he said, nodding. "Now I know why you like that book so much."

"That's right."

"Well, okay," Tony said, standing up beside her. "All right."

FOURTEEN

ᕬ

Friday, on her way to pick up Eric from school, her belly close to the steering wheel, Stella thought about what Felice and Helen were planning. She knew she should help them, but the memory of Doris's face, the thought of seeing Grace down flat on her bed, the pressure from this new child in her womb made it easy for her to say no.

As she waited at a stoplight, the baby kicked her side, and Stella smiled, saying, "Holy cow. Already a princess and you're not even born yet." She placed a hand on her side, thinking of the baby's room, the lush pinkness, the quilts, the little dresses, the black patent leather shoes with bows her mother bought at Nordstrom. "They were on sale," Joyce had said sheepishly. "But she'll be able to wear them in a year or two."

Stella had held the shoes in her palm, the light glinting off the toes, and wondered if her girl would be the type to wear these shoes. *What if her body is like mine when I was a girl?* Stella thought. *What if she's round and tubby and feels ugly all the time? What will these shoes say to her then? That she's not right? Not girlie enough? Would she put them on and feel like she didn't deserve them?* Stella wondered if her own body, her slimmer adult body, and the amount of time she spent on her hair and her clothes would send the wrong message to her daughter, a child born in the new millennium, after the women's movement. This child could have anything despite thick thighs or a round stomach, couldn't she? *All this girl needs,* thought Stella, blood flushing her face, *is me. And love. And Aaron and Eric. Us.*

Stella accelerated at the green light and headed down toward Broadway and Eric's school. If only labor and delivery weren't so awful. She remembered a point with Eric when she believed she could just get up off the hospital bed and go home, imagining she could leave the pain behind entirely, as if it were something simply in the room and not a force in her body. And then there was the delivery, so much blood and worry and sadness. For years afterward, Stella imagined she would never forget it, but it all began to lessen as Eric grew. "That's why people go on to have a second," her mother said. "And a third. It's adaptive. Otherwise, no one would ever have more than one. We'd be crazy to." Only Stella wasn't supposed to be able to have a second. She figured no one would ever forget a labor and delivery so difficult, so God just said, "No more for her."

Stella rolled down the window and wondered what her friends would discover about Grace and if they could help Celia. Stella remembered Celia's impassive face that day in the locker room, even then hardened against her mother's illness. "Think of what she'll have to tell a therapist," Helen had said yesterday at the restaurant.

Everyone had laughed, but Stella knew it was true, childhood, even in the best of circumstances, lurking behind everyone like a shadow. If Grace was lying, Celia had endured nothing short of torture, watching her mother shrink and wither and dry up, Grace lying flat and stiff in that bed like a stale gingerbread cookie. Stella remembered the first time, years ago, that she saw Grace. As always, she had been in her chaise longue by the side of the pool, but soon was paged to the front desk for a phone call. Grace pulled herself up, muscles in her thighs flexing, her arms slim but firm and strong, her walk like an athlete, sure and steady. Stella had followed her with her eyes, wondering how she could feel as good as that walk looked. Now, so many years later, Grace was only and simply her childhood shadow, something so brief and flickering, Stella didn't know if anyone could see the real Grace at all.

* * *

When they arrived home, Stella discovered Eric had hours of homework before him, as if his teacher Mrs. Randolph had suddenly realized that Christmas vacation was less than a month away. He pulled pages of grammar and spelling, a sheet of multiplication, and the detailed plans for a California mission he needed to finish before next week out of his backpack when they came home, looking at her and rolling her eyes. "I'll be doing this until I die," he said. Stella shook her head and laughed, fixed him a tuna sandwich, and then let him watch a half hour of cartoons. Sometimes she wondered how everything ever got done. As she stood at the kitchen counter, she imagined trying to carry towels and swimsuits, diaper bag, and baby carrier out the door while setting the burglar alarm. Stella laughed, thinking she just wouldn't go anywhere at all.

"What?" Eric asked.

"Huh?"

"You laughed? What's so funny?" He put his plate on the counter.

She rubbed his head and he leaned into her, sliding his hand just under her belly button. "I was trying to picture getting out the door with you and the new baby."

"I can't believe you can get out of the door now!" he said, rubbing a widening circle on her belly.

"Gee, thanks, you little rat. You aren't supposed to ever comment on a woman's weight. Or looks. Or clothes, for that matter. Don't you forget that. Now get to your homework," she said, pushing him gently off her.

"Okay, fine." He walked toward his room. "Mom, I was only kidding, you know."

"I know," she said, but she knew he would avoid so much trouble later with girlfriends and then wife if he could just remember what she said.

Stella bent down to pull a head of broccoli out of the vegetable drawer, her stomach fitting like a small basketball between her chest and thighs. Stella stood up and patted herself. At one point, she'd thought to name the baby Grace, hoping that her child would have the strength of her friend. She had always admired Grace's nerve, even before the new cancer, when all Stella saw was a survivor; a woman who raised her child alone for a while; a woman who loved another woman when the world made it so hard to do so; a woman who could laugh at it all. Grace had lived through God knew what as a child and in her first marriage, but now Stella could only see weakness and suffering, tragedy and lies. That was nothing to name a child after.

She thought about her mother and remembered Joyce bending over Stella's bed, tending to her when she had a fever, handing her baby aspirin, holding a bucket as she threw up. It seemed to her that it had always been this way, her mother leaning over her, smiling, her mother helping her, her mother wanting to know what she could do. Even now, when she was frightened or happy or nervous, she called for Joyce, sometimes even before Aaron.

She knew that if she couldn't give her baby the exact ingredients Joyce had given her, she could still give her this, this warm mother flesh. It would be different because Stella was different now and knew, especially after Grace, many things simply didn't matter. It didn't matter that hair turned gray or bodies changed. It wasn't the vanity table and perfumes and cold creams that brought Joyce and her together. Instead, it was the closeness of their two bodies, of looking, at least for a moment, at each other.

I'm going to name her Joyce, she thought, knowing that she could give this baby nothing better than her mother's spirit. It was the gift mothers could hand their daughters, and then that the daughters could pass to their own. Stella put the broccoli on the cutting board and thought about Doris and Grace and Celia. Something had happened so long ago in Doris's house, with her husband, and her children, and now it was showing up on Celia's face just like something inherited through blood and bone.

As Stella cut the broccoli into florets, she knew she couldn't do what her friends wanted her to, skulk around looking for clues, but she couldn't just do nothing. It had gone too far. Stella put down her knife and called to Eric. "Pack up your homework, honey. I'm taking you to Grandma's."

"Did Grace call you?" Doris said at the door.

"No," Stella said. "I just thought I'd drop by. To see how she is."

Doris didn't budge, holding the door firm. "I haven't seen much of you all since that . . . that day. Grace thinks you've all forgotten her."

"I've left about ten messages. I kept calling and no one called me back."

Doris stood silent, a different woman from the one who'd sat with them around the table at the Chinese restaurant, begging for help and advice. It was as if another, harder mother skin had been slipped over her, one that wouldn't let in one single thing. Not help. Not kindness. Not this visit.

"Can I come in, Doris? I just want to talk to her for a while. I can't stay long. Eric's at my mom's."

Doris slowly pulled open the door, and Stella walked in, seeing that Grace's house had never looked so clean or organized. Before, Grace and Kathleen both busy, there had always been clothes everywhere in clean and dirty piles, books and papers, and an inch of dog hair on the floor. Doris had changed all that, the floors gleaming, the windows washed, the smell of something cooking on the stove.

"I guess you've figured out that stove," Stella said. "I tried to help Grace bake a cake here once and it was a disaster."

Doris finally smiled. "It hasn't been easy. I had to call a repairman. And once it was fixed, I realized they didn't even own pans. I had to go out and buy a whole set."

Stella took off her coat. "How is she?"

Doris turned toward the kitchen. "About the same. Her doctors have her on the same medication. I . . . I don't think it's working too well."

"Why?"

"It's not as aggressive as it should be. She's not feeling any better, up and around, eating a bit more. I just don't know what to do. She's getting skinnier and weaker. I don't know how she even manages to get up from bed to go to the bathroom."

"But, Doris, why don't you have hospice in here, then? If she's that bad, you need someone taking care of her all day long. I know her doctors would want her to have all the help she needs." The words she didn't even believe felt like snakes on her tongue, but she knew she had to say them, or she wouldn't get past this room.

Doris waved Stella's question away from her face. "But the next thing I know, she's out running. So sometimes the medicine seems to be working."

"Oh." She moved slowly toward Grace's bedroom door. "I'm going to go in, okay?"

Doris shrugged and went into the kitchen. She breathed and pushed open Grace's door. "Grace? Hon? It's me. Stella."

She moved into the room, and there Grace was, asleep, so tiny she looked like a girl younger than Celia, but tall, her bones long even under the blankets, her skin that same strange orangey tan, her hair a red straw halo around her head. "Hey, girl," Grace mumbled. "I had a dream about you last night. I'd knew you'd come. I knew you of all people hadn't forgotten about me."

"How could anyone forget you, Grace?" She walked toward the bed and sat down, noticing the vial of clear medicine and the same big syringe on a towel at the side of the bed.

Grace laughed softly and pulled herself up against the pillows. "How are you feeling? How's the baby?"

Stella looked down at her stomach that rested roundly on the tops of her thighs. "She's really starting to swim around. Maybe it's all the time she's already spent around a pool."

"Tony will probably want her on the team when she's a year old. I can see it now, his pet project," Grace said.

Then they fell silent. Outside, the dog whined against the glass, hitting the door with his wet nose.

"Grace." Grace closed her eyes, but Stella kept talking. "I just have to tell you how worried I am. I really think there should be people, nurses, taking care of you if you can't get out of bed. Maybe it's time to call in hospice."

"I'll be okay. I just need my rest," Grace answered. "It's not like I don't get up, you know. Felice saw me at the club a while back. She told you, didn't she?"

"She did. But what about now? Are you eating enough? Oh, hon, you seem to have lost so much weight."

"My mom has been making me lots of steamed rice. I've been eating that and . . . other things . . ." Grace rattled off a list of awful food, cold and canned and poison.

Stella grabbed Grace's hand. "That's not enough if you are fighting cancer. It's not enough if you want to beat it."

"If?"

"Whatever you are fighting. If you want to see Celia grow up. You've got to take care of yourself in other ways," Stella said, her heart pounding in her throat. "You can't let her see you like this week after week and not try harder to live. You owe it to her, if no one else. Even more than you owe it to yourself."

Grace was quiet, avoiding her gaze. She pulled her hand away from Stella's. "No one gave me anything, ever, and I did okay."

"Did you? Really? Wouldn't you want it to be easier for Celia? Really! Listen to me!"

"She's fine. Celia's okay."

"She's not okay, Grace. She can see what's going on. How this has gotten so . . . so out of control. If you really had cancer, there'd be hospice nurses here right now. You'd have an IV. You'd be admitted into Stanford at this very minute. Don't you see that we don't believe you anymore? Who is this cancer for, anyway?" Stella felt faint, her voice high and whiny.

But what she said didn't matter. Grace just slowly slipped

down into the bed. "I'm tired now. I need my rest. Karl says I need my rest."

Stella put her hand on Grace's bony knee. "If you don't help her, someone else may try to. Someone else may think Celia needs better care. Someone may want to take her out of here."

Just then Doris opened the door and stared at Stella. "I'm taking care of Celia, you know. She's getting three squares and arriving at school on time. We do homework at night. And she's with her mother. We don't need any help. And no one else needs to come in telling us what to do."

Stella stood up, facing the same monster mother Felice and Helen had talked about. "But who's taking care of Grace? If she were my daughter, she'd be in the hospital right now getting the right medicine. She wouldn't be here with a used hypodermic needle on an old towel."

"How dare you! How dare you just drop by and tell me I'm not taking care of my own daughter! What do you know about it anyway?"

"You asked *us* for help at first. Try to remember that. But now you won't take what we have to give."

"We don't need it. We're fine the way we are."

Stella looked back at Grace, wondering what her face would say after listening to these words, but Grace was asleep, her thin white lids pulled over her eyes. With a jab of pain, Stella imagined that's what her friend would look like in a casket. "You aren't, Doris. No one's fine here. If you were, you would have never stopped the intervention. You wouldn't keep her here. You wouldn't let Celia see her mother like this. You're letting her die! You're letting her die right now!"

The baby kicked as she spat out words, stood up, and pushed past Doris. In that second Stella was scared that she'd put herself and the baby in danger, saying things she probably shouldn't have to a sick, dying woman and her terrified mother. She imagined that Doris might come after her, lunge at her with a heavy object to keep her from telling anyone else about Grace. But Doris didn't rush after her, and as she walked out the front door and down the steps, she finally knew what Felice had been talking about: the fierce fire of love for a child turned bad, the monster that would hold a dead child over dangerous waters. Doris was finally fighting for Grace, now that it was too late, now that Grace could never be saved.

FIFTEEN

ᴄᴈ

HELEN SAT BEHIND THE WHEEL OF DARRYL'S COMPANY CAR, the large, billowy Ford Taurus that Livie called the Tuna Boat, parked in a dark corner of Grace's street, her teeth chattering, her fingers frozen on the steering wheel, her foot poised above the accelerator. She, like Drew and Felice, was dressed in dark clothes, a sweatshirt hood over her hair, her face all but obscured.

"Relax," Felice whispered, putting a hand on her shoulder. "It's not like Grace has even left the house yet."

Helen uncurled her fingers. She leaned back in her seat. "God. I'm just so nervous. I feel like we are the ones running away from something. I feel like something really bad is going to happen tonight."

Felice laughed quietly. "Of course you're nervous. I'm scared to death. How many times do you think any of us have done this?"

"I feel like I'm in some terrible television show. This is probably the stupidest thing any of us has ever done," Drew said.

"I wouldn't count on that," Helen said. "I think I could match this."

"Well," said Felice after a pause, "no one has ever done this particular stupid thing."

"Well, this is what a private investigator would do," Helen said. "It's not as if people don't do stuff like this."

But Helen knew that before tonight none of them had tailed anyone, much less at night, in a car, to who knew where. She felt the adrenaline pull surge in her stomach even more intensely than when she knocked on Pablo's door or when the phone rang in her house when Darryl was home. How could her life had gotten to this point, she wondered, where everything was filled with guilt, dread, and electricity, her head an expanding instrument, thrumming away to everything? How could it have been Pablo's words and not anyone else's in this car or at home, that inspired her to form tonight's plan, this attempt to save Grace and Celia?

"I can't help but think Grace would have wanted to be in on this," Felice said. "She was always the instigator."

"You're right," Helen agreed. "She's the one who always arranged all the surprise birthday parties. Remember how she had to call Stella and force her to come up to the club after we kept postponing her party? The poor thing had a bad cold. What did Grace tell her? That Tony had to talk to her about Eric? Stella was almost in tears until we started singing 'Happy Birthday.' "

Felice sighed. "She's good at sneaking. Look at what she's been able to carry off so far."

The women were silent, and Helen knew Felice was right. It was as if all the things they loved about Grace, her surprises, her jokes, her smarts, were colluding and bringing forth this sickness, this masquerade, this deception that went far beyond parties. It reminded her of what Babe used to say when Jackson punished her as a child: "Your father doesn't like how stubborn you are now, Helen. But what makes this annoying now will make you a strong adult. Don't forget that." But everything was inverted here: Grace alone and dying and crazy, Celia stuck in the house or left alone for stretches at night when Doris wasn't there and anything could happen. It was Oakland, still, even here in the hills. There was fire or robbery or worse, any day of the week, anywhere in the city, and Grace didn't seem to care anymore at all.

"You know," Felice said, "I was searching a database, and I came upon this article on Munchausen's syndrome. I kind of wonder if Grace has that."

"Isn't that the thing where mothers make their own kids sick?

Injecting stuff into them? I saw something like that on *Sixty Minutes*," Drew said, rubbing her hands together. "God, it's cold."

"I can't turn the heater on without turning on the car." Helen breathed into her cupped palms, feeling her breath warm on her fingers. "But that's not what Grace has. She's not hurting Celia . . . well, in that way."

"No," Felice said. "That's the by-proxy kind. This is where you make yourself sick for attention or whatever. Some people actually have operation after operation."

They were all silent for a second. Eucalyptus leaves fluttered outside the car like night moths. "Well, look at all the attention she has gotten," Drew said finally. "Look how she's made Kathleen take care of her. Look at Doris. Look at what we're doing right now."

"There she is," Felice hissed. "Look, coming out of the house."

They ducked and peeked up just over the seats and dashboard, all watching as Grace's flickering black form skirted the side of the house and wisped down the back steps. They heard the Land Rover car door close, and then the car backed silently down the driveway, the motor off, leaves and branches crackling under the tires. When she was on the street, Grace started the Rover and began driving, waiting until she passed her house to turn on her lights.

"Go," Drew whispered. "But don't turn on the lights yet."

Helen's stomach lurched as she started the car, almost forgetting where to place her feet, gulping down air as if it were guilt. "Don't worry," Felice said as Helen pulled onto the street. "It'll all work out."

"I hope Doris is there," Helen said, thinking of Celia asleep, a nightlight on, her pillow squeezed in her arms. Maybe, she thought, one of them should stay with her.

"She is. Stella told me," Felice said.

"How does she know?" Helen asked, the car creeping forward.

"Don't ask. I'll tell you later."

Helen nodded, following the red flashes from Grace's brake lights, leaning forward as she drove, like some little old lady, she thought. "Turn there," Felice said, still whispering. "See?"

Helen turned right onto MacArthur, then followed the arch of the 580 entrance, pulling behind Grace in the fast lane, the freeway empty. "Stay back a little," Drew said. "There's no one else out here."

"Except snipers," Helen said.

"That's great," Drew said. "I can see the headlines now: 'Women on mission of mercy killed by freeway snipers.'"

Helen laughed, then pulled into the right lane and then the next as Grace moved over. "What exit is she going to take?" Helen asked.

"She might not even be going to Oakland at all," Felice said. "Who knows where we'll end up."

"We'll end up at a hospital where we'll find out this is all true. We'll charge in and she'll be lying on a table, an IV in her arm," Drew said flatly. "And then we'll feel like the biggest assholes."

Helen shook her head, pulling over into the farthest right lane as Grace did. Already, they weren't heading toward Stanford or even Kaiser, the two places Grace mentioned throughout her illness. *West Oakland*, thought Helen, *Richmond, San Pablo*. Places where people could be anything at all, take anything they wanted, no one asking for one damn piece of information. Just the opposite of Helen's life, in which everything seemed accounted for, everything but her happiness. These past months she'd found it with Pablo, but she knew it wasn't real. In fact, everything about their relationship reminded her of glass—strong but transparent and potentially dangerous, ready to crack with one hard blow. But how beautiful her reflection was in the glass, how mysterious, how wicked, everything she wished she could see when she looked at Darryl and saw reflected who she really was—a mother, a homemaker, a no one.

"Look! There she goes," Drew cried. "San Pablo exit. San Pablo exit."

Helen pulled off, staying just far enough behind Grace. Grace whipped around a corner onto Thirty-second Avenue and headed down the street. On the sidewalks, women and men grouped and strolled, one woman pulling up her skirt as they passed by. "Jeez," Felice said. "How sad."

"At least she's working," said Helen.

"Oh, come on!" said Felice. "You don't mean that."

Helen was about to say, "Maybe I do," but before she could, Grace made another right, and Helen turned and suddenly shut off her lights as Grace pulled to the curb. Helen yanked the car to the curb as well, and all of them ducked down again, watching Grace move toward the door of a small house and ring the bell.

"Where is she going?" Drew whispered. "Who could she possibly know down here?"

Helen shook her head in the darkness. "I don't have a clue. But this isn't a hospital or a doctor's office or even a friend's house. She's been lying—that's for sure."

"What are we going to do now?" Felice asked. "This is a dangerous place."

Outside, there were a few pedestrians, men and women walking the sidewalks, some heading to the same door Grace disappeared behind. The door would open, a slim flash of light, and then close. Helen felt her body moving to a certainty she knew her mind wouldn't agree to; something older than thought or fear or friendship was pulling her out of the car, toward Grace, toward a woman she'd loved for years who needed her, who needed to live if only for her daughter. Her friend was hurt, hurting, scared, and Helen's hands moved to her seat belt, her purse, Darryl's digital video camera. "Drug house," Helen said. "No question. I'm going to video this whole thing."

"Don't do that!" Drew looked out of the window. "It's too . . . scary."

"How else are we going to prove this? We can't call CPS and say we followed her to a house and then left. We have to show where we are and what type of place this is."

"Let's just call the police," Felice said. "They can do that."

"What will we say? 'Help! Our friend is inside that house?' "
Helen asked.

"I don't know," Felice said. "I don't even like being parked
here."

"You'll be fine. Just let me catch some footage and then we'll
go. We have to have proof. That's what we asked Grace for and
she couldn't produce it. Why do you think anyone would believe
us without it?"

"You're right," Drew said. "And Grace is so smart, she could
convince anyone we were lying, crazy friends."

Helen put the video camera around her neck and punched the
overhead light so it wouldn't go on when she opened the door.
"I'll just be a few minutes. I promise."

"Be careful!" Felice said, clutching the dash in front of her.
"Don't let anything happen."

"Too late for that." Helen opened the door and stepped out
onto the pavement. The air was soft with fog and full of freeway
noises, 580, 880, and 24 all converging just to the east. The sidewalk was empty for the time being, and she walked quickly
toward the house Grace had slipped into. The house was small
and white and the paint was peeling, but there was a garden behind the chain-link fence and a cat sitting on the porch. She
turned on the camera and put her eye to the viewer, the hum of
the camera obscene in the silence. For the first time since leaving
the car, Helen felt her heart skip beats, lurching and pulsing
under her jacket. If anyone was paying attention, she didn't have
much time.

She kept the camera to her eye and moved carefully to the side
of the house, closer to an unshuttered window. The window af-
forded only a view of an entry hall, but she could see shadows and
hear voices. If only someone would come and do something, offer
money, hand a bag, shoot . . . what? Heroin? A gun? Their
mouths off? Helen was thinking she needed some clue as to what
Grace needed in this house when she felt a hand on her shoulder.

"Who are you?" asked a man from behind her.

She pulled the camera away from her face, tucked it under her coat, and felt immediate tears in her eyes. Her stomach clamped down on itself as she turned. "I'm . . . uh . . . I'm . . . ?"

The man pulled her shoulder again, spinning her to face him. He was the same height as Helen, dark, and wearing a baseball cap, a jacket covering his large stomach. "What do you want?" he asked, still gripping her shoulder.

As she stood facing him, her lungs empty, her body suddenly light and worthless, she wondered why she was here. Why had she gotten out of the car? Why had she risked everything for Grace when what was really important was at home, asleep, in bed? Livie. And Darryl. Why had she not talked to him before it was too late? She'd done nothing and now this man had her, and he could do anything he wanted.

"I'm looking for a friend," she said softly. "I'm trying to find a friend."

The man let go of her arm and looked at her. "What's under your jacket?"

Silently, Helen pulled her coat open and showed him the video camera.

"Shit," the man said. "Goddamn shit!" He took the camera from her neck, and she smelled sweat and something sweet and herbal.

"She's lying to us," she said, the story on the tip of her tongue, all of it, from the day she met Grace to the very car ride that led her to this man on this dark street in the middle of no good.

"What do you mean?" The man moved closer. She could see the whites of his eyes, a thin mustache, not enough to recognize him again, notice him in a crowd of strangers. She wondered if he saw her more clearly, learned Grace's story, he would let her go back to the car without doing one more thing.

"She says she's going to the hospital, and we didn't believe her. We followed her here. She says she's getting chemo treatments at night, and she leaves her daughter all alone. She's been doing it for months. We think she's sick. Mentally. She doesn't have cancer. She has anorexia. And maybe something else. But she's lying to us. To us all."

The man didn't say a word but dropped his hand from her shoulder. Helen breathed in deeply and all at once her breath caught on mucous and fear. "Her daughter is only twelve. There's still time," Helen said, pushing out the words. "There's still time for my friend to get help."

The man said nothing and Helen wiped her face with her sleeve. She looked over her shoulder and saw Felice and Drew walking up the sidewalk, clutching each other but moving steadily toward them. "My other friends—her other friends—are here, too."

The man turned to them and shook his head. "You all need to go *now*," he said loudly.

Helen stepped back but then asked, "Do you know my friend? Do you know what she's doing? Her name is Grace."

The man took off his hat and scratched his head. "Get out of here."

She slowly began to move away, taking small backward steps, feeling somehow lighter now that the camera was off her neck. "She needs help. She needs a lot of help."

"This ain't no place for you. I don't want to see *none* of you here again." The man stepped closer to her and Helen turned and ran to Felice and Drew, who grabbed her and pushed her toward the car. None of them said a word as they closed the doors and Helen started the car and pulled out into the street. As the Oakland streetlights shone and changed and the nightlife passed by them, Helen heard the man's words, "You all need to go now," and she knew he was completely right.

When Helen dropped off Felice, her friend turned to her before getting out. "What are we going to do?"

"What can we do?" she said, biting her lip. "I guess it's over. We don't have anything. No proof. No video. That man probably told Grace what happened, and she'll be more careful."

"Doris?"

"Doris is lost. It's over. Now all we can do is wait."

They hugged, and Felice got out, closing the door, and Helen drove up the hill, the night dark all around her.

At home, she put her keys in the bowl on the entry table and closed the front door behind her. Helen crossed her arms and shook, fear pushing up her chest as she remembered the man holding her shoulder, taking her camera, telling her to go home. She knew so much could have happened in that instant that might have changed everything for good.

In her room, she sat softly on the edge of the bed. Darryl had left the curtains open, and Oakland lay before her, alive and restless, so much going on down there she could barely imagine, thinking about the house, the man, the people on the streets. When she and Darryl had bought this house, this is what she saw first and liked best even though she had no idea then about what was really going on downtown or in her own heart. As she had looked out the window, the real estate agent behind her, talking about square footage and school districts, Helen stared, loving the way she could see everything, three bridges, the bay, San Francisco, Oakland's downtown glinting in the morning sun. It was almost as if she could see her future, something shining and beautiful, and she imagined the mornings she and Darryl would lie in bed together, watching the city before them. Why had it come to seem so ordinary, for so long?

Turning her head slightly, she looked at Darryl asleep on his stomach, his arms in triangles on his pillow by his head, his smooth back uncovered. She thought to touch him, to reach out and stroke the soft skin just over his butt, but she knew she didn't deserve it or him, so eager to let him go, so eager for Pablo or the man tonight to take her away from everything. But for the first time in months, she wanted him back, wanted to feel her cheek rest there, wanted to touch something known. Something she loved.

As she took off her shoes, she thought of a dream she'd had at the beginning of spring. In her dream she had been put in a room with a pile of beans. There were mounds and mounds of them, black and red and white, and at first she had company, women who were helping her sort and separate the beans into orderly piles. Helen had bent down and begun to arrange them, but as she looked up, she realized she was all alone and there were more beans than ever, the piles pulsing closer to her, more beans than her fingers could sort, the room filling and falling down upon her, her legs, body, arms surrounded by the smooth flesh of the seeds, finally filling her mouth, covering her eyes, the world a sea of legumes. And then she had awakened, gasping for breath, her tongue still trying to block beans from her throat, her hands over her eyes.

When she had awakened from the dream, she knew it wasn't too hard to analyze. After all, she'd taken Psychology 101 in college, just like everyone else. Freud would say it was her repressed sexuality forcing its way to her mouth so she finally had words to say. Jung would say the beans represented archetypal issues she was dealing with, the mountains of problems Helen had yet to confront. A gestalt therapist would ask her to become the beans, voicing their concerns. Everyone else would say it all went back to her childhood and Jackson's harsh criticism about her inability to organize. It was also probable it was just an anxiety dream about the classes she was taking at San Francisco State, all the papers and homework assignments and books she had to read. But as she had lain awake staring at the arched and painted ceiling above her bed, she had wondered if the beans represented the countless things she filled her life with in order to stop thinking about her marriage, her life, the mundane day-in-day-out of everything.

What had happened to her? Helen wondered now, pulling off a sock. Where had all that hope gone? When had she started dreaming about beans and longing for a boyfriend? Why was it that her future seemed hazy still, covered in summer fog? Why was it she still imagined her life had yet to begin? Helen sighed and then almost jumped as she felt Darryl's hand reach for her thigh.

"Did you find out anything? What did you get?" he asked quietly, rubbing her leg lightly.

She thought of the man holding Darryl's video camera, the way her life almost disappeared. She didn't know when she'd ever be able to tell Darryl about the way everything almost evaporated, about how the man could have changed both their lives.

She swallowed, realizing that there was another man, a man who had put more than his hands on her. How could she not have seen how dangerous Pablo and her attraction to him were? How his touch and his youth were as destructive as a drug dealer's harsh words and serious threats. She'd put herself in Pablo's arms, willing to be taken away from everything she'd chosen long ago for good reasons. How could she not see that all she had to do was sweep away the beans? "Not enough," she said finally. "We didn't really get anything to go on. She went to a house. That's it."

Darryl rolled onto his back. "Are you ready to give up now? Are you ready to let this go?"

At his words, she felt anger in her throat. What a question. How could she just give up? How could she just stop? How could she or any of them forget about Grace and Celia? But she swallowed and realized that she had let something go when the man asked her what she was doing and then took the camera from around her neck. It was as if he was taking Grace away from her and keeping Grace and her cancer or whatever for himself.

"Yeah. I am. I think we all are."

"Good. Come to bed."

"I'm having an affair." The words slipped out of her mouth like snakes and slithered into the silent room. Darryl didn't breathe. The only thing Helen could hear was her heart in her temples. Outside, the lights stayed on, cars crossed the bridge into the city, ships still slipped darkly on the water, the drug addicts skittered back and forth on dark streets.

For the next few seconds Darryl was silent, Helen's heart strung on the wire of no sound, but then she heard him crying, a quiet movement of salt and sadness. And then she remembered sitting next to Jackson as they cried together and drove through Berkeley, all the pain of their life together converging in that one isolated instance of tears. But nothing more ever came from that day, and Helen was now sure that her marriage was over. Darryl, like Jackson, would never move toward her again.

"Darryl."

"Stop," he said, rubbing his nose with his hand. "Don't. You can't say anything right now."

"But I want to explain everything."

"I already know everything! I've talked to him. Your friend. Pablo. A couple of days ago."

"You what?" she said, her mouth open with a puff of surprise.

"I found his number in one of your textbooks." He turned on his side. "I knew I was looking for something. I knew I would find it."

She wondered how he could even say the words. How could it be that she hadn't come home to overturned furniture, broken glass, or, worse, emptiness? He should have been furious, enraged, striding up and down the wood floor, pointing his finger at her, his eyes sharp and mean.

"Oh." She was unable to find a sentence in her mouth that would make sense.

"He said it was up to you. He said he knew it probably wouldn't last."

At Darryl's words, Helen wanted to cry out, not just because he was actually saying all this as the sky was lightening to gray, one last star still visible. It was also because of Pablo's shrugging her off, letting her go, allowing it all to end. The truth was, she had never wanted to call, knowing that she would eventually do just as she was doing now, let go. But she had wanted to decide when and where it would happen, be in control, move back to Darryl when she felt good and ready. Like always, she knew, she wanted to be in charge, counting out feelings in their exact and perfect piles.

"Why didn't you say something to me first? Why didn't you come to me?"

He sat up and leaned against the headboard. His skin glowed pale, a thin streak of blond hair running from sternum to groin. He pulled the sheet over his lap. "How could I? I haven't been near enough to you to say a word in months. You don't talk to me. You don't tell me anything. It's either been school or Grace taking up all your time. And Pablo, too, but I didn't know that then. How could I get close enough to ask you anything, Helen? Pablo at least was honest. Pablo didn't lie. Pablo didn't make up stories."

Helen wiped her face with the back of her hand. "What do you want to do?" she asked, thinking he might want her to leave. He would be right. She was the one who betrayed him, the marriage, the family. He had all the right in the world to point to the door and say, "Go!" She knew that if she were in Darryl's position, she'd want to rip something in half, maybe him, maybe his heart. But he had always been calmer, more deliberate. She thought, *That's why I fell in love with him in the first place.*

"I shouldn't forgive you, Helen. I've tried for months to bring you back. I didn't even know at first how far away you were. But you've been with someone else. You've forgotten about me. Us. Livie even."

"I haven't. I haven't forgotten," she cried, feeling again the man's voice next to her face, smelling his sweat and heat. "I was . . . I don't know what I was. Darryl, I'm sorry. I am. I can't explain it, but . . ."

"You'll have to explain it. You'll have to tell me everything. I have to know, Helen. If I'm going to stay, you need to tell me why you wanted to ruin our life."

"I'm not sure why. I think I was . . . empty."

He didn't say anything for a minute and then shook his head. "You refused everything I had."

"What should we do?"

"I don't know. What do you want to do?"

Helen thought of the man at the house again, his features black in the darkness, his hands taking things from her. Just a video camera, something she didn't care about, but it scared her, handing over what she believed was hers, knowing if she didn't, she would pay for it, and she thought of what she had handed over to Pablo, almost giving him her entire life, her child, her husband. She wasn't willing to give up anything, not when she really had what she wanted all along. "I want to sleep. I want to be here, with you." She turned to him. "I'm so sorry."

Darryl didn't say anything, and Helen could tell she would have to say those words over and over until he could really hear them, until they could sweep into the dark fissures of hurt in their marriage and carry the pain away. She would say them until she forgot about Pablo, until she learned to take the newness he'd given her and press it into her old life. She would have to remember the man tonight, his taking, how it could all have been over. She would tell Darryl about it later, when he wasn't so raw, when he had begun to forgive her, after he'd become angry, after they moved into their new life that was already cracking open on the horizon. Helen would say she was sorry for so long, Darryl would wonder why she was saying it at all.

Darryl slid down on his back and flipped back the sheet. He looked up at her, and Helen almost wept again, because his gaze was so tender, so loving, so happy that she was staying. She knew for certain she didn't deserve it. How could she? She had never believed in herself, despite what her mother had said. Always, it was her father, his voice, the way he shook his head and closed his eyes as if she were too ugly to even look at. But she remembered Jackson sitting behind the wheel, the tears on his face, the way the morning light reflected on the seat beside her. If she had just slid over to him, touched his arm, said, "Thank you," said, "Help," said, "I love you," said, "Why?" her whole story might have been different. It wouldn't have been that hard, sliding across leather into the body she'd always known. But she hadn't, her father hadn't, and that had been it.

Without taking off her clothes, Helen slipped into the bed beside Darryl, and pressed herself against his pale flesh, thanking God for him, this dark night and the man outside the house, Pablo, Livie, her father, and the rest of her life.

SIXTEEN
❦

NOVEMBER SLIPPED INTO THANKSGIVING, and Thanksgiving slid into December's middle, the world outside light and then dark and then light again, the days full of sounds Grace noticed but shrugged off. There were closing doors and car engines and telephones, but she didn't care about any of them, moving only once or twice a day, bending down to pick up her last vial, which lay on a towel by her bed, or sitting up for the rice cakes her mother brought in at night.

With everyone gone except Doris, who moved silently in and out of the room, she had floated in her bed, allowing Doris to sponge her back, change the sheets, drive Celia to school and swim team. Each night after her dinner of green beans and rice cakes in bed, she would stagger to the bathroom to pee, a harsh, dark yellow trickle, and throw up, not needing to use her finger or even lean over the rim, her stomach pushing up everything the second she looked at the toilet.

So it was just another day like the ones before it when Kathleen opened the bedroom door and sat on the edge of the bed. Seeing her, Grace imagined it was years ago and Kathleen was bending over her to wake her for their morning run. She knew they would put on their shoes in the five a.m. darkness and head for Wildcrest trail above the house, the flicker of rufus-sided towhees and Oregon juncos underfoot, the sky pink as new skin, Kathleen's arm rubbing against hers as they pushed up and over the ridge.

But now Kathleen sat still, not speaking. Grace opened her

eyes fully, seeing more than just Kathleen's silhouette. "Hi," she said weakly. "I knew you would come. I was just thinking about you."

"Hi," Kathleen said, putting a hand on Grace's foot. Even through the quilt Grace could feel her heat. "How are you?"

"Not good." Grace wondered if that was true because she often couldn't feel a thing but her heart, heavy in her chest.

"You've got to take care of yourself." Kathleen rubbed Grace's foot, moving up toward her ankle. "If you don't eat, your heart could stop."

Grace considered this. Her heart, heavy and full for years, the organ that had pushed her up hills and on the StairMaster and through miles of bike trails, was all she had left, damaged as it was by too few electrolytes and the wrong kind of people. Why would Kathleen care now? *Guilt*, Grace thought. *She doesn't want to feel guilty when I'm gone.* It had nothing to do with real concern. "It's too late for you to care now. You've missed everything. You don't know what everyone has done to me. Even Stella came over."

Kathleen took her hand away and Grace felt the empty space on her leg like ice. "I do. It was all my fault. Ruth . . ."

Grace shook her head. "Don't blame Ruth. You didn't have to let my mom know. You didn't have to stay away while everyone came over and confronted me. *You* could have made them stop. You haven't even called Celia. She's been missing you so much."

Kathleen was still and silent. Grace wondered how she could sit up and pull her lover to her, wrap her in her arms and make Kathleen love her again. That was all she wanted. That was all she needed. Why couldn't Kathleen see that, see her as she had been all those years ago in the clinic with Jimmy? Kathleen had loved her then, wanted her, touched her gently with soft hands. Why not now? Why not again? And for a second, it seemed that there would be a chance, a moment to make it all happen, Kathleen's face cracking open, the pain of the last months, maybe years, on her face. For a tiny moment, Grace could see Kathleen as she had seen her that first time in the clinic, concerned, open, happy, eager to help, wanting to be next to Grace. Kathleen's eyes looked like they carried the whole world in them and there was still space in her gaze for Grace. *She looks old*, thought Grace. *She needs me.*

But even as Grace thought that, Kathleen's face shut down and she stood, pulling her purse strap over her shoulder, her face as hard and closed as when she first walked in the room. "I can't save you. I never could. I've tried everything I can. I don't know what's going on with you, but you need help. You've got to want to get healthy. I've talked to Doris already about it. I'll pay for everything."

Kathleen backed away toward the door. "I'm going, Grace. You know you can call me. Your mom can call me. But don't until you are ready for help."

"I'm dying," she wailed. "How can you be ready for that?"

"I don't know," Kathleen said. "No one does."

Day sailed into night. Doris talked on the phone for hours; the front door opened and closed. Celia walked in and out of the bedroom, whispering and then picking up Grace's hand, warm fingers pressing on her skin, and then there would be nothing but remembered pressure, fingerprints of care. Sometimes she felt her chest constrict as if someone were pressing steel bars over her, and she imagined she heard Miller's voice coming down the hall toward her, his steps, like they'd always been, soft and quick. But then the bars lifted, and she felt a lightness over her head, a clarity, joy really, and then she slept again, waking to hear nothing but water running in the kitchen. Celia came and sat by the bed for hours, holding her hand. Grace talked back to her, but Celia didn't seem to hear, her grip silent and steady. The television's muffled noise slipped under the bedroom door. She remembered when she was three, running across the beach, her parents sitting on the dry sand smoking cigarettes and laughing. Her dad wasn't crazy then and was so handsome, like Clark Gable, dark with a black mustache, her mother auburn-haired and thin, leaning on him, smiling her red-lipsticked smile. Her brothers splashed in the water, twirling Grace in circles, loving her flesh the right way. The sun sat on the horizon like a persimmon, settling into ocean, and then they all ate at a restaurant, Grace in a booster seat. The waiter smiled at her and gave her a lollipop. At night everyone stayed in his own room.

"Grace," someone said. "Are you awake? What are you thinking about?"

"I'm thinking about summer," she imagined she said, closing her eyes, suddenly back on the beach with her brothers, smelling the Sea & Ski lotion her mother rubbed on her arms and face. Her brothers batted a large beach ball between them, and the seagulls flapped white wings over the water, squawking and calling to each other. Grace found a shell and held it up to the sun, her mother clapping and putting it in a pail full of clam and mussel shells. Grace thought to tell this all to whoever asked, to ask this person to take her to the beach, but when she opened her eyes, it was dark and the person was gone.

When she opened her eyes again, lights were being pulled over her face. She thought she heard Doris and Celia in the background crying, and she tried to speak, but she could barely breathe in. Something was over her mouth, on her face, in her nose. Her body was being bumped and jostled and there were clacks and bangs beneath her. Something stabbed her in the arm, and she heard ripping cloth, ripping plastic, the whine of machines. A voice said, "She's brachycardic."

Another voice said, "I can't get a reading," and then there was something cold and wet on her chest and then a flash, and it was late in the fourth quarter, fifty-six seconds left, and the Trojans were behind by one. Grace's chest pounded from the elbow jab a Cardinal shooting guard had given her in the ribs. She was so tired, barely able to move up the court, and sweaty, the hair along her cheeks deep red and wet, her white skin shiny under the fluorescent lights.

Then Grace had the ball, dribbling it fast down the court, and she saw a flash of blond hair and blue shirt, and bounced the ball hard and quick into her best friend Drew's hands. Drew jumped up and let the ball fly, the ball swirling around the metal and slipping in. Up by one.

"Time out," Drew called. The Trojans clumped together in a circle around their coach, long bones leaning against each other, those who came in from the court panting, chests rising and falling, their breaths mingling as they listened to the coach for direction.

Then everything was movement, and Grace could feel her teammates work with her, all of them pressing, pressing, stopping number 14 from action, fighting for the ball to stop, for 14 to give up and pass it to 19. She forgot about anything but this, moving with the rhythms of the other girls, floating in the air, thudding down, her legs and arms, her whole entire body, perfect for this very thing.

In those last seconds, the lights flashing in her eyes, the electric current of the game in her body, her chest aching from breath and movement, Grace wasn't conscious of the throb in her ribs or her sweat, but only of the next pass and moves, and then number 19 had the ball and made an awkward jump, the ball hitting the rim of the hoop, lurching on the metal, and then falling to the floor, the buzzer going off as the Stanford women closed their eyes and the Trojans jumped up and around Grace, their captain, their friend, and she felt their hands, all of them, on her body as she was lifted up and over and into the bright light of the gym.

Y OU HAVE BEEN AWAKENED AT 5:00, 5:14, 5:29 A.M., the phone jangling in your hand like something alive, your nerves somewhere outside your body. You've listened to the other voice, the voice of one of your best friends, telling you Grace has finally died. You want to cry and maybe tears come, but you already feel you've said goodbye during the months you tried to help her, where she went from someone strong and brave and amazing to someone who was simply in pain.

You confer with your friend, decide to meet later that morning, and lie back against your pillow. There is a body next to you, a man, and you pull him close after you've hung up the phone. He's half asleep but knows what has happened because he, too, has lived through the months of your crusade. He pulls you close and kisses your forehead, telling you, "It will be all right," and you know he's wrong but you want to believe him anyway.

Later you talk to your friends, ask about funeral arrangements and memorial services. You all wonder about an autopsy, but surprisingly, Doris has not asked for one, so no one will ever know the truth, the real story, and you learn that you will have to accept that, even though at night you play the last few months over and over, looking for clues. And later still, you find out Grace has been cremated, so whatever Grace knew, whatever secret she kept, has been scattered in the Pacific Ocean and fallen to the deep sandy floor.

At the memorial in Southern California, sitting with your best friends, you realize that Doris seems to have forgotten about the intervention and all the lies and the anger, bending over each of you, murmuring, "Thank you so much for coming. It would have meant the world to Grace." You breathe in sharply, then exhale, and gently wrap your arms around this mother, this woman, a story you understand.

While Grace's brothers speak about Grace's strength, her courage in the face of terminal illness, you look over your shoulder, wondering if any of these men in the pews behind you is Dr. Karl.

Could you flip through the guest book? Could you find him later and ask him why the treatments had to be so convoluted, so secret? Could you tell him how the secrets ruined everything? You wonder if the man from the West Oakland house would come to a funeral, his hands full of the secrets that might have changed everything. But then you shake yourself, remember the lies, the sad syringe at the side of Grace's bed, the green beans, the rice cakes, the NutraSweet.

Later, at the reception at Doris's house, you watch Grace's brothers, Miller and Frank, move through the room, and you wonder about the story of some kind of abuse. But how could it be true when nothing else seemed to be? How could these men—tall, almost cheerful, handsome in the same way Grace used to be pretty— talk to strangers and shake hands and well with tears, when one of them might have touched her in ways no one ever wants to be touched? Even though you now think nothing she said was real, you recoil when Miller approaches you but manage to stick out your hand, pretending, like everyone else, that everything is finally at rest.

You look toward the corner of the room, and there is Celia sitting next to an older woman, her ankles crossed, her face serious but calm. She is busy listening, pushing a strand of red hair behind her ear. For a second you imagine Celia is Grace, just as Grace must have been in this very house. Celia stands, and you see she has her woman's figure now, her breasts moving well past a training bra, her hips just under the fabric of her dress. You look down at the rolled salami and cheese on your plate and hope that this girl makes it, that her flesh stays her flesh, that her mother left her only her courage and tenacity and nothing else.

Late in the afternoon, you find yourself overwhelmed by the noise and sadness, and you slip upstairs past the bathroom and into the attic, realizing that this was Grace's childhood room, the place where everything started. You sit on the bed and feel the light on your shoulder. You wonder again if you and your friends were wrong, if Grace really did have cancer, if she actually was abused, if there truly was a secret protocol no one could know about.

The light shines hot on your face and you sigh, knowing you will never understand, and you look up and there is Grace, ready for a basketball game, her face full and happy, her arms strong and ready for action. You want to wave, to send her off, but you know you need the encouragement now more than she does, so you stand up and walk out of the room and close the door firmly behind you.

ભ

Jessica Barksdale Inclán teaches composition, creative writing, mythology, and women's literature at Diablo Valley College in Pleasant Hill, California. Her short stories and poems have appeared in various journals and newspapers. Ms. Inclán holds bachelor's degrees in sociology and English literature from CSU Stanislaus and a master's degree in English literature from SFSU. She lives in Orinda, California, with her husband and two sons and is currently working on her next novel.

Visit Jessica Barksdale Inclán's Web site:

www.jessicabarksdaleinclan.com

THE MATTER OF GRACE

Jessica Barksdale Inclán

This Conversation Guide is intended to enrich the
individual reading experience, as well as encourage us
to explore these topics together—because books,
and life, are meant for sharing.

A CONVERSATION WITH JESSICA BARKSDALE INCLÁN

Q. Although Grace's illness is the central mystery of your novel, it's not the thematic core, is it?

A. No. What I wanted to focus on in this novel is the gift of friendship. Like most of us, I've had some friends who were struck by serious illnesses. And what I noticed during those times—especially during the most anxious moments of uncertainty, during testing and surgeries—was the way we all naturally banded together. Each of us no doubt had our own personal problems at home, yet friendship caused an almost organic reorganization of our priorities and we all pitched in together to support our ill friend.

Q. Grace's friends seem to realize how lucky they are to be part of this circle of friends, even though, at times, they neglect their own issues to be there for her. Is this because they realize their friends would do the same for them in crisis?

A. Well, that's part of it. But I tried to make the characters conscious of how important the friendships are for them on a daily basis. In my own life, my women friends have supported me through emotional distress, job, family, and creative issues.

Q. The irony, of course, is that Grace seems to be the one person who doesn't truly benefit from the friendships. Can you talk about that?

A. Sadly, Grace is so emotionally damaged that she can't feel the love of her friends. She needs their attention and their concern, yet she can't really feel lucky to be so loved and supported. Friendship is a daily thing and maybe a crisis rallies the troops, but the community created by a group of friends who care for each other is something to take strength and comfort from every day. That's why the swim team is as important to the mothers as to the kids.

Q. Why did you choose to make Grace's illness more than meets the eye?

A. What really interests me about people is what they hide inside. Grace is an extreme example of this, but Stella, Helen, and Felice also have feelings and needs they can't face. I wanted Grace's illness to be a turning point for all of them—in which, sensing their own mortality, they finally confront their own problems. Because Grace's illness is so much more complicated than the cancer she claims, her friends use the heartbreaking experience of not being able to reach Grace to help themselves reach within.

Q. It's interesting that you made the character who most seems to "have it all" one who also struggled with food and weight issues. Why did you do this?

A. I guess, in a way, Stella represents the flip side of Grace. She didn't have everything easy as a kid but she certainly felt the same need to transform her personal appearance. She was able to make this tremendous effort without letting it become her only priority. Her relationship with Aaron is the most open and communicative one in the novel. They talk. They support each other. Grace's relationship with Kathleen, however, seems to have always been doomed by Grace's intense neediness, her desire to be fixed by someone else's love, her inability to get out from behind the mask she wore.

Q. Why did you make food issues such an important part of the story?

A. The ways women treat their bodies shows what an intense preoccupation we have with our looks. Sometimes it seems as though we believe that, if we could only look great, everything else would be great, too. *I will be different. I will be happy. So-and-so will love me.* While most of us do not go to the extremes that Grace does, I think we all have this reaction at one point or another. I have had to learn to love my body and I sometimes still don't think I fully do. This issue is important to me—somehow girls have to learn early on to love the bodies they have, not try to change what they become as women.

Q. Approaching this story from multiple points of view was an interesting idea. Why did you decide that was the best way to tell this story?

A. While multiple points of view can be a little more challenging for the reader (you feel you are getting to know one character when I move you on to the next), I love the idea of knowing a story from all angles. It's my inherent nosiness. I also think there was great value in having Helen, Stella, and Felice share both their inner viewpoints and their perspectives on Grace. I feel that, in a way, each of them is bearing witness to Grace's mystery, each of them holds pieces of the Grace puzzle.

Q. And yet the puzzle is never fully solved, is it?

A. No. And that's the way life is sometimes. All of the love they feel for Grace isn't enough because Grace can't love herself. And when you can't love yourself, warts and all, it's almost impossible to really love other people. I mean, does Grace really love Kathleen? I don't think so. Real love involves exposing yourself to someone else and risking rejection—not manipulating or deceiving someone into caring for you.

Q. What about the other characters and their relationships? What did you most want to convey in their stories?

A. I am fascinated, as most writers are, by relationships. Sometimes I think we all forget how fluid they are, ever moving and changing. What I have seen again and again is that couples who can confront that shifting landscape with honesty and openness are much more likely to weather life's bumps in the road—and even to be enriched by them. For instance, James and Felice may have been able to make it if they had been attuned to the growing distance between them. But by the time we meet them, it's way too late. On the other hand, Helen and Darryl stand a real chance, despite the affair, because she is able to recognize what's important to her in time to be honest and recommit herself fully to making her marriage work.

Q. Mothering is another theme throughout this book. What did you hope to convey about the bonds of motherhood?
A. I wanted to show, first of all, how strong that bond can be.

Doris, for better or worse, is an example. Even though she has done a lousy job of protecting her child in the past and even though she makes a poor choice in siding with Grace against her friends, most of that comes from a fierce loyalty. I also think that we tend to believe what we want when the truth is too painful and Doris certainly showed that kind of blindness in Grace's childhood and continues to show it during her illness. On the other hand, Felice's mothering shows that a mother can be imperfect, can make mistakes and repair them. Though she loses James, she gains a whole new relationship with her kids.

Q. What about Celia? It seems unnatural that Grace doesn't care more for her, doesn't it?

A. Well, Celia's story is as sad as Grace's. Just as Grace spent her childhood feeling unloved and unprotected by her mother, so does Celia. And when you look at the other mothers in this novel, you see how much they *derive* from the love they give their kids. Poor Grace is caught in—and continuing—the same cycle she knew as a child. And Celia is as innocent as Grace once was, and she's liable to need a lot of help in understanding that she is worth something, even if her mother is too damaged to reach out to her. But I hope I leave readers with the feeling that these women who love Grace will try to help Celia feel loved.

QUESTIONS FOR DISCUSSION

1. Motherhood is an important topic in this novel. How does Doris fail as a mother, despite her maternal drive to protect Grace? Discuss the ways in which she duplicates the same mistakes she made when Grace was a child.

2. Why are the friendships in this circle so important to Helen, Felice, and Stella? What qualities do they find in these relationships that sustain them as meaningfully as—and sometimes more meaningfully than—their marriages?

3. Grace is the one character who fails in her friendships. Why? How does she let the group down? And how is this similar to the way she lets Kathleen down?

4. Kathleen is initially a very unlikable figure. Did you find yourself becoming more sympathetic to her as you learned more about Grace's manipulations? Do you think Kathleen could have handled some things better or did she merely take what steps she could to protect her own well-being?

5. How do you feel about Helen's relationship with Pablo? Why does she have to turn away from Darryl in order to come back to him? Do you think she could have found the desire to try again without having this affair?